Not Quite Broken

Theresa Kuhl-Babcock

Not Quite Broken

Theresa Kuhl-Babcock

Dedication

When seeking my passion, I did not walk alone or without the brilliant memories of my youth. To my friends and loved ones whose shadow made it into this fiction, I love you all.

To Bob,

I hope this book is as witty as I hear you are. To a noted clever man.

Prologue

"Anna, let's pretend you are the princess and I am your maiden." I curtsy holding out my tank top. "We are lost in this magical forest and need to go on a journey to another land in search of your true love." I excitedly hold my arms out and spin in a circle while looking to the sky. I am invigorated in this new place.

"Ella, they shouldn't have left us. My mom is going to be mad if we don't get home." Anna does not join me but stands with her arms crossed at her chest in this large field. Narrow biking paths split every so often throughout this area. The boys are always out here pretending to be pro mountain bikers.

Jake and Craig goaded us to this very spot by stealing Anna's private journal then heading into the field behind her house. "Let's see who finds your diary at the flats."

We never come back here, but Anna was scared that her journal would fall into the wrong hands. We chased the boys for quite some time. When we arrived at this spot, the boys dropped Anna's journal and took off on their bikes. I heard Craig from the distance, "Good luck finding your way home."

Anna retrieved her journal just after we arrived, but now she is stuck in a funk.

I accept the challenge. I will change her mood. "Stop worrying. We'll go home eventually. We don't need those stupid boys." I grab Anna by the hand and drag her into my spin. After some initial resistance, Anna drops my hand, laughs, and spins joyfully with me. Anna is my cousin but we look like twins.

Today isn't as hot as usual because of a constant breeze. Magic fills the air. "We are free." Anna squeals. I know she means free from the boys, but I engage her in role play.

"We must start our journey to the land of Aramos where your handsome prince is waiting for you." I brazenly command. I can see the water tower in the distance that gives us a general idea of which direction to follow. "Head east, fair maiden. We shall follow the sun." I point my finger toward the sun.

Anna is all in. "Alas, we have to make the journey or else the evil queen shall lock me away never to see this beautiful sun again." We both hold hands and giggle as we start our journey.

After a long walk, we come to a clearing with wild flowers mixed with sting nettle. "Careful, though we walk in beauty, danger is ever present." I say pointing out the nasty sting nettle. We return to spinning until the earth seems to tilt sideways. Time stands still.

When we stop spinning, we reach for each other's hands clumsily. We fall to the ground and look to the heavens.

"Someday we will escape from this land and live together as sisters." Anna says.

"But you are a princess. How can we live as sisters?" I question.

"When I am queen, I will marry you off to a prince and give you a title. Then we will be equals." Anna squeezes my hand tightly.

"Anna, I love you."

"I love you, too. I wish we were sisters and I could come and live with you. I'd never have to see my brothers again."

"Except at the holidays, but they wouldn't be your brothers. They would be your cousins."

Anna jumps up. "Fair maiden, we must continue our journey. The evil swine Craig and Jake must be held to account."

"Yes. Let's continue on our way, for great things lie ahead."

We run for a bit before we hear the boys' bikes. "Oh no! The swine have found us." Anna yells.

I feel a ball in my throat. Craig spins around behind me and hits me in the back of the head. I throw my hand out in retribution but miss completely. "Jerk!" I yell.

"Mom is mad. What is taking you so long?" Jake is talking to Anna.

"You left us out here. I'm telling on you when we get home." Anna is back in her funk.

The boys circle us once more throwing dirt in their wake then proceed back toward the house without saying anything else.

Anna and I run behind them, unable to keep up. Anna is no longer interested in our magical adventure. When we arrive, she runs straight into the house.

My parents are standing outside waiting for me, "Ella, we need to go." My mom holds her arms out and I fit nicely into her embrace.

My dad reaches over and brushes my mangled long dirty blond hair out of my eyes, "Wild thing. Did you have fun?"

Before I can answer I am in the car headed home.

Chapter 1

Subtle hints of rosemary and thyme strongly assault my senses as I pass the scented soaps which is preferable to the combination of perspiration and tobacco from the general patrons. The Swap Center is open Friday to Sunday weekly. The large grey warehouse is home to a congested maze of small booths mostly owned by first generation Hispanic families who sell knockoff boots, purses, jewelry as well as imported hats, rugs, clothes, furniture and guns. The crowd enjoys the traditional homemade Mexican foods from the Palateria. The smell is enticing. I have a strong desire for a Carne Guisada taco with hot sauce, but I am not here for the food or the shopping.

Shopping has never really appealed to me. Silly girls with their silly expensive purses and shoes. I prefer the casual look. The weather is generally hot in South Texas, so a tank and shorts with comfortable walking shoes is my preference. I blend in with the environment, even though I am a dirty blonde with a significant number of freckles. I've been told that the right makeup would cover my freckles, but I like my natural face. My wallet, cell phone, and keys are in my pocket. I only carry a purse on special occasions and this outing does not qualify. My sun glasses hang from the front of my tank.

Out of the corner of my eye, I see him. He is a six-foot-tall Hispanic man built like a WWF fighter with a crew cut and chaotic tattoos covering his arms. Based on his driver's license from his rental application, he is 28 years old. He wears ripped men's skinny jeans that hang too low on his hips, a black wife beater shirt with visible underarm hair, and obnoxiously white high-top shoes; a total douche bag look. I haven't seen him since he moved out under the shelter of night.

The police have not been any help. When they came to the house, they didn't see any evidence of wrong doing. The officer looked around and decided that the tenant had simply violated our lease agreement. He did not notice the strong smell of marijuana. The unusual number of holes in the walls, clearly for ventilation and heating lamps, did not rouse any suspicion from the officer. The alarm system was dismantled and obviously replaced with another system that had been ripped out of the wall in a hurry before this man abandoned his lease. Rather than acknowledging that the bastard was using my inheritance as a drug house, this amazing peace officer asked how much I was asking for rent.

So, it is up to me. All 125 pounds of me. I am not sure what my intentions are, but I just can't let it go. He didn't leave a forwarding address and suing is more trouble than it is worth. He is meandering outside of a pipe store; apparently, calling your store a bong shop is illegal in Texas. This is the very pipe store he put on his rental application. In retrospect, this should have alerted me to continue looking for a tenant. From the looks of what was left behind, he was growing a large amount of marijuana in my house. He is likely the supplier for this grand business. Sometimes I wonder if Colorado has it right, just make marijuana legal and tax the shit out of them. While I am deciding on my next course of action, the decision is made for me.

The bastard walks straight towards me. "Hey girl." His arrogance and bold stance only serve to take my anger and boil it into a rage.

With my heart pounding, sweaty palms, and clenched teeth, I lean towards him with my hand propped on my hip to show him that I am not intimidated or okay with this situation. I hold my shoulders back to raise my gait. Standing tall, I still fall a foot below his natural stance but I have no intention of backing down. "Remember me. You skipped out on your rent. And can you tell me what you were doing in the house?"

He smiles. That I'm-a-total-asshole smile. "Don't know what you are talking about. I even painted before I moved out."

I retort with all the vigor I can muster, "You were growing pot in the house. I've called the police. This isn't over."

In the middle of my grand stand the son-of-a-bitch looks up and turns. He doesn't move away. Just stands with his back to me. I can feel the rage burning in the pit of my stomach. Even with the rage, I realize that he is strong and my options are minimal. Just then I see an officer walking by the next aisle. I call him over. "Officer, I would like to report this man. He was trying to sell me marijuana."

The goon turns around and now his anger matches mine. "You little bitch."

The officer asks him to step outside and for me to follow. On the curb the officer searches my foe. He is clean. I mention the shop in The Swap Center. Within minutes, police cars arrive and converge on the small shop. The goon is placed in the squad car.

I am so proud of myself. I mouth, "Fuck you!" It feels good. To celebrate, I buy myself a Carne Guisada taco and a large unsweet tea with lemon.

Unfortunately, I can't celebrate all day. I have to get to work at Taylors Grocery before three. I need to head home. My all faithful decade old Nissan Altima only has 120,000 miles. The air conditioning is cold so the fact that the window does not always roll up is acceptable. I'm not into flash, thank goodness.

∂∂∂∂∂∂∂

I clock in 10 minutes late. Rob, my front-end manager, notices immediately, "No first break for you." I don't really care. The store is busy which helps the time pass quickly.

Greg is working. That brings a smile to my face. Greg is a shy guy a few years older than me. He always jokes around when I bag at his station. I think he has a crush on me, but he hasn't made any kind of move. I'm not sure he has any game. Which is good because I'm not sure I am even ready for dating.

Everyone flirts with everyone around here. When I first started, I had a crush on Dean, but I quickly realized that he is just an egomaniac whom I now find completely unappealing.

"Hey Greg. Rob is a jerk."

"He isn't so bad. Maybe you should just get to work on time?"

"Thanks a lot. Glad to see you are on my side."

I finish bagging the next order and help the stocky overwhelmed mother of four out of the store. What a weird experience pushing a cart with an unknown scared child staring

4

me in the face. "Hi there." I cheerfully attempt interaction with the small child.

Tears.

The mom puts all the kids in the car while I put the groceries in the back hatch. "Here, thanks for the help." She offers a two-dollar tip.

"Sorry, no tips allowed. This is a free service. Good luck with your crew," I nod toward her four children who are currently slapping at each other and arguing loudly about who will get the front seat. I give her an empathic smile.

The sweet mom looks at her obnoxious children and gives me a half smile. "Thanks, this was my break. No one to help get them and all these groceries in at the house."

The exhaustion is obvious in the deep circles under her eyes. I am definitely not ready for kids. I quickly abandon her hectic life. I am an only child who has never understood how a large family functions.

The evening moves along quickly. At the end of my shift late in the evening, Rob tells me to clear the parking lot of any carts. Happy to breathe some fresh air, I head to the lot. I wander slowly around gathering the random carts left throughout the lot.

Generally, I enjoy walking the empty lot late evenings, but tonight I see a serial murderer van between me and the store. White, large, covered windows. I don't know why those always freak me out. I make a wide circle while I watch four guys coming out of the store. They appear to be in good spirits and approach me. "What's up, cutie? When do you get off tonight?"

The big one holds onto the cart I am pushing and the other three surround me. An unfriendly gesture towards a small built 19-year-old female in a dark empty parking lot. My gut instincts kick in. These guys are not good guys. "I am working an all-nighter."

The big guy pulls a little harder on the cart and the group tightens the circle around me. We are headed toward the creepy van. I scan the lot, but no one is around. The guys have realized that I am scared and have only increased in their aggressive attention.

I consider my options. Shove the cart and attempt to run...no. Politely mention my discomfort...no. I decide to attempt to hide my fear and fake interest in the goon standing to my right between me and the store. I smile and look up coquettishly. "What's your name?"

"Carl. You want to party with us?" He relaxes, releases the cart which creates an empty space. I take the moment to dart toward the store. As I am running, they do not pursue.

While guffawing the thugs yell out through laughter, "We just wanted to have some fun with you."

Tears come to my eyes as I enter the store. The store is relatively dead. Rob and Greg approach instantly, "What's wrong, Ella?"

I give a befuddled explanation of the four thugs trying to pull me towards a van. Rob and Greg immediately run to the parking lot. I am flattered to see the machismo working on my side.

When they return, Rob tells me. "The guys and the van are gone."

Greg responds, "Probably just some guys joking around. Nothing to worry about."

Being dismissed so easily after experiencing profound fear undoes any feelings of gratefulness towards either Rob or Greg. Luckily my shift is over. I happily clock out. Greg offers to walk me to my car as his shift is over as well.

I guess the action of the evening has invigorated him. Greg has never offered to walk me to my car at the end of my shift. He has handsome hazel eyes and long lashes. His face is strong, but very approachable. His glasses make him look a little nerdy, but the overall look I must admit is appealing. I feel safe in his company. "Will I see you at Del Mar tomorrow?" Greg asks.

"Yeah, I have morning classes Tuesday and Thursday."

Greg awkwardly stalls at my car. "So, yeah, would you, um, want to watch a movie after classes tomorrow?"

What? No way. Greg and I have worked together for over a year now and tonight, he picks tonight. I have butterflies in my stomach, despite my disappointment with the short length of his protective response to my parking lot confrontation. My initial thought is *no*. I don't really date, but I do friends really well.

I decide to pick a safe movie that I actually want to see. "Sure, I want to see *The Depth*." *The Depth* is a movie about a young girl going to work for a powerful internet company and finding out that with unlimited information comes scary power. Not romantic, but definitely a fascinating theme for friends.

"Yeah, that looks really interesting. The book *1984* is starting to sound like fact these days. Should we just drive to school together tomorrow?"

Again, Greg is surprisingly showing some game. His passive sweet personality is beguiling. "Sure, we can grab lunch too. I play cards with a few friends between classes. Have you ever played Spades?"

Greg looks embarrassed, "My family never really played card games or board games." After a pause, he adds, "I played *Hungry, Hungry Hippo* as a kid."

I can't help but laugh out loud in an unladylike manner. I catch myself. Greg looks like he is shutting down a little. I'm such a jerk.

"I'll teach you. Join us. I pretty much taught everyone else how to play. I think you would really enjoy cards. My family played tons of games. You've been missing out." I realize that I am blushing. This is weird. Good weird, I think.

On the way home, I find myself thinking of Greg. Mostly that he isn't my type, but then my subconscious keeps reminding me of my autonomic nervous system. My heart is racing, my cheeks are blushing, and butterflies are fluttering deep inside my belly. Then I float back to how he isn't what I'm looking for. Shut up, subconscious. I need to rest.

Chapter 2

Greg shows up right on time with breakfast tacos. Damn, I love potato, egg and bacon tacos. Classes start in 30 minutes and the drive is 20 minutes. I hate mornings. No butterflies today, just a strong desire to crawl back into my comfortable bed.

"Sorry I'm not ready. Five more minutes. I promise I'll hurry." Greg is very accommodating considering I am in a towel and look a mess.

Greg takes a long look. I realize that I am underdressed and start to feel a little self-conscious. Greg smiles broadly, "No hurry. We can eat breakfast before you get dressed if you like."

"Funny." I take my taco and head to my bedroom where I quickly pull my hair back in a pony and put on a little eye shadow, mascara and lipstick. Good enough. I throw on a pair of jeans and a tank. I get cold in classes so I grab a sweater that I tie loosely around my waist.

Greg drives a beat up old black Jeep. The soft top does not suppress any road noise and the ride is bumpy. Even though no window is open I feel a hot breeze simultaneous to the cold air coming from the vents. Talking is difficult due to the loud road noise so I yell a little, "Nice ride."

Greg smiles a sexy smile that makes me react in a way a friendly smile does. Damn it. The butterflies are back. I am not use to these feelings. I've only ever kissed one guy. I was sixteen. A girlfriend and I snuck out to the Padre Island National Seashore our junior year in high school. We met two college guys who took us on a romantic walk down the beach. I realized that I was not using the best judgment when they separated us.

When Joel started walking into the water, I put on the breaks. I couldn't get wet as I had told my parents we were going to the mall. About knee deep into the shore, Joel held both of my hands and kissed me. Gross. The saliva kiss had more water than the ocean. I wanted to spit, but that would be unladylike. I then walked straight back to his truck to meet up with my girlfriend. She was apparently delayed. Joel asked if I'd like a back rub. How could that go wrong? He first rubbed my shoulders then moved his hands stealthily to my breasts.

"Stop." I grabbed his hands and threw them off of me.

Joel looked hurt. Pig. "What's wrong?"

"I'm not easy."

"We can have some fun without you being easy."

"Consider me difficult." I sat there not speaking for the next five minutes until my friend arrived. Before quickly departing, the jerk even asked if we'd meet him at the beach the following night. We didn't.

My first experience offered little romance and turned me off dating ever since, though Greg has this amiable quality that I find endearing, charming. Shit, why did I agree to see a movie?

We arrive at Del Mar West campus and park in the student center which is actually a really great centralized spot. I step out of the Jeep and awkwardly start towards my first class. Greg quickens his stride without comment and walks me to my first class.

I have never had anyone walk me to class. I think back to all the cute popular girls in high school. I was such a loser.

Greg continues to make small talk all the way to class and I make sure to keep pace.

"Do you like your classes?" Greg asks.

"They are okay. I'm working on my basics. My art class is fun, though I am not a great artist."

"I'm finishing my basics and have started a few upper level courses. I'm a computer science major. You?"

"Oh, I put down psychology as my major but I'm not really sure. I was considering physical therapy but I'm having a hard time in chemistry."

Greg shakes his head, "I've gone through several majors. I think that is pretty common."

Once we arrive at my class, we agree to meet up in the student center between our next class for the break.

The student center is busy, but my best friend, Tiffany, her boyfriend, and several other friends are sitting at our usual table already playing Spades. I sit and wait to take the place of whoever leaves.

Tiffany wears very little make-up, has a slight build and a short pixie haircut. She dresses more girly then me, though neither one of us is up on the current fashions. Her boyfriend is Hispanic, a little husky and relatively her same height. He dresses very casual in cargo shorts and various logo t-shirts. Today he has chosen, *I like you but if the Zombie's come, I'm tripping you*. Charming as always.

Greg saunters over. He doesn't speak and looks intimidated.

"Greg, come sit with me." I take the time to teach him the game from an outsider's perspective. He understands the basics. Two players have to go to class, but there is only ten

11

minutes until our class starts. "Want to skip class and play?" I ask.

Greg cautiously sits without verbally confirming. I pass out cards while adding a little strategy.

Greg tries his best. Tiffany and her boyfriend are patient. Tiffany comments, "Having fill-ins is great. Sucks when we can't find a fourth for a game." The conversation is light and enjoyable.

In the hour and half time to our next class, Greg improves but struggles with strategy. Time passes quickly. After looking at the time, I interrupt our fun, "I can't skip my next class."

Tiffany agrees, "I know. I have to go too. Greg, are you going to become a regular?"

Greg looks thrilled to be invited back. "Yeah, this was fun!" Greg and I agree to meet at the Jeep when class is over.

English lit is boring as usually. I hate old English tales. *Gunderfoot* just does not interest me. The story of a hero who sails to save his king from a terrible beast who threatens their lives and their way of life… blah blah blah. I hate it. Half asleep I realize the class is finally over.

Greg is standing by his Jeep when I approach. I decide to give him a good look-over as I approach. I mean I should take it all in if I am considering dating him. He is six-foot tall, slender but not skinny. He obviously has some muscle tone, but not a goon. At work, I always check out the dent between his shoulders where the material from his shirt relaxes. Absolutely sexy. I don't know why I like shoulder blades, but damn. All in all, I must admit, I like.

"How was your class?" I smile.

"Boring. I am ready to grab something to eat."

"Where to?"

"How about Boat and Net? The French fries and tartar sauce are awesome." I lick my lips. Boat and Net is a small box where you drive up and order fried fish and chicken. Quick, good, and cheap.

Greg shakes his head, "How about I treat you to a lunch with air conditioning? It is a hundred degrees out today."

"I don't mind paying for myself. How about Senior Lupe's? I love the salsa and the enchiladas."

Mexican food in Corpus Christi is a local favorite. Senior Lupe's has a 7-foot chicken out front. Greg smiles when he sees it, "Classy."

I giggle and we take a quick selfie with the giant orange fowl. As we enter, the bright colors of orange, yellow, and dark blue along with grand chandeliers definitely overwhelm the senses and create a warm feeling.

Greg gives his opinion, "I have never eaten here. I like it. Is the food good?"

"Great," I reply.

Our waiter takes our drink orders and leaves a large basket of chips and fresh salsa. After a minute of devouring the chips and salsa, both Greg and I are in desperate need of fluids. While the salsa tastes amazing, the heat is intensifying with no relief. Laughing we gesture to the waiter who brings our drinks to the table.

Greg orders mini tacos and I order my usual, cheese enchiladas with rice and charro beans. Greg asks, "So how are you doing now? I know last year was hard on you."

"I guess you know my parents passed a year ago in a car accident. I feel luckier than most people in a similar situation. I was almost done with high school and my teachers really helped me get through to the end. Graduation was the hardest." I pause to collect myself. "I miss them every day. I inherited our house, but it was too much for me. I put it up for rent last year. The rental was going pretty well until my jerk renter just up and left in the middle of the night. He did quite a bit of damage."

"Just now? That just happened?" Greg asked.

"Yeah. I guess my savings will go towards fixing it up." I steady my emotions.

"I am pretty handy. I learned a few things from my dad. Maybe we can do some of the work ourselves." Chivalry is not dead.

"That is too much to ask. I'll figure it out."

"You make everything difficult. Why not accept help from a friend?" The honest nature of his retort unsettles me. I was already feeling emotional. Greg is sympathetic, "Sorry, that wasn't my place."

I shake it off and put back on my hard veneer. "No, I mean, maybe. You could help me paint. I guess."

Both our meals have long been gone. The conversation flows easily with Greg. Part of me is mad at Greg for pushing through my protective walls, but another part of me wants to invite him in. What is it with Greg that makes me want to tear down my walls?

Growing up I realized that most people are opportunists just waiting for the moment they can take advantage. When my parents died, several relatives were willing to take me in. All I had to do was sign over the house and they would take care of me. I'm nobody's fool.

At 18, I was fully capable of taking care of myself. I was already working at Taylors, the local grocery store chain in Corpus Christi, and read online about how to rent out a house. Settling my parents' legal affairs and estate took forever. I moved into a low-rent apartment close to work. I felt uncomfortable keeping my parents' furniture, so I put a few pieces of furniture on layaway while putting my parents' stuff in storage. I drive my mother's decade old car and live off my wages. Self-sufficiency has been my mantra. I don't share these thoughts with Greg. I'm not ready for that kind of intimacy.

By the time I focus back on Greg, he is already paying the bill. I tell you. I don't know about this guy. Too good to be true. Yeah, keep those walls up.

Greg is willing to skip the movie and go by the rental house. His curiosity is peaked after I describe the damage.

When we drive up to the 1600 square foot red brick house in the Turtle Cove subdivision, memories of my parents and growing up engulf me. My mother loved to garden. She had a cushion she would place under her knees as she weeded and planted. My dad didn't help, but would sit on the cement bench which sat in the entry way and talk with her for hours. I remember wondering how she didn't get mad at him for not helping. They made each other happy, for the most part.

I choke down tears that threaten and steady myself for an emotionless tour. The front yard looks fine, but only a few overgrown plants survived. My mother would be displeased.

When we walk up to the door, alarms go off in my head. I know I locked the door before I left yesterday. So why is the door ajar? Greg senses my apprehension and steps in front of me. I don't think so. This is my house. Back off the gallantry. Greg concedes as I bully myself past him.

The immediate pungent smell of marijuana assaults us upon entry. "The master bath closet and the guest bedroom are the worst," I inform Greg, but there is more damage than yesterday. Every cabinet door in the kitchen is open and one is hanging crooked off its hinge. "That is new." I point out. "The alarm system is no longer working. Maybe I should get that fixed first."

Most of the damage was here before. The scorched wires from the main living room outlet suggest my renter had a small fire that he didn't report to me. The bedrooms have several fist holes in the walls. The house has tile for the most part but the bedrooms are carpeted. Strange circular nicks are all over the living room tile. The carpet is dirty from soot in the master bedroom and guest bedroom. The most severe damage is in the master closet where there is a partial patch in the ceiling which I assume was for a heating lamp installed to grow the pot. The entire carpet in this area is discolored from potting soil. At least another dozen holes are scattered about. Frustration and anger emerge in an unsettling part of my mind.

The attached bathroom is another area with new paint on part of the ceiling which begs the question, "Why paint there when the house is in such disarray?" I say this aloud to myself while gesturing to the ceiling. There are two dents in the walls over the garden tub. I am guessing they put a bar here to hold the hanging pots of marijuana in front of the glass bricks. Bastards.

My parents designed this bathroom themselves several years before passing. They chose a mosaic glass tile around the garden tub. The neutral stone tiles on the floor are laid in a Versailles pattern. The hard wood cabinets have a dark rich color. The stand-up shower uses the same natural stone tile with a glass door, and river stones for the flooring. My mother loved to soak in this tub. When I was really young, I would join her in lavish bubble baths. I have to suppress the emotions that are bubbling their way over my walls. Not today. Walls sturdy.

My childhood bedroom smells the strongest of marijuana. I've never tried marijuana and to me it smells of feces. The tenant changed the basic lock to a keyless deadbolt. Someone obviously attempted to kick the bedroom door down along with the closet door as they are hollowed out and broken. The soil on the carpet is extensive and again tons of one-inch holes are found throughout the ceiling and walls.

I can barely think of this ugly room as the pink and mint green room covered in stuffed animals of my childhood. I still have some of my stuffed animals in a box in my bedroom closet. Who needs knick-knacks when you have a thousand stuffed animals?

Greg looks appalled as he wipes his hands across the holes. He is taking in all the damage. I'm pleased he is not saying his opinions aloud. I might lose it.

Finally, the garage. A large opening in the ceiling appears to be from a foot that stomped through when someone was in the attic. The attic ladder is partially detached and unstable. The ventilation shaft in the attic is torn down.

There is no way this kind of damage was done accidentally. The worst smell in the house comes from a pile of trash in the middle of the garage. The side door jamb has been knocked in and a considerable amount of oil covers the remaining floor. My dad taught me the many values of cat litter including absorbing emollients. I already poured cat litter over the oil but I just couldn't bring myself to start working on anything else.

Greg looks disgusted.

I explain, "Most of this damage was here before, including this." I point to the pile of trash. "I am guessing someone came back looking for something."

"Obviously not in this pile." Greg pulls out a bag of watches. Upon inspection there are several Rolex, Breitling, and TAG Heuer watches. Greg is impressed, "These are either expensive watches or really nice replicas."

"Maybe that is what they were looking for. Assholes. I'm glad they didn't find them."

I decide to check my cell and realize I have several missed calls from an unknown number. Usually any calls I get are from work or Tiffany. I hit the button and my voicemail begins. The calls are from a detective regarding the events from yesterday at The Swap Center. He is asking for me to come by the station today.

"I have to go to the police station. Can you drop me off at my apartment so I can get my car?"

"I'd prefer to come along. Nothing exciting in my plans today. Remember I still live at home with my parents."

Chapter 3

Detective Haas is a husky man with too much facial hair. He is wearing a suit which looks sloppy. He has a stain, ketchup I think, on his shirt. He has a jarring manner when he introduces himself and appears to have the intention of intimidating me.

"Well, you have opened a can of worms, young lady. Big John says that he was your tenant and your report of misconduct to officers was retribution." I stay quiet. "We have your call to police two days ago where you claimed he was growing cannibis in your home and moved out without notice." I continue to stay quiet. "Do you stand by your report of him trying to sell you marijuana?"

"Yes. I confronted him and he offered to sell me marijuana to calm me down. He pointed to the store." I am fully aware of the repercussions of false reports to police. I am standing by my report. Detective Haas responds with a closed lip half smile. I get the impression he is holding something back as he strokes his awkwardly long discolored mustache.

"We need you to write up a statement for the official record." He hands me a notepad and points to a table outside his cubicle. No privacy around here. The office is stark with pale blue cubicle walls and old mismatched office furniture.

I sit to write my statement. Detective Haas gives me a general format which I follow. Greg stands protectively over me, though Detective Haas all but ignores him. Within ten minutes I have completed my task and committed my statement into memory. I hand the statement to Detective Haas. "By the way, we went by the house before coming here and someone entered the house. No significant additional damage, but it appeared they were looking for something. In the garage, we found these."

I hand the baggie of watches to Detective Haas. He peruses the bag and after a time responds, "I suggest you change the locks and alert the neighbors. We will have to process these to ensure they are not stolen. If they are not stolen, abandoned property belongs to the homeowner in a rental situation like this." He pauses, then adds, "Look, I know you lost your parents. That shop in The Swap Center was a front for the Syndicate. Be careful. No reason to believe they will bother you, but no guarantees either. If we are able to make a case, the prosecutor's office may be calling to interview you. They would love to be able to take this to court."

I have an uneasy feeling. I never considered getting involved in a significant drug case. I decide the best course of action is to... ignore. Don't think about it. Nothing I can do. I can't just up and leave. I won't just up and leave. I'll be fine.

Greg puts his arm around me. I balk at his touch. I didn't mean to, but I've hurt his feelings. All this is more than I can handle. I'm ready to go home.

The ride to my apartment is quite. I am happy that I don't have to work tonight. I exit Greg's Jeep and walk around to the driver side door. Greg starts to get out, but I stand, holding his door, blocking his exit, "I think I need time to process. Thanks for the company today."

Greg nods slowly and shuts his partially opened door. When he drives off, I feel a sadness fall over me. I'm not sure if that is because he is leaving or just everything.

After taking a shower, I call my old neighbor, Rene, at the rental house. I've known him all my life. A good family. Not sure how they didn't realize my tenant was a drug dealer, but good people. They are sympathetic and agree to keep an eye on the house.

There is so much to do. I have to figure out how to quickly and cheaply get the damage in the house fixed so that I can get another renter. I hate the idea of using my savings. Juggling these responsibilities with work and school is a lot.

The overwhelming truths of the day overcome me. Heavy tears roll down my cheeks. Before I know it memories of the time I had a mom and a dad to hold and comfort me come flooding in. Damn it. I don't want to be alone.

After a hard cry, I search the television for a sad movie. I settle into another viewing of *Steel Magnolias*. My mom and I would watch this and cry together. I miss my mom and break into heavy tears.

At some point I must have fallen asleep. I awake with thick sleep in my eyes and the harsh sound of banging on my door. My body is sore from sleeping on my sofa.

Greg stands in the doorway. "What?" I ask, confused.

"You were suppose to be at work two hours ago. I only have a few minutes but I was scared something bad happened to you after yesterday." Greg looks weary and tired.

"I'm sorry. I fell asleep on the couch and didn't set my alarm. I'll be in shortly. I'm surprised they didn't call me." I pull out my cell and see that I missed several calls from work. Why does my cell always go to silent? Shit.

I rush to shower and make my way to work. When clocking in, Rob approaches me. "I'm cutting your hours. If I

21

can't count on you, I will give the time to someone who shows up. Consider yourself on probation."

I'd quit except I have a scholarship from Taylors. Seventy-five percent of tuition and fees. I can't screw this up. I am contrite when I tell Rob, "I need the hours to keep my scholarship. Please, I'll do restroom duty. I had a rough day yesterday. I can show you the police report."

Rob relaxes and curls his lip. "Fine. You're still on probation and I'll take you up on restroom duty."

Maybe Greg is right and Rob is an okay guy. I appreciate him giving me another chance. I clean the restrooms. A dirty job but I do it with pride.

When I'm finished, I have to make change for one of the checkout girls. Dean is working the front counter tonight. I use to make excuses to go to the front counter and flirt with Dean, but now I simply ask, "Can you give me quarters?" and hand him a twenty.

Mr. Ego takes his opportunity, "What will I get if I give you quarters?"

Part of me still responds. He's a babe, but I know that he does this to all the girls. "Your paycheck." I'm proud that no one could confuse my response as flirting. Mr. Ego hands over the quarters, defeated. I feel a little guilty, just a little.

When I look up I notice Greg is watching me from his checkout station. Wow, my day just keeps getting better. I make sure to monopolize Greg's checkout aisle. Everytime a patron wants a carry-out I feel disappointed only to be reinvigorated when I see Greg smile as I come back to his aisle. What a difference Greg is from Dean. Karen keeps making her way to Greg's checkout aisle, but I notice he has been saving that special smile for me. Butterflies are back.

Greg finishes his shift several hours before mine ends. The rest of the evening drags. When four o'clock arrives I eagerly ask to clock out. Rob points out that I was late and owe him the time. Back to thinking Rob is a jerk.

Finally the end of my shift arrives and I am able to go home. As I go to unlock my apartment, my elderly neighbor Mr. Ed comes out onto the stoop. "Ella. I wanted to let you know that several not so reputable looking guys were hanging around here today. I thought they were checking out your apartment. I sat on the front stoop and stared until they left."

I love Mr. Ed. He brought me yummy tacos when I first moved in. I lost my family, but I found Mr. Ed.

I spend a little time letting him know about what happened with the house and the possibility that I might be mixed up with the Syndicate. Mr. Ed looks worried, but lets me know that as a good Texan he keeps a loaded gun in his apartment. Yeah, I love Mr. Ed. I give him a kiss on the cheek. His blush makes my day.

Or so I thought until Greg's Jeep barrels loudly into the parking lot. After putting the car in park, Greg jumps out wearing tan slacks and a slightly tight rust t-shirt which shows just a little of his dark chest hair. He looks dashing. My heart skips a beat. Walls, Ella, walls!

"Do you want to go to the beach?" Greg asks holding his arms out wide with a big smile.

I consider giving him the cold shoulder. I don't think I'm ready for this, but somehow I succumb. It takes me a few minutes to jump in the shower and wash off the smell of work.

I put on a tiny red two piece, short denim shorts, and a button up white shirt that shows my red bikini top. I look hot. *YOLO*, I tell myself.

When I come out of my room, the look from Greg awakens parts of me. My precious parts tingle a little. I am surprised and excited by my physical response. Greg is speechless and smitten. "Well, let's go." I catch myself swinging my hips. Man, I've got it bad.

The weather is perfect. The sun is setting and rays of various shades of violet shoot from the horizon above the crashing waves. The temperature is still warm with a soft wind. The surf is rough at high tide and the waves rush onto the shore. A few surfers are taking advantage. North Padre Island allows you to drive and park on the beach.

Greg offers to take me 4X4ing. I've never gone 4X4ing before, but I'm up for it. Greg takes down the soft top and plants his foot heavily on the gas. As we swallow the dunes, I feel my breasts rise and fall. My hair is blowing in the wind. This is sexy. Who knew driving on the beach could be this sexy?

We are far enough out that no one else is around. Greg takes every opportunity to catch a glimpse of his companion. I notice the wind blowing my top loosely open, but I make no effort to correct the situation. I am, afterall, wearing a bikini top underneath.

After a few miles, Greg stops the Jeep. "Do you want to take a walk?"

The sun is mostly down but the sky remains bright from the moon's reflection on the water. I have never felt this excited before. Why do my senses feel so intense? The idea that he could touch me feels like it will be my undoing. I step out and take off my blouse covering my bikini top. Greg gives me that look again. I'm a virgin, but I feel dirty. My mind keeps wandering to thoughts about how his touch would make me feel. Just then I notice my hard nipples. I am embarrassed, until I notice he has his own issues to hide.

"Let's walk along the water," I suggest.

The water is warm and the waves crash over my feet that sink a little into the moist sand with each step. While we walk, I avoid looking at Greg. He moves to grab my hand. I splash him. His smile is warm and genuine.

Without asking he lifts me into the air. I squeal in delight. He threatens to throw me in the water and I jokingly threaten his life. When he places me gently back into the surf, he leans in to kiss me. I turn away. I don't know why, but I turn away.

The moment passes. What did I do? Chickened out... that is what. To recover, I splash him again and run towards the Jeep. Greg beams and follows me. The drive home is quiet and Greg breaks the silence. "Describe yourself in three words."

Surprised but intrigued. I feel the need to answer carefully. After a time thinking, I answer, "Difficult, intelligent, careful. Your turn."

Greg smiles his sexy smile, "Easy."

I laugh out loud. "And?"

"Let's see," after a short pause he continues, "adventurous, wanting love."

"Suppose to be one word."

"So I'll go with wanting."

God he looks sexy. Every part of my body responds. Message loud and clear. He hasn't given up. That makes me happy. A warm glow takes over my body and I relax into the seat of the Jeep. Best ride home ever. When we pull up to my apartment, I am hoping he will try to kiss me again but he just looks at me with kind eyes and says, "Sleep, I'll pick you up for class in the morning."

There is not one part of me that wants to get out of the Jeep. This is my new happy place.

Chapter 4

I take a shower and as soon as my wet head hits the pillow, I am deep asleep. My dreams are erotic. I have never had such intense sexual dreams. I awake to a strange noise coming from my front door. I look at my alarm clock which says three o'clock. Who could be at my door at this time? Focus.

My door knob is moving. My small apartment amplifies all noises and I can hear the clinking of the door knob like it is right by my bed.

When my wits come back to me, fear hits me. There were strange men watching my house? Could it be the Syndicate? I go to the wall shared with Mr. Ed and start banging. The noise abates.

After a minute, I hear a knock at the door. I can't move. I hear Mr. Ed's voice, "Ella, are you all right?"

I head to the door. Mr. Ed is standing at the door with a large caliber pistol in his hand. I throw myself into his arms still wearing my night clothes. I whimper, "I heard someone at my door."

"Same guys here earlier, Ella. I'm sure of it. My eyes are too old to get the license plate, but I sure scared the shit out of those punks. They are gone. I think you should call the police."

When the police finally leave, the sun is coming up. Nothing they can do but take a report. The young officer recommends I use my keyless deadbolt and stay alert. Duh.

Going back to sleep isn't as easy as earlier. I lay in bed trying to sleep but my imagination keeps running scenarios where I end up dead. I've never been happier to have my trusted retiree next door. Love you, Mr. Ed.

Too soon, someone knocks on the door. I bolt upright. No longer trusting, I move to the window and peak out. Seeing Greg standing on the front stoop with tacos makes me happy. I could get to love this guy.

I open the door, "Are you trying to fatten me up?"

"No, I like what I see, but I am trying to win your affections." That smile again.

"Food is an effective means of winning a man's affections but not so much the ladies."

Greg nudges his shoulders, "I'm famished. I can always eat both tacos."

Giving him a disapproving look, "You wouldn't dare."

"Tell you what. I'll take my time while you take a quick shower. Then you can retrieve your taco in that cute little towel you had on the other day. Fond memories." Greg pretends to remember the image from Tuesday.

I blush, "Give me ten minutes and I'll be fully dressed and ready for my taco."

"I guess that will have to do."

When I get into Greg's Jeep, I notice paint cans, brushes, as well as putty and tape to fix the holes in the walls. "What is this?"

"We agreed to get that house of yours ready for re-renting. No time like the present. Thought we could get started after classes."

Classes fly by today. Playing a game of Spades with Greg and my best friend Tiffany between classes is the highlight. I feel a heightened sense of awareness. Every guy who walks by seems to be watching me. I know I am being paranoid. I have not told Greg or Tiffany about last night.

Tiffany offers to walk me to class. "What is up with this Greg guy?"

"I like him. I like him a lot." Tiffany smiles, but when I explain everything else that has been happening, she is angry.

"Why wouldn't you tell me? I can sleep over tonight, or you can stay at my house?"

"Tiffany, I can't intrude on you and Bob." I laugh whenever I say Bob's name, sarcastically. She never appreciates this. Out of all the sexy names in the world, she falls for Bob. I like Bob. He is by far the best guy she has dated, handsome and good to her.

"Bite me." She smiles then changes the subject, "We can come help paint today."

"Really, I'd love that. I'll get pizza." I feel blessed to have such an amazing friend in my life.

We meet at the rental house after our classes. Greg and I pick up pizza and a cold 12 pack of Coke. None of us are drinkers. Plus, I need to keep everyone working. We didn't consider the stench when deciding to eat at the house, but we quickly remedy the situation and decide to have a picnic on the front lawn.

After lunch, Bob and Greg start working on the holes putting spackling in each void and wiping it with the putty knife. Tiff and I go for cleaning supplies.

Outside is smoldering and we are already overheated from lunch. We are appreciative that the electricity and water have not yet been turned off. We turn the a/c down to 65. Not my bill, not my problem. With everyone's help, by early evening the house looks and smells better.

I realize I will still have to find a handyman to fix the doors and the attic issues as well as a professional cleaning crew before anyone moves in, but the improvement is significant.

Tiffany looks tired. She approaches, "I love you girl, but we are going to head out."

"Are you kidding? Go home. Thank you guys so much for all the help. I think the place looks amazing, especially considering what it looked like when we started." I hug her tightly. Tiff and Bob leave.

Greg walks out to his Jeep and returns with two folding chairs. "How about we take a break?"

I'm exhausted and ready to call it a night, especially since I have to work tomorrow. Luckily not until the afternoon.

"Thanks, there is no way I could have gotten this far along without all the help. I was starting to feel overwhelmed." I look around the house. "Now I can imagine someone being willing to pay rent to live here again."

We both open a Coke and relax. Greg starts, "Seems strange to think that we were in the same high school for one year and never met."

Greg was a senior when I was a freshman in high school. "What were you like in high school?" I ask.

"Shy. I had my friends, mostly girls. We would dance on Friday nights at Club XS. I definitely would have had a crush on you."

"You think. I wasn't really into boys in high school. All my friends were dating. I don't know. I had a few crushes, but no one ever asked me out." Talking to Greg is easy. I don't feel any judgment.

"I went out with a few girls, but mostly just friends. I think I liked them more than they liked me. I had one girlfriend but she had so many rules. I like the way you just go with the flow." Greg leans his shoulder into mine and nudges me playfully.

Without thinking I put my hand out. Greg holds my hand. My body responds to his touch with electricity. Is this what people are talking about when they talk about chemistry? Greg starts to stand while he is holding my hand.

Oh shit. He is going to try to kiss me again. I'm not ready. I quickly shake off his hold. "We'd better seal all this paint and clean the brushes. I don't want to buy more. How much do I owe you?"

Greg looks disappointed, "My treat."

"No, this is a business. I will need the receipt for my taxes."

Greg looks annoyed and fishes through his wallet. "Whatever." He hands me the receipt. We don't talk as we finish putting the supplies away. "Ready to head out. I'm tired."

The drive home is equally quiet. I regret my retreat, but can't make myself take any other course of action. I guess this is the way it needs to be for now.

When I get home, I start registering the rental house on various home buying and selling sites using the pictures I had prior to this renter. I know the house still needs repair, but maybe I can luck into someone needing to move in quickly.

While searching the internet for a local handyman, my cell dings indicating a new message. I hope that Greg is checking up on me, but instead I look at a picture of me on my laptop. I am wearing the same clothes and realize someone has taken a picture of me through my front window. The number is unknown.

Fear takes hold. This isn't funny. I cautiously move to the window and close the partially open blind, then look through. I can't see anything. The lights in the parking lot are on but I don't see anything or anyone. My cell dings again. I am afraid to walk to my cell which sits next to my laptop. The entire scenario feels like a set up.

Screw this. I open the door, stand on my front stoop and give the finger to the night. I still see nothing of concern but my brazen gesture makes me feel strong and, strangely, safe.

I go back inside and lock the door. Slowly I move to my cell which continues to ding. Ten pictures of all my movements. That feeling of strength subsides and is replaced by my inner scared child. Tears come to the surface. Who would do this? Why would someone do this?

Chapter 5

Work. I'm going to concentrate on work. I am scheduled to work from ten to six for the next two days. I make sure I am on time today. I clock in and start bagging groceries right away. Put in large items, fill the middle, separate the cold items, meats, fresh items, and fragile items. I take pride in my work.

Rob approaches me. What now? I'm on it today. "Ella, do you want to move into a checker position?"

"No way. I like the exercise I get moving all day. If I become a checker, I'd have to stand in one spot." I have turned down the two dollar an hour promotion three times already. I could use the money, but I would hate it. I think I'm officially the oldest bagger on the line.

Rob shakes his head. "You will never grow up, will you?"

"I hope not. Certainly not by your definition of growing up." Prick.

"Take lunch."

I'm hungry so I head over to the deli. They have a chicken and fries employee special for four dollars. Extra dollar for a Coke. Cheaper than McDonalds, though no healthier.

The patrons in this place are interesting. One toddler is throwing a fit after demanding a well-placed toy at the front of the store. While this technique to increase impulse buying is brilliant, I feel bad for the frustrated mom. I secretly urge her to hold out. The man going around her is in a hurry. His facial expression is priceless, but again I feel bad for the mom, always judged.

Bored watching passer-byes, I look out the window and notice the serial murder van from the other night. Abandoning my food, I run to the front of the store with my cell. I'm going to take a picture of the license plate. If these are the douche bags that have been stalking me, I plan to turn the tables. I take a quick picture as they are turning out of the lot. Fishy. They never stopped, just drove through the lot.

"What's that about?" I hear Greg's voice behind me.

Happy for the company, I explain about the pictures texted to me last night and my new found paranoia which has me taking pictures of my own. When we return to the deli, my overly efficient co-workers have already cleared my lunch while cleaning the table. Oh well, so much for lunch. At least I had a few bites.

"Wish I was off tonight to keep you company, but I just got called in. Figured I could use the hours. If you'd like I can come over after I get off, around ten?" Greg wiggles his eyebrows suggestively.

Part of me, that special part, wants to accept the offer, but I have those walls to think about. Being a strong, independent woman is important. I don't need a prince charming. I don't need anyone. "No, I have plans."

"Really. With?" His attitude immediately changes.

Ugh, I didn't consider he would think I had a Friday night date. "I have to work on the house."

"Alone. That is not a good idea."

"Don't underestimate me. I don't need your permission."

"All right. I have to clock in." Greg walks off clearly frustrated.

34

What right does he have to be upset? I have been on my own for a year now. I don't need him or anyone else. I finish my shift and avoid Greg's checkout aisle.

I head home for a quick shower. My pride is diminished slightly and my trepidation over going to the house alone is increasing. I decide to call Tiffany to come with me. Tiffany doesn't answer, not my call or text. I listen to a few messages on my cell from interested renters. I will have to call them and arrange to show the house, but not before giving it a once over. I'm off on Sunday.

I call the interested parties and arrange to show the house between one and three to three different callers. Two callers ask the wrong questions, "Why would my credit score matter?" and "I have a bull mastiff, is that okay?" Everyone has to do the credit screening and no large aggressive breeds. I've done my homework. I don't want another hoodlum renting the house. Been there, done that.

I decide the best course of action as an independent woman is to buy a gun. I head to the local gun shop. They require an online background check and to be eighteen years of age. After about an hour of paperwork, I am the proud owner of a Springfield XDS. I like that it is unobtrusive for open carry and the small size suits me. The cost is just over $500 with another ten dollars for a box of ammunition and $50 for a holster.

I am officially broke. Between fixing up the house and this new purchase I will be eating ramen noodles for the rest of the month. Good thing I love ramen.

I don't have my open carry license, but I don't actually expect to use the gun. Just have it with me in my house, my rental house. My father taught me to shoot when I was younger. We would go hunting. I am a pretty good shot. I remember the basics, but the class is probably still needed.

My cell goes off. "Hey, Tiff. Where are you?"

"Bob and I just got out of the theater. Watched *Guarding Amy*. It was really funny."

"Oh, are you guys on a date night?"

"Yeah, first in a while. We are headed to dinner if you want to join us?"

"No, have fun. I was just looking for company. I'm good. I have a lot of reading I need to finish before Tuesday anyway."

"Love you." Tiff is always inviting me out with her and Bob. Sometimes I impose, but I can tell that Bob gets annoyed. I have things to take care of anyway.

I hold my hand over my new purchase and protector. Pulling up to the house, my chest feels tight. I have to get this anxiety under control. I can see the neighbors are home, so I visit each side neighbor to let them know I am having some trouble and will be in the house alone. They are nice, but don't appear to take my concern seriously. I'm sure they just think I'm a scared kid. Oh well, onto working on the house.

The evening goes by quickly. I still have electricity, though the water has been turned off. Luckily the neighbors are okay with me using their outside faucet. Not convenient but it gets the job done. The house looks clean. The smell of marijuana is still there but not as strong. Nothing I can do about that other than adding air fresheners that only slightly mask the smell.

When I finally have time to sit in the bay window it is 10:30 pm. My back is aching so I do some stretches. While up, I open all the windows to air out the smell. A nice breeze runs through the house.

My mind wanders to old memories of sitting on the couch with my mom watching television. She smelled like flowers and always had a hot mug of tea. She would ask about boys. I would wish I had a boy to tell her about.

Now, I could tell her about Greg, about how stupid I am, and how incapable I am of acting on my feelings. I imagine her telling me to open my heart and follow my instincts. She would say I was too tough for my own good. She wasn't tough. She was kind and soft. My cell goes off. I jump back into reality. The neighbor is calling.

"Hey." I answer.

"Probably nothing, but a Jeep has been sitting in front of your house for at least ten minutes."

Surprised I think of Greg's Jeep. "Is it black?"

"Yes."

"Thanks, I'm guessing it is a friend of mine. Sorry to worry you."

"Don't be sorry. We will always look out for our Ella."

Tears threaten to come to my eyes. "Thanks. That means more than you know."

I head to the front window and peer out. Sure enough Greg is sitting there, but why would he be sitting there for ten minutes? I turn on the porch light and yell out, "You're scaring the neighbors."

Greg exits his Jeep and walks toward me. He looks tired, not like himself. "Hey."

"What are you doing?" I ask.

"You make everything so hard. I drove over here to surprise you then found myself remembering that I was specifically not invited."

Shit. I am not in the mood to feel bad. I have a lot going on. This isn't even about Greg. "Look, I need friends, but I have so much on my plate. I don't think I can be what you're looking for."

"Friends. Got it." Greg looks like I smacked him. Bullshit really.

"I'm headed home. I'm beat. I told you I wouldn't be up for anything."

Greg smiles, not the smile that makes me feel things, well, actually it makes me feel bad. "Okay, sorry. Good night." Greg walks back to his Jeep and leaves quickly. My heart sinks.

I go into the house to lock up when a feeling hits me. That feeling of not being alone.

A rustling noise outside the bay window where I had been sitting catches my attention. The neighbor's dog starts barking frantically. The hair on the back of my neck is standing up and I am hyper alert. I feel in my pocket securing my fingers around my new gun. Screw that. I pull out the gun and yell, "Show yourself! I have a gun!" Yelling only increases my fear and panic. My hand is shaking.

I hear hushed talking from the backyard. I move toward the kitchen grabbing my keys while in route. Slowly I walk backwards toward the front door. I decide that I will be safer in my car. I can't lock up the house as I would have to go closer to my intruders in my backyard.

At the front door I can see a shadow standing outside the back door. The shape stares at me. I yell out, "Open that door and I will shoot you!" The shadow bolts left then disappears.

I fling open the front door and run to my car. Highly alert and scanning my surroundings I clumsily open the car door, get in, and quickly lock the door. I turn on the car and spin out of the driveway. As I make the turn off my street, I see it. The white serial murderer van is pulling out from the street before mine. My heart is racing so fast I fear it will explode. Shit, something is very wrong.

I call 911. "Operator, what is your emergency?"

In a haphazard manner I quickly spew, "I'm being followed and they were outside my house. I need the police right away."

After taking my address, the operator recommends that I stay in my car until officers arrive.

The patrol vehicle drives up after I had been waiting in my car for nearly an hour. My neighbors hear the patrol car and stand on their front lawns. I am embarrassed. I am making trouble. The female officer is dismissive when I start to give my play-by-play of events. She condescendingly asks, "Why are you working alone at night? Why are the windows open? "

I defend myself, "I need to get my house ready to rent. There is a smell in the house. I was trying to air the place out." With each defensive statement I get more frustrated. I try to explain all that has been happening. "I am being stalked by a white serial murderer van." I show the officer the picture I took of the van in the Taylors Grocery parking lot. "This same one was here tonight. I am not positive, but I think this same van was at my work the other night when four men tried to pull me into a van that looked just like this." I go on, "Then my neighbor, Mr. Ed, saw several men watching my apartment. Later that night, someone tried to open my apartment door in the middle of the night. My neighbor chased them off after I banged on his wall." The officer is writing down my statement but shows no real interest. "Here. Someone sent me these pictures. I am being stalked."

The officer does not soften toward me. She finishes taking notes and gives me her email address to send the pictures. She then advises, "Don't work alone in the house anymore." Feeling like a scolded child, I don't mention my gun that I hid in the locked glove compartment of my car. The officer walks the property, while I lock up the house.

I am finally walking to the car to head home when Rene my old neighbor walks towards me. The officer drives off. Dread overwhelms me. I feel like my dad is coming to scold me. When he reaches me, he holds out his arms and says quietly, "Oh sweetie."

I crumple into his arms and weep. Realizing that no one has held me since my parents died, I cling to him, keep my eyes closed, and imagine my dad hugging me, calming me, reassuring me, protecting me.

When I finally convince myself to reenter reality, I pull back. "I am so sorry. I don't know what overcame me. I don't mean to make trouble."

Realizing I have built my walls back up, Rene steps back and simply says, "You're not making trouble. We are here for you. Do you want to spend the night?"

"No, I have my apartment. I'm going home. I have to work in the morning." I leave as quickly as I can.

Getting home, I scan the parking lot, put my new gun in my holster, and walk brusquely to my apartment. No sign of trouble. Once inside, I lock the doors and go room to room making sure I am alone. This process only increases my fear. Once I have the house secure, I fall onto my bed and sleep, hard. I awake to my alarm going off. Everything is as it should be.

Chapter 6

I arrive at work on time. Rob smiles when I clock in. Greg is already working. I want badly to bag at his station, but I just can't. I keep busy. On my break, Dean, aka Mr. Ego, sits with me. "Why are you always so mean to me?"

Really. Maybe because you are absolutely in love with yourself. While I let this thought run rampant in my head, I actually reply, "I'm not mean to you."

"So why don't we hang out sometime after work?" I am flattered until Greg walks in. Then I realize Dean is sitting very close to me. Greg notices immediately. I can tell he is angry. So can Dean. Dean leans closer, wrapping an arm around me, "So tonight?"

Greg opens his locker, takes something out, shuts his locker and walks away without any comment. My heart falls. I shrug Dean off. "No! My break is over." I walk out in a huff.

Greg works for another two hours and leaves. He never looks at me again the remainder of his shift.

At the end of my shift I clock out and walk to my car. Greg is sitting on my car. I vacillate between feelings of giddiness and fear of rejection. He cares. He wouldn't be sitting on my car if he didn't care. I approach with trepidation. Greg stands as I approach. I speed up, walk straight up to him, wrap my arms around his neck, and kiss him.

Greg responds. Oh, how he responds. My brain swirls. Emotions I have never felt overwhelm my senses. I never want to stop. So much time passes. We just continue to kiss until the need dissipates. When I finally withdraw, Greg catches me and pulls me close. We fit. Our bodies fit together like a puzzle. A warm, cozy, puzzle… if a puzzle could be warm and cozy. I laugh at my silly thought.

Greg smiles that sexy smile, "Not this time. I'm holding on."

Eventually we make our way to my apartment. We talk for hours about everything and nothing. Time moves slowly when I am with Greg. We sit entwined on my bed with classic rock playing in the background. I can remember no time in my life where I felt this happy, content, safe… in love?

When I tell Greg about the van and the events after he left last night, Greg insists on spending the night. "How do you feel about me sleeping over tonight?"

I respond with a smile and a kiss. I have no complaints. The idea that he would leave me is inconceivable. We are both off tomorrow. I only have to show the house tomorrow afternoon. We spend the evening talking, kissing, holding, and watching romantic movies.

As it gets later, I realize I need to change into something more comfortable. For the most part, I don't have anything cute to wear to bed. My negligée collection is mostly tank tops. I get up from the bed and choose my cutest tank top and soft shorts. When I return from the bathroom after changing, I comment to Greg, "So are you wearing that to bed?"

"Umm." Greg blushes. Damn he is sexy. He pulls off his jeans and t-shirt. He stands there wearing only his bikini briefs. I can see his excitement.

Watching Greg watch me is the sexiest moment of my life. Part of me wants to rip off my clothes, but the other part is more pragmatic. Instead we gently lay beside each other on the bed. Greg kisses me. His hand is on my thigh. He moves his hands under my panties rubbing and squeezing my bare buttock. My breasts rise with excitement. In response, Greg thrusts his body up against mine. We don't sleep. Every move, every touch only serves to rouse us. The night lasts forever. Touching, kissing, teasing. Desire keeping us both awake, alert, excited.

In the morning, I feel as though I have slept hard. Unexpectedly, I am rested, happy, and still in Greg's arms. Strong, virile arms. "Good morning," he says.

I give him a sweet peck on his cheek and squirm to remove myself from his embrace. I desperately want to brush my teeth.

After freshening up, I return to bed to plan for today.

Greg offers, "Why don't we just stay in bed and see where that takes us."

I redirect him, "How about making breakfast and taking a walk on the Bayfront before going to show the rental house."

Greg agrees to be in charge of breakfast. That is until he looks through my kitchen. "Not much to work with here."

I agree. Typically, I either skip breakfast or grab a taco. "Maybe we should go out for breakfast?"

Greg has other ideas, "Why don't we jump in the shower?"

This time I blush. "Why don't I jump in the shower, first?" Greg pretends to frown, but his smile still peaks through.

Greg pulls me to him, pressing a hard kiss onto my lips. "Let me know if you reconsider."

I do. I reconsider. I want him. I so want him, but then I run to the bathroom and shut the door. I'm such a chicken. I emerge from the restroom wearing my towel. I have a full face of make-up and straight ironed hair. I even sprayed my Sweet Pea Body Spray lightly all over. I am in the mood to look and feel beautiful.

Greg stares with a wild smile unable to hide his excitement as he is still in his briefs. He has a heavy five o'clock shadow. His features are sharp and his deep hazel eyes are looking more green then blue today. Even his hair looks a deeper shade of auburn.

He approaches and places his hands under my towel. I hold the towel tightly in place while he explores my body with his hands, starting with my thighs, then buttocks, and then gently touching my pubic hair. His hands rise across my belly cupping my breasts, then gently squeezing my nipple. His lips part.

I rise to my tippy toes and meet his lips with my tongue. I am still clutching my towel. My last figurative wall. Greg has torn down most of my walls, but this towel remains in my control.

"Your turn." I whisper as I pull away nodding toward the shower.

Greg remains erect. "You know you're killing me, right?" to which I smile and head toward my closet.

When Greg comes out, I am dressed in a short flowy summer dress that shows off my legs. Greg almost approves, "Looking that good is not helping me."

I laugh. "Looks like we have to stop by your place if you want fresh clothes."

"You mean my parents' house. I really need my own place."

I suggest, "Maybe you should keep a few things here. With all that is going on, I like having a house guest."

We stop by Greg's parents' house. "Coming in?" Greg asks as he gets out of the car.

"I need to check my email." Greg is disappointed, but I do not have it in me to meet the parents. I see Greg's mother looking out the front curtain. Not wanting to engage, I pull out my cell and busy myself online.

Greg returns relatively quickly with a small duffle bag. "My mom wants to meet you."

"Not today. It is too soon." My anxiety is rising. I feel the need to bolt.

"Calm down, Bambi."

"What does that mean?"

"Look, I don't care if you meet my mom today, tomorrow, or ever. Well, someday would be nice. She asked that I ask. I don't want you leaping off and away. Yesterday you changed my life. You became part of my life. Don't push me away."

Greg has this way of coaxing me off the cliff. "...became part of your life?" I smile.

"Yeah, stupid."

I uncontrollably laugh. The perfect answer. I can't help but lean over and kiss him. He is a good kisser.

When Greg returns I mention, "I think we missed breakfast. How about lunch?"

Before Greg answers, my cell goes off. I look at the caller ID. Detective Haas from the Corpus Christi Police Department is calling. I answer, "Hello."

Detective Haas curtly asks, "Can you come by my office after lunch today?"

"Sure." I respond. I hadn't realized the police station was even open on Sundays.

Greg and I decide to stop at Boat and Net for a quick lunch.

"I love the French fries with tartar sauce. I can't believe I haven't ever tried this. Good choice for lunch," Greg compliments.

We eat in the parking lot. While not fancy, just being together is nice. Several alley cats circle the car. We are more than happy to share our inexpensive lunch.

At the station, we are brought into Detective Haas's cubicle. The suffocating 3X5 space is filled with old furniture. There is no real personalization. Detective Haas has only one picture frame with a homely woman sitting at a table. I am saddened that he doesn't even display an attractive picture of the woman I assume to be his wife.

Detective Haas doesn't mince words. "We will be returning the watches you turned in. They have not been reported stolen or missing. We have them in the database, but you need to understand they are valued at over $300,000. Somebody is missing these and not reporting the loss." After a pause, he continues, "Big John has a long criminal history and connections to the Syndicate. We have an active, ongoing case based on the drugs found in the shop at The Swap Center. I pulled your file."

47

"I have a file."

"Yes, as a victim. You have made several reports in the last few weeks. I am concerned whoever left these watches could return or may already have been making contact with you. We looked up the license plate on the white van you took a picture of and it does not belong to the van. It is a stolen plate. A dead end. We have an APB out for the van, but we don't expect a hit."

"What does this mean for me?"

"CCPD does not have a reason to put you on protective status. I see you purchased a gun yesterday?"

Greg sits up, "What?"

"I've always had shooting as a hobby. Is there a crime against me having a gun?"

Detective Haas answers, "No ma'am, but if you don't have an open carry license then it should not be on your person."

I left the gun in a drawer in my room. I feel safe with Greg. "Are you accusing me of having the gun on my person?"

"No ma'am. You made it through the metal detector and you don't seem to be a complete idiot. I would have been surprised if you had brought it into the station. Just giving you the facts as I understand them. I am concerned you are mixed up in something."

"I am concerned I'm mixed up in something. I have been followed. Someone tried to get in my apartment, and someone stalked me at my rental house. Knowing that something is wrong doesn't help me. Tell me something that will help me."

"Look, here is my card. You can call me if anything else happens. The district attorney's office is bringing charges and intends to call you for an interview. Keep your head straight and be careful." Detective Haas then looks sternly at Greg. "You her boyfriend."

"Um, I'm trying." How Greg could make me smile in this moment flusters me.

"Keep an eye on her. Watch out for yourself as well. These guys are violent and not afraid of the law."

"Thanks." I say sarcastically. "Is that all? Now that I am aware that I am a victim, violent fearless men are out to get me, and the police have no reason to protect me, can I go?"

Detective Haas apologizes and allows us to leave.

Chapter 7

When we arrive at the Jeep, I vent to myself under my breath. "This is such bullshit. I don't have the time or the energy for any of this. I have to get to the rental house for the showing." Greg listens without comment. I then turn my attentions to Greg, "I don't need or expect you to protect me. Got it?"

"Geez, you make everything difficult."

"I told you I was difficult on the front end." We drive silently. When we pull up to the rental house I soften, "I want you here. Not to protect me. Just to be here."

Greg responds with a simple smile and holds my hand tightly. His response calms me.

Heat assaults us as we enter the rental. The electricity has been turned off. Greg and I open the windows resulting in a slight improvement. A hot breeze blows through the house. I spray some air freshener. The house smells of a warm meadow, or at least that is what I hope my potential renters will think. With the windows opened and air freshener, the house smells okay.

Greg takes this time to follow up with a handyman his dad recommended. "Hi, this is Greg. I was told you would have a bid for me today."

I walk around the house tidying up. When I return Greg tells me the estimated bid which sounds very reasonable. I am feeling good about the house being ready. I sit as Greg calls the handyman back and arranges for the repairs to be completed next week.

My first prospective tenants are a young couple with two kids. After a brief look around and very few questions they leave. I mention to Greg, "I can't imagine they will be back."

An hour later, a husky bald man with a tattoo on his scalp shows up. He aggressively stares at Greg as he enters. Without asking, Greg protectively takes over the showing. "Hi, how are you today?" With everything else, I calm my inner feminist and allow Greg to show the property.

The man ignores Greg's outstretched hand. Instead of shaking hands he gives a nod of his head in Greg's general direction in acknowledgement as he proceeds to walk around the house. When he returns, the man walks directly to me. "So how much is rent?"

I review rent and the required background and credit check. I am brief, hoping to discourage his interest. The man is obviously annoyed but states he will call later as he leaves.

"Let's hope we don't see or hear from him again." I comment.

Greg agrees.

The final woman is a well-dressed older woman of slim build. She is easy to talk to and explains, "I am trying to find a place for my newly married son's family. I have a new grandbaby. I can't wait to spend time babysitting. They are moving home from San Antonio. I am very excited about having them home again."

I like her very much. She reminds me of my mom. She has no concerns with the background or credit check.

"My son is a district manager for an oil products distributor. I love the house. I live only a few blocks away. I'll have my son, Joe Magnum, call you to settle things."

Greg is more excited than me when we lock up and head to the car. "I think the last one was perfect. You?"

"Don't count my chickens before they hatch. She seems great but it could take a while. It would be nice to have someone move in quickly and start paying rent."

"How are you doing on money?" Greg asks.

"Okay, I have savings. I also have the last tenant's deposit. Asshole won't be getting that back."

"Dinner is on me. Where should we go?"

My cell dings. There is a text from Detective Haas. "Pick up watches at station between 9 and 5 any time after next Tuesday. You will need your ID."

Greg reconsiders, "I don't know with $300,000 maybe you should pay for dinner."

"I don't think so. Your offer stands." Just then my cell dings again. I look down to see a picture of Greg and me in the Taylors Grocery parking lot kissing. Ten more pictures follow.

Greg looks distressed. "I am starting to understand why you bought a gun. By the way, we need to talk about that."

For the moment I ignore Greg. I don't plan to explain myself to him on the subject.

We decide to stay in for dinner and invite Tiffany and Bob to join us. Greg cooks. Steak, garlic potatoes, and Brussel sprouts. The man can cook. So much better than the microwave mac and cheese to which I have become accustomed. My mother had been an amazing cook. I guess it skips a generation.

We play Spades while I bring Tiffany up to speed.

"You should have told me you were going to the house alone when you called me. I could have come." Tiffany is upset that I did not mention my plan to work alone when I called her the other night.

"Tiff, I know you would have been there for me, but I didn't want to intrude on your date night. Plus, I have not had time to think anything through. Everything is just happening so quickly."

Tiffany's mood elevates after beating us in both of the next two rounds. "Well, I doubt you guys want us to beat you again. I think it is time to call it a night." Tiff gives me a hug and whispers in my ear, "I like Greg. I'm glad to see he is staying with you. You will need to fill me in on the details later."

I leave her to imagine details that don't yet exist. After a few minutes of snuggling and making out, Greg and I both fall asleep. My sleep is restless and the night is long.

In the morning, Greg goes into work before I fully wake up. He encourages me to sleep in and tries to make as little noise as possible while getting ready. I appreciate the effort. I spend the next few hours having a lazy morning in bed.

ೲೲೲೲ

When I clock in, Rob asks that I come into the office. This is new. I assume I have been late for the last time, but today I was on time. Rob asks me to sit. "Greg mentioned you are being stalked."

Oh no he didn't. I am furious. This is my personal information. "I am having an issue, but you don't need to worry."

"I've discussed this with the store manager. We would like to offer you the open position in GM, General

53

Merchandise. Terry would be your new manager. You would not be stuck in checkout. Your job would be organizing shelves, returning product, and keeping the GM department looking good. The position includes a two-dollar raise."

As mad as I am at Greg for interfering, I had not thought moving to another department was an option. I have been starting to feel uncomfortable in the parking lot, especially with the van coming around. "Okay."

"Alright. You are starting today. We already have your shift on the front end covered."

I get up to walk out. Then stop, turning to look at *Rob the Jerk*, "Thanks. I don't think I say that enough. Really, thanks." Maybe I have to change Rob's nickname.

My shift goes by quickly. GM is awesome. I miss all the people in the front end of the store, especially Greg. In my head, I run through a conversation I intend to have with Greg about boundaries. I am not his problem to solve. That said, this worked out pretty well.

When I get to my car, Greg is sitting on the hood. While still feeling annoyed, I am pleased to see him there. "Nothing better to do." I joke.

"I can think of a few more fun things to do. You being one of them." Greg returns wagging an eyebrow suggestively.

I roll my eyes. "Coming to my place?"

"That is the plan."

"We are going to need to talk about the plan. While I like GM, you should have brought the idea to me. Going to Rob was not okay."

"Sorry."

I accept his apology for the moment. We both recognize that this subject is not closed based on my facial expression. I head straight home and wait on the front stoop for Greg.

Greg makes a pit stop to grab a pizza and Coke. When Greg arrives, he joins me on the front stoop. We eat straight from the box and chug straight from the 2-liter Coke bottle. With dirty hands and burping bellies, we laugh heartily at this little aside from decorum. Behaving badly is a freedom. This is the best pizza I've ever eaten, or maybe that is just what it feels like in the moment.

I tell Greg about how when I was a child my family would have carpet pizza night. "Dad would bring home a pizza and we would sit on the carpet in front of the television watching *Big Bang Theory*. I loved watching *Big Bang Theory* with my parents. Sheldon was my dad's favorite. Sometimes I thought he was a little like Sheldon."

I privately consider how I have not felt that comfort of family for some time, but sitting here with Greg reminds me of family time. I feel more like myself then I've felt since my parents died.

Greg reminisces about how his mother would cook amazing big meals when he was a kid. "Now she makes chicken or burgers with fries or I fend for myself. I guess it is different now that I am not always home."

"I'll cook for you some time." I say.

"Looking forward to it." Greg responds.

"Don't look too forward to it. In all truth I am a horrible cook. I've tried to recreate the television idea of cooking with ambience and fresh foods, but in the end, I don't enjoy cooking. Usually I wish I had just picked up a burger."

"Maybe it's an issue of the company. I'm great company." Greg grins.

He is great company, I think. With everything that has been going on, Greg makes me feel happy, peaceful, and safe.

We make our way inside and I check my email. I have two completed background and credit checks to review from Experian along with two rental applications.

I figure that is pretty good for three showings. The first is the man with the tattoo on his head. His report shows that he has one arrest for disorderly conduct and a low credit score. The second is the older woman's son, Joe Magnum, whom I'd hoped would send an application. His credit is adequate and no concerns on the background check. The application shows that he works for a business serving the refinery. He has references.

I call Joe immediately. "Hi, this is Ella Fontana. I was able to review your application for the rental house on Blue Jay."

"Hi Ella. Nice to hear back from you. Did I pass inspection? My mom really liked the house. My best friend's parents live around the corner, so I spent most of my childhood in that neighborhood."

"Everything looks great from this end. Rent is $1600 a month with a $1600 deposit and non-refundable pet deposit of $500. Do you have any pets?"

"Yes, a standard poodle. Rent sounds reasonable. Lease is for one year, I'm guessing?"

"Lease is a minimum of one year. You can choose multiple years to lock in the rate or go month to month at the end of the lease."

"I need to move by the end of the month. We hope to build a new home eventually. A one-year lease sounds perfect. Mom said there were still a few repairs pending?" Joe sounds a little hesitant.

"I have a repairman coming by this week. Everything should be ready by the end of the month. I know your mother was able to see the property. Are you wanting to see the property prior to signing the rental contract or should I email it to you?"

"We'll be down visiting my mother next weekend. We definitely want to see the property."

"Keep in mind I will still be showing the property as it is still on the market until the rental contract is signed, and I have first and last month's rent."

Joe is more eager, "Okay, I'll see what I can do to make it down sooner. I need to ensure we have a place. I start work on the first. I have a place up here until the end of next month but we are eager to get into a semi-permanent place in Corpus."

I feel excited, "Sounds great. I'm looking forward to meeting you and hope this works out for both of us." I am proud of my professionalism, considering all my knowledge comes from Google. Greg waits patiently while I finish the call.

When I hang up, my mood is lifted. I am ready for a steady stream of income again.

"I'm still hungry. How about I cook dinner?"

I head into the kitchen to see what is available. Sadly, there is very little to choose from. I find some rice, a can of mushroom soup, and some frozen chicken. My mother would make a casserole from this stuff when I was a kid.

I pick up my trusty cell, hit the google microphone and ask, "Chicken mushroom casserole." *Any Recipes* has a simple recipe with my ingredients. I don't have any paprika, but how much could that matter? I turn the oven to bake 375. I mixed in my ingredients and add some Nature Seasoning to replace the paprika. I place the dish in the oven and return to Greg.

Greg had been sitting watching me cook. When I return, he has a big smile on his face. "What?" I ask.

"You really don't know what you're doing in the kitchen, do you?"

"Shut up. Smell that delicious meal. You're going to eat your words, literally." I laugh.

I am looking forward to my successful meal. I playfully punch Greg in the arm. He thwarts me off with a block and wraps his arms around my waist pulling me to the couch. I don't know what it is about having his arms around my waist but it feels amazing.

Greg looks more serious. "Have you noticed anything else strange lately or gotten any strange texts?"

"No. But I've been with you or at work since we met with Detective Haas. I don't want my life turned upside down by whatever is happening." After a pause, I bring up the work issue, "I like having you around, but I also need to make my own decisions. It really wasn't cool you going to Rob." I start to pull away.

Greg gently holds on then releases as I persist in my push away from him. "I didn't think it through. The idea of you in the parking lot, at risk, was too much. Rob asked how you were doing and the conversation just sort of happened."

I hadn't thought about anyone at work going to Greg to see how I was doing. I feel somehow violated. Greg and I have only been hanging out for a short time. "You shouldn't be talking about me or my issues with people at work. We are still new. I'm not even sure how I feel about everything between us."

"It wasn't like that."

"You are not my father. I am on my own. I don't need the stress of wondering what you are saying about me."

"Hold on a minute. I'm not out there gossiping. I definitely don't want to be your parent, but I was under the impression that we were getting to be..." after a short pause he continued, "a couple."

"We're not a couple. We're not anything official. We're just..." I feel overwhelmed. I miss my walls. I want to run away. I guess my body language shows it, because Greg starts to get defensive too.

"This together not together thing isn't working for me. I want to be a couple. I like you so much. You don't feel the same?" Greg looks sad. It hurts me to think that I am hurting him. Greg attempts to put his arms around me, but once again I push away.

I need to feel strong, independent. Greg is pushing too fast. "I need time. I don't rush into things. Either that works for you or it doesn't." I sit waiting for his answer with my stubborn face on and arms crossed protectively across my chest. Part of me wants him to storm out and part of me knows that I will be heartbroken if he leaves.

Greg looks down, pulls out his cell and starts pushing buttons. Within a minute, Bruno Mars belts out criticisms of my inconsistent love from Greg's cell.

"You are so stupid." Greg looks so sexy as he sings along to Bruno Mars while ignoring me. I cannot help but let go of my anger and join in.

For the next 20 minutes, Greg plays song after song as I lay beside him on the couch. We are interrupted by the buzz of my oven. Dinner is ready.

I set out the table including candles. I turn down the lights. My tiny apartment looks cozy and warm. Just how my mother served dinner, I place the chicken and rice on the plates. Greg walks over, "Wow, this looks amazing."

We both take our first bite. Greg continues to chew with a slight frown on his face. I spit it out. "Okay, this is awful."

Greg quickly spits out the bite he is working on. "Thank God you called it. I wasn't sure I was going to make it."

"Ha-Ha. We can go get something?"

"I'm fine really. We had pizza after work. How about we just lie down and talk?" I assume Greg has more in mind with this *lie down and talk idea* but in all reality that sounds perfect.

Greg helps me clear the table. With a little sadness, I throw out my creation.

We settle in my bed with Pandora playing in the background. We hold each other and talk more about our lives. Greg's voice is deep, soft and rhythmic. He sounds like an audio recording reverberating throughout my room. While talking, Greg gently strokes my lower back as my t-shirt rides up. Greg starts, "I have a fairly traditional family. I'm the oldest of four.

My parents moved from the east coast when I was in middle school."

"That is a hard time to move," I say.

"I had a hard time. I didn't really make any friends. I felt like I didn't fit in here. I had wanted to return to the east coast. That was until I met you." I lay imagining young Greg. I wonder if we had met when he was in middle school if we would have been friends, but then again, I was never really friends with boys. Actually, I would have been a long skinny awkward elementary school kid when he was in middle school.

"Do you still want to move away?"

"No. I'm quite happy right now as long as you don't keep trying to break up with me." Greg kisses me gently.

Now is my turn. "My parents lived here their entire lives. They met in high school and married a few years later. They were happy together. They fought sometimes, mostly about my father's brother, Uncle Billy. Billy is a little rough around the edges. He isn't married, but he and my Aunt Donna have been together forever. I don't like her."

"They still live here?" Greg asks.

I continue, "Yes. Their kids, my three cousins, also live here. I was close to Anna when I was a kid. We are the same age and even look alike. She kind of moved toward the wrong crowd in high school."

I privately think about how Anna's choices make sense considering her family. Uncle Billy is nice sometimes, but he smells bad and chews tobacco. I was always grossed out when he would spit in cans and leave them around the house. He would try to hug me, but I never really felt comfortable with him. He worked on and off in the oil fields. He talks a big game about what a hot shot he is, but in truth he lives in a shanty house and constantly complains he does not have any money. I decide not to share these details with Greg.

Greg interrupts my thoughts, "I didn't realize you had family in town."

I grimace, "My Aunt Donna is just plain mean. She was always yelling about something and hardly ever smiled. I don't remember her ever really talking or interacting with me. Anna would sleep over with me all the time. I would visit her house with my parents, but they never let me spend the night. Craig and Jake, Anna's brothers, are a few years older than me. I still see them around. Both of them work the oil fields with their dad. Sometimes they have good income and sometimes they are bums. Both are very good looking and have lots of friends. In high school, all my girlfriends had crushes on them. For the most part, they have good personalities but, like Anna, the crowds they hang around with are a little rough for my taste."

"I can't wait to meet them," Greg says nervously.

"When Mom and Dad died, Uncle Billy and Aunt Donna offered to adopt me. They said they would handle the probate. They wanted to put the house in their name. I think the whole family planned on moving in with me. When I let them know I had other plans, they were really ugly. Uncle Billy actually called me a 'little bitch.' The funeral service was hard. No one was talking because I was such 'a spoiled, entitled brat'."

"That's awful. I can't even imagine." Greg looks bothered.

"My parents had a will, thank God. The probate took forever. I struggled while I waited for my parents' funds to be released. I felt very alone. Friends of my parents offered to help, but I really didn't know them. Plus, I think their offers were disingenuous and only served to make them feel better. When I told them I was fine, each and every one of the offers flew away in the wind. No one followed up with me, which is fine. I'm doing pretty well on my own. My parents raised me to be independent."

Greg waits without comment. I think he doesn't know how to respond, but he does seem interested.

"I was already working at Taylors. I stayed in the house for a few months, but it was too much for me. I couldn't keep up with the lawn, bills, and, more difficult, the memories. I miss my parents every day." I pause to regain my composure. "I had expected to go away to college. I had put a deposit down on a dorm in College Station. I remember my dad was really proud when I got my acceptance letter. Neither of my parents went to college. I will be the first college graduate in the family."

"Wow. Both my parents have bachelor degrees. Going to school was always just assumed for us. Your parents would be proud of how great you are doing. I'm totally impressed." Greg praises.

Hoping Greg is right I continue. "My dad worked on the military base for the Army Depot fixing helicopters. My mom worked all over. For a while she worked at the day-old bread store. That was great because she would bring home all sorts of treats. She also worked at Michael's making flower arrangements. They both worked hard and wanted me to finish school. When they passed, I didn't go to College Station like I planned. Instead I started at Del Mar. I wasn't derailed. I was just taking another path, a more comfortable path. I already had a job and knew the area. I guess I was scared to leave."

"You don't have any other family?" Greg asked.

"My mom's sisters live on the east coast. I never really knew them."

Greg holds me a little tighter, "I can't imagine being alone at 23, much less at 19. I still live with my parents. I can't imagine losing them, though getting my own place sounds good." Greg is sincere. I like that he doesn't say too much. Too many people say too much. We fall asleep while talking with the music playing in the background.

At midnight, I wake up with music still playing and the lights on. I get up to turn everything off. My mouth is dry. I head to the kitchen for some water. For no reason, I decide to look out the front window. Something seems off. Mr. Ed's front porch light is on. Mr. Ed never leaves his light on.

I open the door and peer out. I squint my eyes. Something is on the front stoop, or rather someone. I swing the door open and run to Mr. Ed. Mr. Ed is not conscious. He is bleeding on the top of his head. "Greg! Greg! Call 911! Oh my God. Oh my God, Mr. Ed."

Greg comes running out the front door in a panic. When he sees Mr. Ed, he turns quickly and heads back into the apartment. I look around but there is nothing to stop the bleeding. I start to stand to go get a rag but Greg emerges with his cell and a hand towel from my kitchen. "Hello, we have an emergency." Greg gives the address and details to the 911 operator.

My heart is racing. The ambulance is taking too long. Mr. Ed needs help now. I can't think of anything else to do to help him. By the time the ambulance arrives and brings the gurney up the stairs, I am livid. I step back to let them get to him on the shallow stoop.

The police arrive at the same time as the ambulance. I focus my anger on them. "What took so long?" I demand.

"Sorry, ma'am. We got here as quick as we could. Can you tell me what happened?"

I explain how I happened upon Mr. Ed and hadn't heard anything, very likely due to Pandora playing. Mr. Ed is taken to the hospital. He is still breathing, but he remains unconscious. The paramedics tell me which hospital they are transporting to and leave.

The officer walks through Mr. Ed's apartment. I hear him radio for the crime scene bus. By early morning, the place is abandoned. I call the hospital and am told that without a patient number the hospital cannot confirm or deny a patient.

Greg sits beside me. My life is a bad omen. Mr. Ed is my friend. He is like family. I don't even know his full name. My brain keeps assigning personal blame. Why wasn't I there for him like he'd been there for me? Is it my fault that Mr. Ed got assaulted? Was it the goons that came to my apartment the other night? Guilt overwhelms me and I sob. Negative feelings swell into my thoughts. I miss my parents. Greg helps me back inside.

Chapter 8

The next week passes in a blur. Each day I call the hospital getting the same non-answer. Without a client number they cannot confirm or deny if Mr. Ed was even brought to the hospital. I am frustrated and scared. Has Mr. Ed regained consciousness or is he lying in a hospital bed unable to connect with the outside world? My thoughts are driving me crazy. I have called Detective Haas several times but he doesn't answer and has not returned my call. I can't think of anything else to do. I feel useless.

Robotically, I just keep going with my day to day schedule trying my best to not think. The days pass without incident or any new knowledge about Mr. Ed. In all my distress, Greg has become part of my landscape. We still have not made anything official, but we have an unspoken understanding. Greg has enough clothes at my house that I give him a drawer, a bottom drawer.

Giving up on understanding what happened with Mr. Ed, I have to get on with my responsibilities. I dress and head into work. Greg went in to work several hours earlier.

Sunday noon is the time all the area drunks come in to buy beer. Texas has a law about not buying alcohol before noon on Sunday. I guess that isn't an issue for separation of church and state. Early Sunday afternoon is always a mix of people from those needing a beer run to those grabbing the basics to head to the beach.

My cousins, Craig and Jake, walk in to buy beer and subs to take out fishing. Apparently, today is going to be a great day for fishing due to the calm waters and cooler temperature. The weather has dropped 15 degrees. Corpus Christi is usually quite hot and windy, but today is a perfect 80 degrees without a strong wind which is rare.

Craig puts a hand up in acknowledgement, "What's up, cousin?"

"Hi guys. Headed out fishing?"

"It's a sin not to fish on a day like today. I heard you had a commotion in your complex Monday night." Jake comments. Carla walks by giving Jake a smile. "She's cute." Jake nods toward Carla.

"I'm sure she's interested. She is interested in just about everyone. What did you hear about Monday night?"

"The news said an older man had a home invasion in your apartment complex. They said he is in critical condition."

"Yeah, my neighbor, Mr. Ed. I found him our front stoop. It was horrible." I shake my head trying not to visualize.

Jake goes on, "Dad says you have no business living there by yourself. He says you are some special kind of dumbass." Craig and Jake laugh heartily at my expense.

"Thanks. Have fun fishing. I have to get back to work." I nod and busy myself straightening shelves. Assholes. I am appreciative that the work in GM is slow and dull. The downtime gives me plenty of time to get lost in my thoughts and not have to interact with anyone. Occasionally, I get a question from a customer about where to find a product which is a nice distraction from the monotony.

Lunch comes late afternoon. I decide to run over to the Sandwich Shop. I am really hungry. On my way out the door, I am abruptly stopped by the man with the tattoo on his head that looked at the rental house. "Hey, aren't you the girl from the house. I haven't heard back from you."

"Yes, sorry. We had several applicants. I have a deposit from another of the candidates. It looks like the property is no longer available."

"It would have been nice to get a call before I put in my $15 for the background check." As he walks off, I hear him sneer, "Stupid little bitch."

I think to myself, today has been a day abundantly full of assholes. I continue over to the Sandwich Shop. While waiting for my order, my cell goes off. Detective Haas is calling. I eagerly answer, "Detective Haas?"

"Is this Ella Fontana?" the Detective asks.

"Yes, thank you for returning my call. Did you hear about my neighbor?"

"Sorry it has taken me so long to get back with you. The assigned investigator is treating the case as a home invasion. It appears someone tried to force their way into his apartment. He was injured during a struggle. The investigating officer believes that the assailant or assailants fled after hitting him. We are searching the camera footage from the front of the complex. I've asked them to go back to the incidents you previously reported. I don't have any further information at this time."

"I tried to call the hospital but they wouldn't give me any information. Do you know how Mr. Ed is doing?"

"I really can't talk about anything else, except the official release that he is in critical condition." The phrase *official release* takes me aback.

"Is there something you are not telling me?"

"Ella, I've already told you I have concerns in this case. Nothing official, but as an officer my experience has taught me to follow my instincts and recognize patterns. You be careful. By the way, you need to pick up the watches soon."

Acknowledging this necessary errand, I hang up the cell. I eat lunch and head back to Taylors. On my way in I run into Greg who is just getting off his shift. "Ella, my mom is throwing a fit that she hasn't seen me in days. I'm going to dinner at home tonight. Do you want to join us?"

"No, with everything that is going on I'm just not up for a meet-the-parents dinner." Greg looks disappointed.

"I don't like the idea of leaving you alone." Greg says protectively.

The feminist in me shoots back, "I don't need you or anyone else to babysit me. I can take care of myself."

"Ella, none of us is an island. Look at Mr. Ed. He knew how to take care of himself and he still got hurt."

I do not appreciate the scare tactic. I know full well what happened to Mr. Ed. "I have a gun. I know not to open the door to strangers. I'll be fine." I dismissively walk away so I can clock back in. Greg appears to consider a rebuttal but walks off instead. A feeling of dread washes over me. I deserve to be alone. The rest of the afternoon goes by very slowly.

Walking to my car I am hyper alert. Every car, every person looks suspicious. I am actually appreciative that my job is no longer clearing the parking lot of baskets. I hold my keys between my fingers. At the Women's Night Out event at the university, the presenter had suggested holding keys in this formation as a weapon. I hurriedly unlock my car and sit inside only to quickly lock the car. Realizing that the world is not a safe place is petrifying. I long for the days when I believed that the world was friendly.

When I pull up to my apartment, I feel a new feeling of dread and apprehension. I use to feel a sense of safety with Mr. Ed next door. I miss feeling safe. I hope Mr. Ed is okay. I fear that his pain is my fault. *Please be okay*. I say a silent prayer.

The walk to my apartment feels ominous. Tonight, I am very aware of the parking lot. I pay attention to the dark area under the stairs, and the cars that seem unfamiliar. Thinking of the cameras at the front of the complex gives me some sense of safety, but then I think of all the uselessly blurry video footage shown during the nightly news. I make it inside and lock the doors up tight only to feel insecure. I pull out my gun, which only serves to further heighten my anxiety. I walk through the apartment turning on every light, checking behind every door, and any area where a person could hide.

The apartment is secure. I put my gun on my nightstand, but still feel unsafe. I hate this feeling. *I am a strong woman*; I tell myself while feeling like an insecure child. Looking through the closet, I notice a box of old photographs. To busy myself, I decide to pull the box out. I turn on the television for background noise. *The Voice* is on. Adam Levine and Blake Shelton have great banter.

I rifle through pictures that bring back all sorts of memories. My mother and father look so in love with each other and me. My dad and Uncle Billy laughing while my cousins and I climbed all over the old cannons in front of the USS Lexington, an aircraft carrier on North Beach. That was a good day. I remember we had taken my grandparents who had visited from the east coast to Padre Island and then to North

Beach. Even though we live here, that day we were local tourists. My cousin, Anna, and I were wearing the same outfit in two different colors. We loved looking like twins.

I giggle at the pictures of my 10th birthday sleepover. We had a water balloon fight. Anna and Tiff were there with some other childhood friends. My parents did not especially like Tiffany. Little did they know that she would be the only person who feels like family now that they are gone from this earth.

The next batch of photos is from when my parents were young. Here is one with my dad and uncle with a group of guys from what looks like high school. I recognize one of the guys from the funeral. I had seen him around as a kid. He was a close friend of my father, but, weird, next to him is my prospective tenant with the tattoo on his head.

I am unnerved. I cannot tell if he is in the group or if he is just randomly standing off to the side. Detective Haas's comment about following your instincts and recognizing patterns reverberates in my head. Did this man know my father? Does he know my uncle?

Chapter 9

I consider going to sleep early when Greg texts. "Can I come over?"

Ten minutes later, Greg arrives with leftover chicken and mashed potatoes. "My mom sent this for you." I hadn't even realized that I was starving. The food is nothing special but certainly better than my attempts at homemade dinner.

"Is this why you went home? To eat edible food?"

Greg sarcastically responds, "Doesn't hurt. Actually, I would have preferred skipping dinner and being with you."

"Luckily, you didn't have to choose. Plus, skipping dinner is not such a good idea."

Greg leans over and gives me a kiss. "My mom isn't sure if she approves of me sleeping over."

I give him a condescending look, "You are 23 years old."

"I think she just has never seen me be this into someone."

I crawl across Greg's lap straddling him. Greg's smile covers his face. I kiss his neck, and then tug gently on his ear lobe with my teeth. Greg puts his hands gently on each side of my face drawing me in for a deep sexy kiss. His hands slip to the back of my neck and wraps into my hair. My body responds to his touch. Greg's hands slide down my back gently to the top of my shorts which he easily slides down exposing my bare buttocks. His hands are soft and warm.

I long for his caress all over. I reach down and pull my shirt over my head. In an unskilled manner, Greg unhooks my bra. Greg tosses the unwanted undergarment across the room.

My body tenses and my breasts rise. Greg takes my nipple between his teeth, gently sucking and biting. The sensation runs straight to my precious parts.

For the first time in my life, I am ready. I rotate my waist to rub across Greg's hard penis beneath his jeans. I reach down and unbutton Greg's jeans. I have never seen an exposed penis before this moment. I reach my hands inside his jeans and feel his erection. I reach further and graze my fingers across his scrotum. Greg's eyes roll into the back of his head.

"Let me get some protection." Greg returns ready. We move to the bedroom where I sit on the side of the bed. Greg leans forward so that I lay back. He removes my shorts which had lain slack on my thighs. As I lay naked beneath him, Greg removes his remaining clothing. He returns kissing my inner thigh. I feel myself becoming wet and a tightness in my groin. Greg takes his fingers and gently messages my tender parts until finally entering me. Initially there is some discomfort but after a few thrusts our bodies move together in sync.

The whole experience is brief but intense. I feel happy. Afterwards Greg holds me. "I guess I am no longer a virgin." I giggle.

"Ditto." Greg's cheeks redden slightly with this exposure. I had assumed Greg knew what he was doing. The thought that we shared this first together makes me feel warm inside. Greg is mine. Loving and possessive feelings overcome me. I have felt so lonely for so long, but in this moment, I am not alone. We are here together. We stay in bed holding each other for several hours before falling asleep.

In the morning, Greg awakes aroused seeking round two. I am game. We start the day exploring each other. I enjoy the playful easiness with which we interact. The way Greg looks at me with big dough eyes leaves me feeling beautiful and peaceful. I want nothing more than to spend the entire day in bed. I have never done that before and, sadly, I won't today. We are both scheduled to work. I have to go in this afternoon and Greg in the evening.

Around noon, Greg releases me. He offers to make us some lunch while I get ready for work. While in the shower I quickly become lost in thought. Quiet moments always lead to old sad memories about my parents or scary fears about my new reality. I am happy Greg is here to make my lonely moments fewer.

Just then, the shower curtain moves. Without hesitation, I throw the palm of my hand out toward the movement. Greg falls backward and blood runs from his nose. "What the hell?" Greg looks emasculated and definitely injured.

"I am so sorry. I didn't think. I just…" I step out of the shower reaching towards his nose.

"Don't." Greg does not want my help tending to his injury. He washes his face in the sink. He throws his head back and holds a tissue to his nose. The blood is already coagulating. Nothing appears to be broken other than Greg's ego.

I turn off the shower and wrap myself in a towel. Greg grunts, "Two punishments, I guess."

"Huh?"

"First you punch me in the face, then you cover up. Don't I get anything out of this?" Greg tries to be charming, though he has obviously lost the mood.

I lean in and kiss him gently on the cheek.

While putting on his shorts, Greg mentions, "Lunch is sitting on the counter."

We eat our sandwiches and mustard potato salad mostly in silence. "Thanks for lunch. Sorry the shower didn't work out so well."

"I guess it gives me some comfort knowing that you can defend yourself from a big, strong man." Greg gives a Cheshire grin and flexes his arms.

Through reddened cheeks I explain, "My dad taught me some basic self-defense moves when I was young. He wanted to ensure that I could defend myself on a date."

Greg flippantly responds, "He was successful. I'm certainly announcing myself from now on."

Before I leave for work, I hand Greg a package.

"A gift?" Greg is genuinely surprised for the second time today.

"Yeah. Open it." I am squirming with excitement. Greg opens the small box which holds a key. "So you can come in when you want and don't have to wait for me."

Greg stands for longer than I had anticipated without comment. Clearly, he is thinking about something I didn't see coming.

After far too long, Greg explains. "I don't think I should have this key unless we are official."

"Okay." I declare. "We're official."

"So that I'm clear. We are officially?" He waits for me to finish his statement.

"Together?"

"And by *together* you mean…?

"Oh my God, are you going to make me say the words?"

"Yes. I need to hear the words." Greg enjoys this moment.

I consider throwing him a sidewinder and pull out the sarcasm, but instead I put on my big girl panties and just say, "We are boyfriend and girlfriend, officially."

Greg does not let me down. The look on his face is pure joy and the passion in his kiss is contagious, until I hurt his nose. "Sorry." I release as he holds his tissue back up to his nose.

"It was worth it." Greg interjects though he does not return for another kiss.

Work flies by as memories of the last 12 hours play in my mind over and over again. I am barely aware of my environment as I mindlessly straighten shelves. This new position in GM is solitary. Today I enjoy wallowing in thoughts of Greg and I. I had started to believe that I was destined to be alone and unhappy after my parents passed. Today, new ideas of a future in connection with another human being flood my thoughts.

My dad would like Greg. They are similar. Good, solid, loving. My dad had strength in his ability to love. His weakness was that he had a hard time saying no. My mom, on the other hand, could be stern. She was much quicker to yell at me and set me straight. My dad was protective but never harsh. They had a weird balance together. When my dad was away for work, my mom and I fought often. When my mom was away, my dad wanted to talk too much. I would pull away. I wish I had stayed more, listened more. The best times, though, were when we all hung out together. Sometimes I think God took them at the same time because they belonged together. I can't imagine either of them being here with me without the other. Maybe Greg and I will be like them.

Before I know it, my shift is over. Greg will not be off for a few hours yet. I decide to buy myself a Coke so I have an excuse to go through quick-check with Greg. The line is fairly long. Greg notices me immediately and is showing off how quick he can run each customer through.

Dean comes up behind me holding a Dr. Pepper. I don't like Dr. Pepper. "I thought couples weren't allowed to check each other out, but I can always check you out."

Dean stands too close as usual. Greg stops showing off and annoyance shows in his eyes. I enjoy his jealousy, but Dean needs to be brought down a peg. "I guess you are right. Now that Greg has the keys to my apartment and we've made it official. I suppose one more time won't hurt."

Dean steps back unconsciously with a disappointed look. Greg immediately notices and smiles broadly at me. When I reach him, I say, "Dean pointed out that couples shouldn't be checking each other out."

Greg smirks, ignoring Dean, who is listening for his response. "Fine by me as long as I'm the only one checking you out outside of work."

"I'll be waiting with excitement, Babe." I blow Greg a kiss and saunter off without acknowledging Dean.

I drive home running the images of Greg and me this morning and even putting Dean in his place in my mind over and over. That is until I pull into my apartment parking lot.

I look up and see Mr. Ed's apartment. I miss Mr. Ed sitting on the front stoop filling me in on the happenings in the apartment complex. Mr. Ed has been like a grandfather to me.

My lovely thoughts immediately change into worry. Worry about my friend's health. Wishing. Wishing I could see him and kiss him on the cheek. Fear. Fear that whoever hurt Mr. Ed could be waiting in my apartment. Panic takes over. Panic and shame. Shame that I am panicking. What is wrong with me? I can feel my heart race and I am breathing far too fast. Searching for air without release. Tears. My hands are shaking. What is wrong with me?

A knock on my car window alarms me. The woman has a concerned look on her face. I have seen her in the complex. I think she lives in my building. "Are you okay? Hey, are you okay?"

I open the door. "I can't breathe." I continue frantically drawing deep breaths without feeling like air is making it into my body.

The woman is very calm. "Put your shirt in your hand and hold it over your mouth to reduce your oxygen intake."

Confused, I do as the woman says.

"Take shorter breaths. Concentrate on my voice and breathe slowly."

I comply. Slowly I feel myself calm. I wiggle my fingers which had begun to tingle.

"My name is Allie. I live over there." She points across the parking lot from my apartment. "I'm a nurse. You are hyperventilating. If you keep breathing at a normal rate into your shirt your oxygen level will balance and you will be fine. I think you are having a panic attack."

Shame fills me again. A panic attack. I've got to get my emotions under control. "Thank you. I'm feeling better."

"Let me help you into your apartment." After a short pause, I conclude the woman is safe. I exit my vehicle. She holds my arm as I walk up the stairs. I feel slightly lightheaded. "You know, if you had continued to breathe that way you would have eventually passed out."

Passed out? That is a scary thought. "This has never happened to me before. Should I go to a doctor?"

"Usually that is not necessary. If you learn to monitor yourself, you can stop yourself. Have you been having a hard time lately?"

Shit yeah, I think. I do not want to air my laundry, so instead I respond, "I guess. Did you know Mr. Ed?"

"Your neighbor? Not so much. He always waved to me and seemed very friendly. I couldn't believe it when someone broke into his apartment. I guess it was more shocking for you since you live right next door."

"I miss him."

"I bet. Do you know how he is doing?"

"I don't. They won't tell me anything. I really want to visit him, but I can't even do that." Tears come to my eyes.

Allie sweetly squeezes my hand and tells me, "Everything happens for a reason. This too will pass."

Screw that. 'This too' is a trigger for me. I feel a rush of anger. God takes everything from me. Through angry tears I spew, "I'd really like to be alone. Thanks for helping me, though."

Allie quickly gathers herself and leaves. I feel guilty for my lack of manners. I'm such a jerk. And that is how quickly the damn breaks and the tears rush in. I start to breathe fast, but this time I stop myself. I certainly do not want to pass out.

At nearly midnight Greg noisily enters the apartment. Greg is concerned as he finds me slouched on the floor in front of the couch. "Ella, are you okay?"

I look up at him with red, angry eyes. "Why does God take everything from me?"

Greg holds me, kisses my head, and says, "Well, he sent me."

Chapter 10

Greg, being a responsible person, had set the alarm for school. At day break his alarm's piercing noise takes over our cocoon. No part of me wants to go to classes. I declare, "You go. I'm staying home today."

Greg gets up, takes a shower and leaves without saying goodbye. I lie in bed feeling like a sour apple. I deserve to be left without a goodbye. I am becoming so pathetic. Who would want this?

In the middle of my self-pity, I hear the front door. "Hello?" I say firmly while moving toward the drawer where my gun is stashed.

"Taco?" Greg yells from the entry.

Shit yeah. I have never wanted anything more than Greg and a breakfast taco. I look at the clock and there is still time for me to get myself together, but not before greeting Greg with a big morning mouth kiss and delving into a chorizo and egg taco.

Classes go by in a typical fashion. Tiffany is in the student center during my break. We spend some time catching up. She listens to me gloat about Greg and I making everything official and becoming intimate.

"I am so happy for you. I thought you would chase him off." Tiffany laughs. Changing the subject she asks, "Did you get a signed lease yet?"

"He was supposed to come down this past weekend, but he didn't make it. The current plan is that he'll be here this weekend to both see the apartment and, hopefully, sign the lease. I did get a handyman. He finished all the odds and ends for a reasonable price. The place is ready. I just have to pay for a final cleaning and lawn mowing but only after I have the deposit. Fingers crossed."

"I really haven't had much other interest in the house, other than tattoo guy who is not an option." I get lost in thought. I wonder if he is connected to my dad or uncle. I should probably visit Uncle Billy, though I never really look forward to seeing him.

After classes, Greg and I drive to the police station to pick up the watches. The process is pretty straight forward. Once we have the watches, I stop by Detective Haas's office to see if he has any new information on Mr. Ed. Detective Haas is sitting at his desk eating an éclair and drinking a cup of coffee. "You picked up the watches?"

"Yes." I hold them up. "I figured I would stop by and check if you had heard anything new."

"Sorry, I have not heard anything." After a short pause he adds, "You are not just leaving those in your apartment, are you?"

I hadn't even thought about what to do with the watches. "What happens if someone lays claim to them now?"

"Depends. If they can prove they are stolen, then we have to investigate. But the reality is big ticket items are usually reported quickly or not at all. Consider them yours. CCPD has determined that they are abandoned property from your rental."

"What do I do with them?"

"Keep 'em, sell 'em, give 'em away. Up to you really." Detective Haas appears to have lost interest in me and regained interest in his éclair.

In the car, I place the watches in my school backpack along with my laptop. I have never carried around anything with this much value before.

Greg mentions that he has a friend whose dad owns a jewelry store that does secondhand consignment. We decide to stop by.

∂∂∂∂∂∂∂

The store is very nice in an upper-class shopping center next to a Mediterranean Café that I have always wanted to try. Greg's friend's father, Mr. Kirby, is as a stout man with a big, warm smile. He is a good salesman and tries his best to have us shop.

"I have some beautiful necklaces. Not as beautiful as you, but they would look lovely around your neck." He looks to Greg, "You should give this beautiful creature a proper present to express your love."

I interrupt to get Greg off the hook, "Not today. These watches were left in my rental house." I sit the watches on the counter. "CCPD gave me this document showing no one has made a claim regarding the watches and they are now my property. I was told I could sell them."

Mr. Kirby takes a few minutes to read over the document. "Good. Good. This is a good document to have. I can't be accused of selling stolen property." He then looks at the watches under a magnifier. "I will need to establish market

83

value. Are you comfortable leaving them here with me for a time?"

"Sure." I respond happily.

Mr. Kirby agrees to follow up with me in a few weeks. He provides me a receipt with serial numbers and pictures of the watches. He explains that this is standard practice. I trust Mr. Kirby implicitly. I feel relieved to leave the premises without the watches.

By this point, I am hungry. Greg and I head to lunch at the Mediterranean Café next door. The atmosphere is very romantic. I immediately worry that we cannot afford to eat in this nice of an establishment. The server sits us in a booth, taking our drink orders and leaving the menu. While having several more expensive dishes, the menu also has a gyro meal we can share and appetizers that fit into our budget.

I offer to pay for this meal as I am kind of the recipient of a large sum of valuables. The watches still feel like dirty stolen property from Big John. Part of me hopes they sit on consignment forever. During our conversation, Mr. Kirby had informed me that in Corpus Christi a long time could pass before getting any offers due to our small market for big ticket items.

The waiter brings our appetizer platter that consists of baba ghanoush, fava beans, dolma, falafel, hummus, and tabbouleh along with fresh pita chips. The foreign flavors are delicious, especially the hummus. We feel very grown up trying the new items.

While tantalizing our taste buds, we are interrupted by none other than my cousin, Anna. She stands by the table waiting to be acknowledged. "Anna, I haven't seen you in forever."

Anna and I had always resembled one another, though today she appears too skinny with dark circles under her eyes. She looks unwell. Her hair looks two shades darker than mine but of the same hue. "I'm here with friends." She points to two large tatted men that stand out like sore thumbs in this establishment. Neither of her motley crew appear friendly.

"This is Greg. We are seeing each other." I pause. "Greg, this is my cousin, Anna."

Greg graciously asks, "Join us?"

"I can't right now. I'm having lunch with my friends." Anna turns to me, "Would it be okay if I stopped by and visit sometime. Are you still in your old house?"

"No, I rent the house out. I live at Bayside Apartments across from Taylors in Flour Bluff."

"Really, I live across the freeway. Weird we never run into each other." I can tell Anna is nervous but I have no idea why.

"Stop by some time. I'm in apartment 110 in the front of the complex." I feel cautious about giving out my address, but she is my closest cousin despite us growing apart. One part of me feels ashamed that I am a snob, while the other part of me does not trust her to come alone. "You and I can catch up on things. Just us, right?"

Anna looks indignant. "Yeah, just us." She waves without saying anything else and joins her companions across the room. The waiter brings the gyro and fries, but I am so uncomfortable. I ask Greg if we can just take it to go. We leave shortly after without further acknowledging Anna or her friends.

In the Jeep, we snack on the leftovers while driving home.

Greg asks, "What was that about?"

"I don't know. I haven't seen her in forever. She's the cousin I told you about. She is so different from when we were kids." Anna is clearly a junky now. When we were young, we had plans to open a pet store together. Be a dynamic duo of sorts. The dreams of our childhood were left behind long ago. We are virtual strangers now. I keep these thoughts to myself.

When we pull up to my apartment, a large grey moving van is blocking Greg's spot which is actually Mr. Ed's spot. My eyes dart to Mr. Ed's open apartment door.

I quickly exit the vehicle hoping to find Mr. Ed inside. I rush up the stairs. Several movers and a woman who identifies herself as Mr. Ed's niece, Tammy are inside.

"Hi. I'm Ella. I have been trying to visit and follow up on Mr. Ed, but the hospital could not confirm or deny if he was ever admitted."

Tammy is very understanding, "Yes, our family opted to not allow visitors. We don't really know what happened. Mr. Ed is out of the hospital now. We moved him to a convalescent home."

"Is he doing well then? Can I visit him?"

Tammy looks uneasy, "He is conscious and talking. The head injury caused retrograde amnesia. He does not remember the night he was assaulted. His old memories are still good, but those from the last few years are still being recovered."

"I guess you don't expect him to return to his apartment?" I ask gesturing to the moving van.

"No. We don't expect he will ever live independently again. He is being moved to a long-term facility that can care for his medical and physical needs."

"Can I visit him?" I ask again.

"Of course, maybe seeing you will help him recover his memories." Tammy then gives me the information on his new residence and a hug.

Chapter 11

The next day Greg goes to work while I have the day off. I decide to visit Uncle Billy's house. Uncle Billy lives across the freeway in the general area Anna reported living. That area has never revitalized and consists of small, dilapidated homes and shanty apartments. Mixed in at the shore are a few larger nicer homes on pier and beam belonging to fishermen who enjoy easy access to the bay and do not mind the hood.

Uncle Billy's house is an average home for this neighborhood. No bigger than my one bedroom apartment, his home is two bedrooms with a window air conditioner unit in the living room. The house smells of sweat and pot. Uncle Billy and Aunt Donna are generally unkempt. They look less than excited to see me, but offer me a beer just the same. I decline.

Aunt Donna's vexed look matches all the memories from my childhood. I cannot remember a time seeing her smile. Uncle Billy smiles easily showing the black tobacco stuck to his teeth, "Shit. Are you surprised Ms. Fancy Pants don't want a beer?" He laughs heartily while insulting me to my face. "You are just like your momma. She always thought she was better than everybody else too." Uncle Billy spits into his red Solo cup. The visual turns my stomach.

"Where are Craig and Jake?" I wish my cousins were here. They might be jerks, but for the most part they are affable and generally better natured in their banter than their parents.

"Nah. They are always out carousing." Uncle Billy says. "Why? Are you afraid to sit with your aunt and uncle to have a talk?"

"No." I lie. I add, "I see them at the store sometimes. I see they still love to fish."

"Got me a freezer full of fish. Going to fry them up tonight. You sticking around for a family reunion?" Uncle Billy is being short with me but not unkind. I appreciate that he is making an effort. Aunt Donna ignores me with a scowl on her face. I can tell she would just assume I leave. "How have you been on your own? Heard there was some trouble in your apartment complex?" He spits into his cup again.

"Things have gotten a little weird lately. My neighbor was assaulted during a home invasion."

"They got any suspects."

"I don't know anything." I don't know why I don't tell him about Mr. Ed. Paranoia, I guess. "I've been okay, but my tenant left my house pretty messed up. I am looking for a new tenant."

Aunt Donna snorts, "That should be a family home. Guess you have no sense of family."

Uncle Billy interrupts, "Her house, her choice, Babe." He returns his attentions to me. "Seems like bad karma though."

"I ran into Anna for the first time in forever yesterday." I state.

Aunt Donna changes her facial expression to interest and fully engages in the conversation.

"Where? Who was she with? What did she want?" Aunt Donna probes.

"In town, at the Mediterranean Café. I figured you guys were seeing her regularly. She said she was living in this area."

"I haven't seen her in over a year." Aunt Donna rebuffs. "Actually, since the funeral."

"She was with two guys." I mention.

"I don't doubt it." Aunt Donna stops herself from saying something.

"You know them?" I inquire.

Aunt Donna's face contorts, and I recognize the transition as anger. Uncle Billy steps in. "Sounds to me like your life is getting a little complicated. You should be careful. If the wrong people decide to take an interest in you, then you will need a little education on the subject." He spits in his cup.

"I don't understand."

"Anna runs with a rough crowd, is all. A crowd that you don't want taking an interest in you."

My mind starts to wonder if she could be involved with the Syndicate. I start to conjecture: my cousin, runs with a rough crowd, shows up out of the blue, after my neighbor is attacked by someone, after I have been accosted a few times by strangers. I stop myself and respond, "She told me she wanted to stop by and catch up." I feel nervous sharing this much. Then I ask, "Who is this crowd?"

Uncle Billy looks pensive, "You mixed up in something? I always said you were a special kind of dumbass. You got everything on a silver platter and you over here asking questions that you got no business asking. What are you after? You've never come to enjoy our company before."

"Actually, I had a guy apply to rent the house, then, by coincidence, I found a picture of you and Dad with him in it." I hold up the picture.

Uncle Billy rolls his eyes, "Would have been nice if you'd come for a visit." He takes the picture while spitting into his cup. I catch a glimpse inside the cup and my stomach turns. "This is Buddy. He is a friend of mine. So?"

"Just thought it was a coincidence." I say aloud while thinking privately, or a pattern of events.

"Ain't nothing wrong with Buddy. He's a good guy. You are just a snob." Uncle Billy sits down and starts watching a show. Aunt Donna joins him, and I realize that I have been dismissed.

I am happy to leave. Between the smells and visuals, I feel sort of sick. I sit in my car and attempt to put the puzzle together, hypothesizing. Buddy was Uncle Billy's friend. I wonder if he knew who I was the whole time: during the showing, when I ran into him at Taylors. I couldn't tell if Uncle Billy knew his friend had tried to rent the house. Uncle Billy acts like typical Uncle Billy, but I start to wonder if he was fishing with his questions. Did he know that I was in trouble? Why would he ask if I was in trouble?

Uncle Billy was right that I have never visited before. Even as a kid, I never visited Uncle Billy's home without my parents. My mom didn't like to visit except when necessary or my dad insisted, which wasn't that often. Family events were usually at our house. Uncle Billy was always friendly but on edge. I guess he was the same today. He certainly lives in a world with people I do not understand.

I start to think about sweet young Anna. We used to be so similar. The idea that she is mixed up in this underworld or worse, that someone might take that kind of interest in me makes my skin crawl. Uncle Billy planted a seed of fear that is quickly growing into a bush. A bush I want to hide behind.

As I am pulling out, Craig and Jake are pulling in. They jump out of the pickup and run over to me. "What the hell are you doing here?"

"I stopped by to see your dad," I reply.

Craig and Jake give each other knowing looks. "Well, you going to start visiting regular or is this a one-time stop? We're going out tonight if you and that boyfriend of yours want to join us."

I don't know why it bothers me that they are aware I am seeing someone. "What boyfriend?"

"The one you are shacking up with regularly," Jake snickers.

Craig and Jake have never been to my apartment and I have never shared anything with them. This knowledge regarding my life leaves me concerned. "Sorry, I don't think I could keep up with you guys."

"Of course, you can't, but we'd love to see you try." Jake pushes his brother and heads into the house. Craig gives a half wave as he opens the door and disappears inside.

Chapter 12

I long for the times in my youth when we all enjoyed each other's company. Being the only child left me alone with time to think, plan, and create in calm and quiet. My cousins' world was simply more exciting. My cousins lived in a tumultuous world that intimidated me, but they also had freedom. Their world overwhelmed my sheltered existence. Craig and Jake feared nothing and were conquerors from an early age. They didn't have a lot, so we spent our time in role plays. When I was with them time stood still, and the part of me that normally stayed hidden took over in their realm of imagination.

When Anna began hanging out with her new crowd a small part of me had wanted to join in like I did in the fields. To live in the moment.

Once in high school, I went with her to a party. The party was in a trailer park. One of the boys from school that I had a crush on was there, Chris. I was excited. He had a floppy surfer haircut and ocean blue eyes. I had seen him in school but had never even had a class with him. The trailer was old with second hand furnishings. Everyone at the party had a drink and cigarettes. I had neither.

I was initially flattered when Chris approached and showed interest in me. I tried to engage him in conversation, but I did not understand the social rules at this type of party.

Chris looked bored with me. He asked, "Are you a stiff?"

I answered "Yes." I was. The party was trashy. No music or joking. Just drinking until a certain time when couples began going into bedrooms. I was appalled.

Chris approached me later that evening and asked, "You want to have sex?"

God no. I couldn't believe that the girls were going with these crude boys. I called my parents for a ride and went home.

The next day Anna asked, "Where did you go last night?"

I returned her question with resounding judgment, "I left. I don't belong at a party like that. Full of trash."

That was the last time we really hung out. Our worlds went in two separate directions. I was jealous at times because I was often alone or with Tiff, my only real friend.

Anna was surrounded by friends; though not friends I would have chosen for myself. She was wild and free. I had never experienced that kind of freedom. Even when my parents died, I think they settled in my brain because I constantly hear them guiding me and telling me what to do. I always ask myself if I am letting them down.

Driving up to my apartment, I see Anna sitting on the front stoop where Mr. Ed belonged. She looks fragile and broken. Not the wild, popular energetic Anna that I envied in my youth. She is different: worn, tired, hungry. At least that is my perception of her.

I remember the two goons at the restaurant. I scan the parking lot. If they are here, I cannot see them. Anna sees me almost as soon as I see her. She nods her head and waits for me. I wish I had my gun. I left it in my dresser drawer. Not because I fear Anna, but I keep thinking about her crowd. Where are the goons?

I feel some relief with the time of the visit. All my neighbors are either coming home or leaving for the evening

94

shift. Early evening is a busy time in an apartment complex. Plus, we have the cameras. I realize if something happens the cameras are unlikely to save me, but it holds some consolation.

I walk up the stairs and stop halfway. "I didn't expect you to actually visit." I say.

"Well, here I am. Should I stay or go?" Anna looks defeated.

"Stay. I've missed you." I finish the last half of the steps and hold her in a long hug. I am surprised that she does not retreat. I do not want to let go. She does not seem like she wants me to let go either.

I completely forget about all my paranoia. We enter the apartment. Anna sits on the couch and I get us each a glass of water. Anna smirks, "Why am I not surprised you don't offer me something stronger?" She puts the glass down without taking a drink.

"Sorry. I don't have anything stronger. I am not 21 yet."

"How about that cute boyfriend of yours? He looks at least 21." Greg is actually 23, but I guess he either doesn't drink or hasn't had a drink with me.

"We've only just started seeing each other. We haven't even gone on a real date." Strange, but we haven't. We are living together but have never been on a legitimate date. We go out to eat while running errands and dealing with all this nonsense.

"Oh. I thought you two were a couple."

"We are. A new couple. I'm still settling to the idea. You wouldn't believe how bad I am at this." I can feel my cheeks turning a warm shade of red.

"I don't know about that. From where I sit, you look like you really have your shit together." Anna looks down and disheartened.

"I guess I got a little help from my parents." I do not want to brag or ignore the truth in the situation. Anna's parents are alive but have never really been there for her. Even in death I have more guidance and financial help than she ever has.

"Hmmm." Anna is annoyed at me. I feel bad but do not know how to make things better.

"I've missed you. I was just thinking about us running around the trails after your brothers when we were kids."

"They were such assholes. Do you remember when they took my journal into that field and we couldn't make our way out?"

"I do. That is actually one of my favorite memories. We pretended we were lost princesses seeking out a new kingdom. We eventually found our own way home." I pause, "I guess they didn't come back for us."

"They got their butts whipped when I got home and told Mom," Anna muses about the boys being punished.

I remember my aunt's anger. She would get that belt and just swing it at any body part. Never at me. My parents would not have allowed it. I always felt bad that the rules were different for me.

"I was always afraid of your mom," I admit.

"Why? She wouldn't touch you. You were the princess."

"I know. I'm sorry."

"Shit, I didn't come here to feel sorry for myself. Let's go have some fun, Ella." Anna immediately becomes her old self. Energetic. The life of the party.

"Greg gets off in half an hour. I think we should wait for him," I suggest.

Anna rolls her eyes and increases her assertion, "Let's go. I don't know him from a hole in the wall. We need a girl's night."

I do not know how to tell her that with everything going on I do not feel comfortable going out. Or more importantly, going out with her. She has started pacing and looks uncomfortable in my apartment. She looks so much older than me. I assume she has already lived a much fuller life than my sheltered existence.

I decide to suggest going for dinner at our old hangout, the Taco Stand. The Taco Stand is always busy. Seating is on the patio. The place is not very pricey, just casual dining at the road side stand with a constant stream of customers at the drive thru.

"Fine, but we have to stop at the liquor store first."

"There is a liquor store across the street." I hold my hands up and make a face. "Do you have a fake ID?"

"Girl, you really need to broaden your world." Anna heads out the door. I grab my wallet, sunglasses, cell and lock the door behind us.

"I'll drive," I say.

"You're also paying." Anna comments without waiting for my response.

While waiting outside the liquor store for Anna, I send a quick text to Greg letting him know that I am at the Taco Stand with Anna, knowing he won't get the message until after he clocks out.

Anna is quick and returns with a brown bag. I am not sure what she purchased but she takes a swig as soon as she sits in the car. Her demeanor changes immediately to a more relaxed state. "You want a drink?" She leans the bottle towards me then snickers while immediately taking another swig. Something about how she looks at me is mocking.

We easily locate a table at the Taco Stand. The drive thru is busy but the seats are empty. The Taco Stand is perfect as Anna is able to bring her bag of booze over without arising any concern. Anna is wearing a red bra with an oversized beach shirt and torn jean shorts. She has several visible tattoos including a medium sized star on the back of her neck and a large vining rose on her right shoulder. I have never been a fan of tattoos. I do not even like my freckles. Anna had the most beautiful unblemished skin growing up. While she has no signs of regret, I have many for her.

"I haven't seen you in forever. Where have you been?" I ask.

"I told you I live across the highway from you. I guess we just have different schedules." Anna chides.

I continue, "I visited your parents. Your mom said she hasn't seen you in a while."

"Quite on purpose. Can't stand her or my dad. I avoid them like the plague."

"But they live in that same area. How do you avoid them?" Privately I also wonder how she avoids me. Flour Bluff is a small community. One grocery store, two liquor stores, some fast food chains, and a few local joints, not much else other than the school. We only recently got a Super-Mart.

"You ask too many questions. This shit doesn't matter. I get on. Okay?"

"Okay. Who were your friends the other day?"

"More questions. Friends. I know them from work."

"Where do you work?" I ask.

"Girl. You don't want to know. I've seen you at Taylors with that guy of yours. He's cute. Doesn't seem like an asshole."

"Greg is very nice. The nicest guy ever actually. I really like him. I've never felt like this before. I guess he's actually my first boyfriend."

Anna loses a little spittle while guffawing. "You've always been such a stick in the mud."

I feel defensive. "Look, we've obviously made different choices. I miss how we used to be as kids. We're still family."

Anna takes a swig from her brown bag. "Yeah. Family. That hasn't been a big part of our life for some time."

"Are you happy?" I ask.

"Ah shit. I don't know if this is going to work. I feel like you live in a fantasy world and just don't get it. Real life is going to sneak up and bite you on the ass, Cousin."

I start thinking of all that has been going on lately. Is she part of all this? Why is she showing up now? She doesn't appear to want to catch up, so what are we doing here?

After a long pause, Anna starts again, "I need something from you." Anna's mannerisms change. She straightens her back and looks me square in the eyes.

Her behavior is reflected in my now upright stance. I feel tension in my stomach. "What do you mean?" My mind is racing. Anna has never asked for anything before. My brain starts spinning with all the puzzle pieces. Anna may be part of the Syndicate. She showed up at the café when we dropped off the watches. Why are we here? Is the Syndicate using my cousin to control me? What do they want? My testimony? The watches? Fear runs through me while I wait to hear her request.

"I need a place to crash for a few weeks. My boyfriend kicked me out and I have nowhere to go."

My mind continues to spin. On one hand this is my cousin and closest childhood friend. On the other hand, this is a young woman mixed up in all sorts of bad things. I am not sure if she is a friend or a foe. I can hear my parents telling me, *absolutely no*, from the abyss. I, too, am mixed up in some trouble. Trouble Anna knows nothing about? Or does she? Her trouble and my trouble might land us in big trouble.

"Look, I need a safe place to reset things. Where better than your place? La la land." Anna looks genuinely contrite, maybe a little scared.

How would this work? I give my strung-out cousin the keys to my apartment, knowing she is probably member of the Syndicate. I have seen her friends and they terrify me. What happens if I say no? Do they go the aggressive route? I sit unable to answer.

The silence hovers like smoke replacing all the air. I fear that I will pass out. If I pass out, will her friends abduct me and take me away? If I take her home, will she wait until I am asleep and let in the very people I bought a gun to keep out?

Anna stands, "I get it." She sends a text to someone. Within a few minutes the goons drive up in a late model black Tahoe and Anna is gone.

Chapter 13

After Anna leaves, I sit stupefied for quite a while. My heart aches for Anna, the beautiful princess of my childhood that no longer exists. I cannot help but erect a new wall to protect myself from this scary version of her that I simply don't understand.

Greg drives up. "What are you doing? Where is your cousin?"

Greg parks and sits across the bench from me. The exact location Anna had been sitting. I try to imagine her perspective. She is a young woman caught in a world of drugs with no one she can count on, not even her childhood confidant and cousin. I didn't even get her phone number. I let her down.

I follow Greg back to the apartment in my car. I do not explain my day. I need to process. I am torn between believing that the entire world is out to get me and that I am a snob who only cares about herself.

Greg and I sit and watch *Scandal*, but my thoughts are distracted by all the events of the last few weeks. How can this be my life? A year ago, I was in high school with two loving parents. Now I have no family connections and chaos is taking over my life. Like this stupid show where every season the good people became bad people to suit the plot line. I don't want a frenzied plot line. I just want to finish college and live a normal life.

I want to cry but then I would have to explain my thoughts to Greg. My thoughts turn into sleepless hours which turn into disturbed dreams with cameos from Mr. Ed, Big John, Uncle Billy, Anna, and my parents.

Morning finally arrives. I am up early. I am exhausted but no longer want the punishment of my sub-conscious mind flipping through random thoughts, fears, and disjointed memories. On our way to classes my cell rings. Unknown number, so I let it go to voicemail.

The voicemail is from the District's Attorney's office to set up a date for an interview. The DA is gathering evidence including interviews for the pending charges against Big John and associates. The word *associates* scares me.

I regret celebrating my winning victory at The Swap Center. I won the battle only to be dragged into a war. A war involving one of the largest drug operations in the United States according to Google. A war I am not going to win. Certainly Mr. Ed had not won anything. I am not sure what my rights are regarding testifying. I am second guessing every decision I have made since that monumental day.

I decide to call back immediately and see how much trouble I am in. Rip the band aid.

"Hi, this is Ella Fontana. I just missed your call about an appointment."

"Yes. Let me see." After a brief pause, "We have you scheduled for an interview at the District Attorney's office next Wednesday at 9 am."

I check my work schedule. I am off in the morning. "I can be there. How long will this take?"

"Expect two to three hours. Meet in the conference room on the second floor of the courthouse. You will need to wear proper attire."

"Got it. Thank you." I put the appointment into the calendar of my cell.

Greg offers, "I want to go with you."

To which I respond, "That's okay. I want to go alone." I'm nervous enough without having a witness.

Greg starts to argue with me, "I really think I should go with you."

I firmly stop him, "No! The answer is no."

Greg recognizes my distress and backs off.

For the rest of the week I experience constant paranoia. I run in and out of campus buildings and constantly think I see goons following me around. I haven't seen Anna again. I am not sure if that is a good or bad thing. I still have moments of heartache for her, but I don't let myself wallow in those thoughts.

I wear my handgun everywhere I go now, knowing I don't have an open carry license. Greg disapproves, but I feel unsafe without it.

"You can get arrested, Ella." Greg argues once again as I strap on my holster.

"So be it." I ignore him.

"Look, here is a Groupon for an open carry class for $75," he says. "I bought one for each of us. Date night."

"We don't do real dates, do we? Sign us up." I chuckle.

My life has changed so significantly in the last few weeks. Greg is basically living with me. He has gained part of the closet and another drawer. I am not the best girlfriend. I am stressed out all the time. All that considered, Greg is very understanding and supportive. I feel safe with Greg here. Not to mention, he makes me laugh despite all that is going on.

Wednesday morning arrives. I leave my gun in my bedroom drawer. Typically, I lock it in my glove compartment, but that would not be such a good idea for the courthouse parking lot. I feel a little naked without my gun.

Greg is working the same hours as me today. Hopefully, we get our break together. I choose to wear a red blouse with tan stretch dress pants and flats. I pull my hair back and tie it in a bun with a few strands framing my face. I want to look sophisticated and strong. Looking in the mirror, I don't see sophisticated or strong. I see a scared little girl in over her head.

"You look very professional. I'm impressed." Greg says from the bed. "Are you sure I can't go with you? I'm just going to sit here and worry about you."

Greg's words help guard me against my self-criticism, but I have to do this alone. "I've got it. Thanks though." I give Greg a kiss and head out to my appointment.

I locate the DA's office on the second floor. I wait in the stale reception area in a large maroon leather chair for what feels like forever.

Finally, a confident slender middle-aged woman in a light grey power suit approaches me, "Ella Fontana?" She holds her hand out. I make an effort to give a strong handshake with my sweaty palm. She introduces herself as Gail Henry. I wonder if she is related to Thomas J. Henry, the big-time personal injury lawyer in town, but I refrain from asking her.

I am escorted to a conference room with many large maroon leather chairs surrounding an impressive hardwood table. The far wall is covered with floor to ceiling windows. The view outside from this floor is not impressive, though the room is intimidating. Along with Ms. Henry is a man dressed to the nines. He introduces himself as Assistant District Attorney George Kemp.

ADA Kemp starts. "Thank you for coming in today for this interview. You should know that your testimony might be unnecessary in court. We need, though, to be ready as the defense is asking to depose you. They have entered a written objection contesting the veracity of the warrant. If the warrant gets thrown out much of our evidence goes with it."

"Okay." I like the idea that my testimony might be unnecessary.

ADA Kemp continues, "The warrant to search the establishment is based solely on you informing the officer that Big John offered to sell you marijuana from the establishment. Detective Haas is expected to testify that you are a credible informant. The defendant has alleged that your statement to the officer was a lie as retribution for him leaving the rental house. Today we need to prepare your testimony as a witness."

Gail Henry hands me the statement I created for Detective Haas. She explains, "Take a moment to reread and reflect on your statement provided to Detective Haas."

ADA Kemp turns on a recorder and begins asking me questions. "What is your name? How did you come to know the defendant? Why were you in The Swap Center that day?" ADA Kemp offers insights as to how to respond as we progress.

I am careful to respond consistently with my statement. I worry that I am not being one hundred percent truthful. I am committing perjury. I feel my breathing quicken. I can't get enough air. I draw in faster and deeper breaths. Then I hear my sweet neighbor Allie in my ear, *If you recognize it, you can calm yourself down.* I concentrate on breathing with my hands over my mouth slowly. I look up to find that everyone is looking at me. I am embarrassed by over-reacting in front of these professionals. Uncontrollable tears flow from my eyes. All I wanted was to present as a mature woman, but I am now a blubbering child.

ADA Kemp states, "This concludes our interview."

Ms. Henry turns off the recorder and calmly says, "Let's give her some time to process. We are off record now." I appreciate her maternal instincts and the almost empty room. Ms. Henry remains and sits outside of my field of vision as I try to calm myself. When I finally feel pulled together sufficiently, I apologize, "I'm sorry. I am very stressed."

Ms. Henry moves next to me and places her hand gently on my shoulder. "It is our intention to involve you as little as possible. We are sensitive to the fact that you are a young adult who recently lost her parents. The good news is we do not intend to call you to testify in the trial. The bad news is the defendant has already notified the court that you will be called as a witness at trial and has requested a deposition."

I ask, "Do I have to cooperate? Can I refuse?"

Gail Henry looks uncomfortable. "The defense is expected to send you a subpoena which requires you to attend. You can refuse, but would be subject to being held in contempt of court. You can request a protection order. The protection order would need to be filed by your attorney separate from the DA's office." Gail Henry pauses then continues. "Consider that we will only ask you to take the stand if necessary and even then, we are only asking for limited, though important, testimony. The defense counsel, though, is expected to call you to stand should we make it to court. That is why we prepared you today."

"Do you know that I've been stalked since Big John was arrested? My neighbor was assaulted. I'm scared."

"Any recent events?" Gail Henry asks.

"Not in the last few weeks." I answer.

"Detective Haas has kept us informed. At this time, the DA does not have compelling evidence that you are under an undue burden. We encourage you to contact law enforcement if any new events occur."

Gail Henry starts to walk me out. Her words offer me no security. My anxiety and feeling of being alone is greater now than before I met with the ADA. Part of me is angry with the DA's office, then I realize that I brought all this on myself.

When leaving the courthouse, I notice two guys across the street that are eerily familiar to me. Their eye contact is a little too intense and I wish I had my gun. The police station is across the parking lot in the other direction. I doubt that I am in danger in this particular location, but worry that I am an easy target generally. I take mental note of the unique features of the guys while moving efficiently to my vehicle, alert to the environment. I am exhausted by the need to be constantly alert.

I am relieved to see Greg when I arrive home. He is dressed for work sitting on the porch. I am heading up the stairs when I hear a loud smashing noise. I nearly fall to the ground before realizing the noise is coming from a garbage truck emptying the dumpster next to my unit. The parking lot is mostly empty. Luckily only Greg sees my exaggerated response. Greg runs to my side. "Are you okay?"

Embarrassed I reply, "I just slipped. I'm fine." I try to hide my shaking hands.

Greg, being sympathetic, does not inquire further but simply says, "I made you a sandwich. I figured you would be in a hurry when you got out of your appointment. How did it go?"

While eating my sandwich, I give Greg a run down. As we are finishing lunch, someone knocks on the door. Greg opens the door. "Ella Fontana?" a strange voice inquires.

"Who's asking?" Greg responds while holding the door protectively.

"I have a package for her." The man holds an envelope with my name on it.

I peek my head around and accept the package. Inside is a subpoena for the deposition two weeks from Friday. Ms. Henry did say the defense had already requested the deposition.

Greg asks, "Do you want to drive into work together?"

I appreciate the gesture, "That sounds good." I will have to ask for a schedule change to make it to the deposition.

On our way over Greg jokes, "It seems like driving into work is the most romantic thing we've done lately."

"Yeah, all this stress has definitely kept us from being romantic. We need a good old fashioned date. Not an open carry gun license class."

Greg agrees, "I accept."

"Okay, I'll plan something. My treat." I say.

"Nope, you're my sugar momma paying all the rent. The date is on me. We're both off Saturday night." Greg's big smile is contagious. I am happy to have something to look forward to on Saturday. Though the deposition still has my stomach tied in knots.

When we arrive at work, I clock in and head to my new manager's office. "Terry, I have a subpoena for two weeks from Friday." I hand him the paperwork. "Right now, I'm scheduled to work."

Terry advises, "No problem. We handle subpoenas like a Jury Duty request. I'll get the shift covered."

I am relieved. One less thing to worry about. I start my shift straightening shelves. Most days GM allows me to pick the time of my lunch break. Today I wait for Greg to be released for his break by the front-end manager.

Feeling amorous, we make out in Greg's Jeep, skipping lunch. Our break passes quickly. Disappointed we have to head back in, Greg quips, "Time really does fly when you're having fun." I enjoy Greg's sappy sense of humor.

To ensure we keep the option of having our breaks together, we make sure to clock in on time. Re-entering the store as a couple after being inappropriate in the parking lot feels a lot like committing a crime. Everyone takes notice. Snide looks, judgment, and jealousy abound. I feel no shame. I deserve these small moments of happiness; we were only making out. Avoiding eye contact, I return to my department.

Chapter 14

Before I know it, we are a few days from the deposition. Between work and school, time has flown by. Greg and I are enjoying taking breaks together. Tonight, we get off at the same time. We clock out.

Holding hands, we walk to the Jeep. The parking lot is relatively empty. The Jeep is in the back of the lot as employees are discouraged from taking close parking meant for customers.

Greg puts his arm out and stops me. He nods toward his rear right tire. Greg walks closer. After inspection he says, "Someone stabbed the tire. This gash is too big for a nail." Greg is visibly upset but pulls himself together.

"It's late. Let's just walk home." Greg suggests.

Due to the hour and the short distance to the apartment, we report the incident to management and walk home leaving the Jeep in the parking lot until morning. We can take my car to school in the morning, then pick up a new tire.

We decide to stop in for a late snack at Taco Bell. While eating his Taco Supreme, Greg shares, "My friends and I would come here all the time in high school. My first date happened right over there." He points across the dining room.

Laughing, I respond, "Our big date better not be at Taco Bell."

Greg assures me, "I've been considering options all night. I have a few ideas but let's leave it a surprise."

With full bellies, we make the final trek home. We head to the curb and hear, "Hey cousin. Why are you walking at this time of night and in your work clothes?" Craig and Jake stop next to us.

I feel nervous, considering we have no idea who stabbed Greg's tire. Detective Haas's words of caution to look for patterns come to my mind. I shake off the idea. My mind just can't accept that my cousins are intimidating me. I respond, "Nice evening and a flat tire."

"Need a ride?"

"Nope."

"Suit yourself." They drive off with a whoop whoop.

Greg questions, "They seem like fun guys?"

"Those are my cousins. I guess I should have introduced you," I concede.

As soon as we approach the stairs to my apartment, I know something is wrong. My apartment door is slightly ajar. I start walking brusquely toward my apartment, but Greg stops me. He is already on the phone with 911. After thinking through my options, I am relieved that Greg is showing caution.

The police take forever to arrive. Greg gives his statement first. "We walked home because someone stabbed my tire. When we got here, we found the door open. We have not gone inside."

Before talking to me, the officers draw their weapons and search the apartment. Within a few minutes the officers return with a relaxed stance. "All clear." The officers suggest I look around to see if anything is out of place.

The door lock is damaged by what looks like a crowbar; otherwise, no obvious items are damaged, missing or out of place. I report my lack of findings to the officers who agree to turn in a report. They do not dust for fingerprints. Once again, they tell me to stay alert, lock the door and contact them if anything else occurs.

Helpful. How many times can I be told the same stupid thing with no resulting action? Maybe I should become a police officer. All they do is take reports and leave scared victims standing alone.

Greg appears to share my frustration. He paces then vocalizes, "This is ridiculous. At what point do the police do something, anything?"

Before they leave, I mention, "I have an open case with the DA's office and an officer I've been working with, Detective Haas. Can you let them know about tonight?"

"Sure," the officer responds.

Once they leave, I encourage Greg to sit with me on the couch and watch television. A new episode of *Naked and Afraid* is on the DVR. Normally, we watch with disbelief. Survivalists sign up for a show where they are starved, eaten by bugs over their entire bodies, and left in the cold and rain for 21 days. Occasionally, participants are severely injured or ill. Tonight, I see a parallel with my life. I too am being watched in a very real and dangerous situation.

I get up to make myself hot tea. I grab my favorite oversized mug, fill it with water, and pop the mug in the microwave. While waiting for the two minutes to pass, I clean up the counters. That's when I come across a strange note, from Anna. Scrawled on the small note pad is a message,

Don't trust him. –Anna.

I cannot be sure if she wrote this note when she visited me or if she broke into my apartment and wrote the note, though that is unlikely. I try to remember our prior conversation but cannot think of whom she is referring. At this point I don't trust anyone except for Greg and Tiff. I fully know that no one else in my life is to be counted on.

If Anna had wanted to tell me something, why didn't she? Thinking back, I presumed she was nervous because she needed a drink, but maybe there was more to the story. I hope she is okay. Sad feelings overwhelm me as I think about her being worried about me. She had needed help, and I didn't help her.

I don't know why, but I hide the note in my junk drawer and do not mention the note to Greg. My deception hangs in the air, ruining our evening together. I feel a new wall growing. A need to keep everything secret. My mind is spinning. Nothing makes any sense. Fear is becoming my constant companion.

I toss and turn all night. Lying awake, replaying all the scenes from the prior weeks over and over in my head. Every hour I open my eyes to see that approximately one hour has passed. Early morning, I open my eyes and watch Greg sleep with his gentle snore. As time passes his snore sounds louder and louder. I cannot turn off my mind. I lie awake trying to stop my obsessing mind, pacing my breathing to Greg's snoring.

Exhausted, I finally fall asleep only to have short bursts of sleep, reliving and rewriting recent traumas in a series of draining nightmares. Three guys in the parking lot pulling me towards the white serial murderer van. I scream but only a whimper emerges. I fight, only to be overtaken by the goons. In my dream they look exactly like the guys at the courthouse. Then these same guys assault Mr. Ed. In my nightmare, Mr. Ed is even more violently injured. He does not awake but lies bleeding out on my porch. Help never comes. I am alone watching my beloved friend die. I awake in a pool of sweat. My mind is confusing reality and fantasy. I decide to check on Mr. Ed after school today. I miss him dearly.

Greg awakes early as usual, surprised that I am awake. Considering my restless night, I am not tired. I am anxious and ready to busy myself and avoid my disturbing thoughts. I shower and get dressed. I put my gun in the holster behind my hip while Greg is not present. He continues to complain about me carrying the gun, especially on the college campus. Even open carry is not allowed on the college campus. Regardless, with the deposition scheduled for tomorrow morning I am not taking any chances.

Before we leave, Greg wraps his arms around me giving me a hug and kiss. He notices the handgun and looks at me sternly. He seems to pick up the idea that I am not in the mood for a lecture and keeps his thoughts to himself, though his look speaks volumes. I admire his ability to read me. I often feel challenged to keep my undesirable thoughts to myself. Greg certainly has more self-restraint than I.

Chapter 15

Classes go by quick enough. After our classes we stop at a discount tire outlet to pick up a replacement tire for Greg's Jeep. While sitting in the car waiting for Greg to pay, I receive a text message from my potential new tenant Joe Magnum. He informs me he is coming in on Sunday with his deposit to take a final look at the house and hopefully sign the new lease. I need to finalize the lease tonight through the online company I use. We have agreed to monthly rent, first month's deposit, and pet deposit. Getting the house rented will take one huge burden off my shoulders.

I contemplate selling the house, but even with my horrible tenant I made money. Plus, it is nice that the equity in the house is increasing. I can always sell at a later date if necessary. Renting is the smart bet, though I certainly need to improve my radar for quality tenants. I am sticking to my guns and only renting to a person or family with a good credit history that makes me feel completely comfortable. I give a silent prayer that Joe and his family are the right tenants.

We stop to eat submarine sandwiches for lunch. I am distracted. Greg asks, "What is wrong? You're not yourself today."

Annoyed, I respond, "Sorry, I guess you can't understand that things are stressful right now."

"The stress I understand but you are pulling away from me. Last night we barely spoke and now I feel like I'm eating alone." Greg looks honestly hurt.

"I have a lot on my mind and a lot I have to get done. Are you okay with me dropping you off at Taylors so you can change out the tire? I need to see Mr. Ed. If I have time, I want to complete the lease before I go into work tonight."

Greg looks anxious. "I don't like the idea of leaving you alone. Why not do that tomorrow after the deposition?"

My heart races and my blood runs hot. "I guess I'm not asking. I'll drop you off." We finish lunch without any further conversation.

I drop Greg off and head over to the convalescent home. I have never actually been inside an old folks' home. The exterior of the building looks much like an upscale apartment complex. Definitely nicer than my apartment complex. I am hopeful that Mr. Ed has upgraded.

Unfortunately, my expectation of an upgrade for Mr. Ed are quickly squelched as I walk through the door. Busy antiquated floral wallpaper greets me first, then a counter with a robust woman with messy curls in scrubs. There are dark settee style couches scattered throughout the otherwise abandoned area. I don't know why but the area looks more like a funeral home then a hopeful place for families to visit elderly relatives with health issues.

I approach the middle-aged woman with an uncomfortable smile. She is friendly enough but the interaction is stale and disingenuous, likely from a day sitting without any real human interaction. "I'm looking for a friend of mine, Edward Whitting." I only learned Mr. Ed's real name from his niece. I hate his real name. Mr. Ed is my friend. I don't feel like I know Edward Whitting. I imagine Edward Whitting working in a suit in a stuffy law office.

116

The attendant looks on her computer, "Room 286." She points, "Take the elevator at the end of the hall."

After signing in, I head down an unusually wide hallway. A nurse pushing a thin, frail elderly woman on a gurney passes me. My heart melts as the elderly woman reaches out her hand. The nurse instinctively pauses, "Ms. Berth enjoys meeting new people. Do you mind?"

I am intimidated to touch Ms. Berth as her skin is very thin. Ms. Berth relishes the moment I put my hand in hers and tell me all about herself. "I was a teacher before the big monstrosities they call schools today. I taught Elementary school while raising three children. I am the great grandmother of ten children ranging in age from 3 to 15."

"Wow. You have had quite a life," I respond.

Ms. Berth has a joyful smile. "I have pictures in my room." She points down the hall.

I stand bewildered and unsure of how to decline this amazing, graceful woman. The nurse, far more accustomed to these types of interactions, graciously interrupts. "Let's thank our guest. We have to get ready for your speech therapy this afternoon. You don't want to disappoint Ms. Letty, now do you?"

The light disappears from Ms. Berth eyes as she accepts that her brief social engagement has ended. "Next time, dear." She squeezes my hand gently.

I feel a sense of shame for my selfish appreciation for the nurse's intervention. Walking away, I consider making a special return visit for Ms. Berth.

Walking past other rooms, I realize that no visiting guests are here. The noise is mostly from loud television sets or nurses checking on patients. I see none of the hustle and bustle seen on sitcoms. No elderly women sexually harassing elderly men, or recreation rooms full of patients happily playing cards, joking about the happenings of the prior day. The grounds in back of the facility are well preserved. They are full of abundant flowers and bushes, but empty of guests.

Mr. Ed's room is to the right off the main elevator on the second floor. I stand too long outside his door unsure if I should enter. I feel like an intruder. I didn't even bring flowers or a gift. What if he doesn't recognize me? His niece said that he has amnesia. I have never met anyone with amnesia. A nurse approaches, "Can I help you?"

"I'm just here to visit my friend." I point to the room and enter.

Mr. Ed, like many of the residents, is watching television from his bed. I barely recognize him. He is thin and has lost so much muscle tone since I saw him just a few weeks back. He has a disoriented look on his face when I enter.

"Mr. Ed. Remember me? Ella." I walk close up so he can see me.

Several seconds pass before Mr. Ed stops looking me over. Mr. Ed appears to be using considerable effort just to sustain his gaze in my direction. I realize that only the shell of my neighbor lies before me. I wipe an emerging tear from my eye.

I want to run from the room, but I hold steady. I pull a chair up close to the bed and sit next to him for a visit. Mr. Ed appears to want to speak and even opens his mouth but no words emerge. I decide to fill the silence telling him about all that is happening in my life. "I have a live-in boyfriend now,

Greg. He's not as good of company as you. I miss you sitting with me after work. I'm still having problems. I have to go to court tomorrow. I'm scared. I wish everything could go back to the way it was."

Mr. Ed appears to be listening. During our conversation he intensifies his engagement, squeezes my hand and opens his mouth to speak but no words come.

We are interrupted by his speech therapist. "Mr. Whitting, time for speech therapy." To me she says, "We have a standing appointment."

I say goodbye and kiss him on the cheek. Before walking out I ask Ms. Letty, "Can he speak?"

Ms. Letty kindly explains, "Mr. Whitting has language issues due to his head injury. He is making progress. He has been able to articulate sounds though he has not been able to form complete words. He can write some."

"Is he going to get better?" I ask.

"It is rare for people with this type of injury to make no progress, though some do have problems that are ongoing. Mr. Whitting needs lots of rest as he had considerable brain swelling. We will continue working with him. I believe he will speak again, but I cannot predict how well." The half-smile is my cue that she needs to get to her appointment.

I decide that I will visit weekly. I owe that to Mr. Ed.

I rush home to make it to work on time. I pull up to my apartment with 20 minutes to spare. Thank goodness, I live so close work.

While parking, I look up. Uncle Billy is sitting on the front stoop. My heart drops. I feel fear. Anna's note enters my mind. Why would Uncle Billy be sitting on my front stoop? I don't have time for this, either way. I have no idea what I should do. I look around. I do not see any of my neighbors.

I yell from the street, "What are you doing here?"

Uncle Billy doesn't respond, rather he just waves for me to come up.

I pretend to get a call from Tiff. I hope Uncle Billy is far enough away not to realize my cell never went off. As I approach, I say loudly into the cell, "Hey, I can't talk. My Uncle Billy is here and I've got to get to work in 20 minutes." I pause, then say "Okay. I'll call you back." I pretend to hang up and put my cell in my back pocket.

"We need to talk." Uncle Billy looks very serious. My mother always argued with my father saying that Uncle Billy was a deceptive person, and she didn't want him around. My father always rolled his eyes and responded, "He's my brother." I am unsure if he was here as my father's brother or as a deceptive adversary.

"I've got to change and be at work in a few minutes."

"I'll keep it short then. Be careful at that deposition. I'd be forgetful if I was you."

I think back to make sure I haven't said anything about the deposition to anyone other than Greg and Tiff. "How do you know about the deposition?" I step back, showing him my mistrust.

"They are watching you. If you say too much, I can't protect you."

I feel betrayed, not protected. "Who is watching me? When have you ever protected me?" My voice is obstinate. I am ready for a fight. Ready to fight the world.

Uncle Billy spits his chewed tobacco into his cup. Part of me thinks that he purposely chose this moment knowing my distaste for his ugly habit. He looks mean. "Girl, I'm your uncle even if you don't see it. I've kept an eye on you. I owe your dad that much. Your mom never cared for me, but we were brothers."

"Alright. I don't know what options I have, but I hear you. Anything else you need to tell me?"

"Have you seen Anna? I need to talk to her." Uncle Billy's mood changes perceptibly. He looks worried. Anna's note comes to mind. *Don't trust him.*

"Sorry, she asked to stay here, but it didn't work out. She left without telling me where she lives." In the end this was the truth.

"I bet it didn't work out. You wouldn't take even one of us in if we were dying, would you?" Uncle Billy's mood tips back to anger. He turns and walks away.

I quickly head into my apartment. I do not have time to think about any of this. I quickly change and make my way to work.

Chapter 16

Despite being moody when I dropped him off earlier, Greg gives me a wave when I walk into Taylors. I feel bad for being short with him. He is looking out for me. I still trust that.

I absentmindedly straighten shelves while reflecting. I try to put the puzzle pieces together. My family knows about my problems without me saying a word. Anna and my cousins keep showing up ever since I turned in Big John. A bag of expensive watches is in my possession, sort of. They are at the jewelry store. Anna wanted to stay with me but I essentially abandoned her.

One of Uncle Billy's disreputable friends tried to rent my house but failed to mention he was an old friend of Uncle Billy. Goons have been following me, sent stalking pictures to my phone, and violated the backyard of the rental house when I was there alone. Someone assaulted Mr. Ed. Someone broke into my apartment after stabbing Greg's tire. What does all this mean? How do the pieces fit together? Who is the someone or group of someones?

I give up on this train of thought as I am getting nowhere and try to change my focus. The solitary task of straightening shelves does not offer any distraction and my mind wanders to the deposition.

I have no choice but to go to the deposition. I received a subpoena. I can't refuse. I would have to get a lawyer if I refuse. I will be lying, regardless. I can't plead the fifth, as that would suggest I am breaking the law.

I try to wrap my head around the fact that I am going to commit perjury. Big John was growing pot in my house and left the house damaged, but he never tried to sell me drugs. I regret being stupid.

I interviewed Big John when he came to look at the house prior to signing his rental contract. He was the first and only prospective tenant. He told me he was working in the oil fields. He was making a good living. I figured having the money to pay the rent was all that was important.

In the end, telling the officer he sold me drugs did nothing other than give me a short term emotional high. I have not gotten any recompense. I certainly have gotten a lot of headaches.

When my shift ends, I clock out. Greg got off work two hours ago, but he is standing by the clock. He has changed clothes and looks very handsome. "Are you mad at me for wanting to see you home safely?"

I don't answer, but my smile surely eases his concerns. I can't kiss him in the store while in uniform. Instead, I push him playfully. Dean barks from behind the office counter, "Take it outside."

I fill Greg in on my visit with Mr. Ed and the visit from my uncle. "Maybe I'm being stupid, but Uncle Billy has me a little freaked out."

Greg ignores me. He pulls out his cell. He is buying something. After putting in his credit card information he announces, "I got us a last-minute reservation at the Ambassador Shoreline."

"You didn't need to do that." I say shocked.

"I can think of many ways you can repay me in a nice hotel." Greg does his signature wiggle of his eyebrows. "Leave your car here. I'm going with you tomorrow, invited or not."

Greg is parked front and center. I am relieved not to have to walk alone to the back parking lot and to get to avoid my apartment too. No surprise guests at a spontaneous hotel.

The drive down Shoreline Boulevard is beautiful. To the right is the sparkling bay with a full moon and stars glistening on the gentle waves. No gusts of wind tonight. To the left are stately homes and mansions.

"That one is the old Taylors family estate." I tell Greg.

A minute later Greg adds, "That one with the tower belonged to a woman's rights suffragette from the 1950's." I wish I knew all the wonderful stories attached to these homes.

"In ten years, maybe we will own one of these houses. I'll be a famous psychologist and you will create a computer program that revolutionizes the world."

"Sounds good, but I think I would want to move. Maybe Colorado?" Greg continues watching the road.

"Or maybe Oregon. We could live on the coast overlooking the ocean." With an unbearable reality upon me, this dream means more to me than Greg knows.

We park in the garage of the hotel. Before walking in, Greg takes my hand, "Do you mind if I tell them we are married?"

A giddy smile takes over my face, "Sounds perfect. Mr. and Mrs. Greg Sparsky."

I am exultant when we approach the counter. Such a change from all the feelings that have dominated the last 24 hours. "Welcome to the Ambassador," says the front counter clerk.

"We have a reservation for Greg Sparsky. We just got married," Greg says.

I giggle and squeeze Greg's arm.

"Honeymoon suite, then?"

"No, we have a last-minute reservation." Greg shows the clerk the confirmation on his cell.

"Complimentary upgrade. We have a four-star steak house on the roof that includes a bar with cocktails open until midnight. In the morning, we have a buffet until 10:30. Check out is noon. Enjoy your evening." He hands us our keycard for room 1822.

On our way to the suite, I share with Greg, "I have not been in a hotel since our one trip to visit my aunts in Maryland when I was in middle school."

"Maryland. Did you have fun?" Greg comments.

"It was a special trip for my parents' anniversary. My mom wanted to see her sisters. Maryland is really pretty. Lots of big trees." I add, "I can't see my mom and dad's faces anymore in my memories. Their faces blur. I'm glad I still have the pictures."

Greg listens as we get to the suite. "During the trip I complained incessantly because I was missing Tiff's 15th birthday party. I nearly ruined the trip. My parents actually grounded me in the hotel on the last day. I'm sure they wanted some alone time from their moody teenager. I have so many regrets attached to the best memories."

I stop myself. I am not going to ruin this evening. I am tired and distracted, but also excited. We have only been together in my apartment. This is a first for us. I grab Greg's hands and stare into his eyes. "This is our honeymoon."

Greg sweeps me up in his arms and carries me across the threshold. The illusion is complete. Greg has successfully taken a night destined to be full of anxiety and granted me perfection and happiness.

The room is warmer then I prefer. I immediately turn down the thermostat. We then look over the room. The suite is elegantly decorated with dark sleek wood furnishings with ambient lighting touching every surface. The bed has luxurious soft white down bedding and looks like a cloud.

Greg asks, "Do you want to go to the rooftop?"

"No. That would be a waste of this view." I stand in front of the floor to ceiling windows overlooking the bay and t-heads filled with sail boats. The sky outside our window is pitch black except for the intense sparkles from the stars. Across the bay, we can see the bridge all lit up and the USS Lexington an air craft carrier, known as the blue ghost, glowing purple.

Greg wraps his hands around my waist and kisses my neck gently. I turn and kiss Greg passionately, wrapping my body around him. I push Greg away, "This room is officially Naked Land."

Greg immediately removes my clothes. We take a shower. Greg role plays spa attendant washing my entire body. We transition clumsily to the bed amongst fluffy feather blankets. My spa attendant asks if my skin is dry then offers a happy remedy. Greg grabs the complimentary lotion from the bathroom counter. He takes his time moisturizing every inch of my body while I lay completely relaxed. His gentle and attentive nature encourages my reciprocation. The night blissfully continues as we envelop one another. If only we could stay in this fantasy. I fall asleep content in Greg's arms.

Greg, being a responsible soul, sets his phone alarm for 7 am, knowing I will need time to access appropriate attire. While I slept well, I awake with anxiety. We quickly check out of the hotel. I am sad to leave behind the magic of our prior evening to face the dire reality of the day.

Chapter 17

We drive to my apartment with only enough time to shower and change before leaving for the courthouse. I throw on a printed blouse and a pair of black dress pants. I wear my hair down.

The playfulness of the night before has passed. I feel the dark cloud of my bad mood return. I play back my uncle's visit in my mind. I have made no actual decisions on how I will handle today, with the exception of knowing I am showing up. That much I am committed to.

The courthouse is the same. Today, though, the courthouse is like an evil fortress where I am approaching my day of reckoning. Such a childish thought, I know, but I feel like a small child. Greg strides confidently by my side like a knight attempting to protect his maiden. At least in this version I am a maiden and not a child. I like that better. We approach the office door. I am pulled from my imagination back into reality.

Gail Henry once again is the first to greet me. She explains. "When ADA Kemp is ready, I will bring you into the same conference room from before. The court reporter, ADA Kemp, and defense counsel will be sitting at the table. You will sit across from them." She pauses then looks at Greg, "You will not be allowed to enter. You can wait here."

"Thank you." I say meekly.

"There will be no surprises." Ms. Henry assures me, then adds, "The entire process will be complete within the next few hours." Her smile is comforting.

When Ms. Henry comes for me, Greg and I stand. My knees feel weak and my hands are sweating. Greg leans over and kisses my cheek. "Good luck. I'll be here when you finish."

I smile and think to myself how this fiasco will be over when I am done. Hopefully I don't leave in handcuffs.

I enter the room and take the seat across from ADA Kemp. This time we stand on ceremony. Official introductions are made by all parties. The court reporter typing every word.

ADA Kemp opens by placing me under oath. Then explains the expectations, "You can say 'I don't remember,' if that is the truth. It is okay to estimate times and dates but comment such if you are unsure…" As he goes on, I think to myself that this is too many rules. I am going to screw this up.

Defense counsel begins, "State your name for the record."

"Ella Fontana."

"How did you come to know John Barrett?"

"He was my tenant for the last year. I have a rental house."

"How did you happen upon John Barrett on the date of July 10, 2018, at the Corpus Christi Swap Center?"

"He moved out of my rental a few days before. He left my house with considerable property damage. I came to ask him to pay for those damages."

"Did you ask him to pay for damages?"

"No, he turned his back on me and would not respond."

"If you did not ask a question, what did he not respond to?"

"He wasn't letting me ask."

"Is that when you called the officer over?"

"Yes."

"So, you called the officer over when you were angry that Mr. Barrett ignored you?"

"Yes. No."

"Which is it Ms. Fontana, yes or no?"

My face is hot like it is on fire. I know the story. I know the truth. I don't want to commit perjury. I want to leave. "I called the officer over because he told me I needed a hit and offered to sell me marijuana from the bong store."

"I thought you just said he turned his back and ignored you." He pauses without asking a question, "Now you are saying that he offered to sell you marijuana?"

"Yes, before turning his back."

"Is that how you described the incident in your statement to police?"

"I think I did."

"Would you be surprised to know that Mr. Barrett says you made up the accusations?"

ADA Kemp objects. "Calls for speculation."

I am instructed not to answer. The defense counsel continues, "Are you lying about Mr. Barrett attempting to sell you drugs?"

I don't want to be a liar. I don't want to make things worse with whomever is stalking me. I sit for a short time before answering, "I'm not lying. I'm sure he was growing marijuana in my house and pretty sure he was selling it to that store."

"That sounds like you are assuming a lot which might explain why you made this false allegation."

ADA Kemp again objects, "The attorney is testifying."

"Ms. Fontana did you make a prior report to the Corpus Christi Police Department regarding Mr. Barrett engaging in illegal activity prior to July 10, 2018?"

"Yes, I reported him for growing marijuana in my house."

"Did the police investigate your report or find any wrongdoing?"

ADA Kemp objects. "Compound question."

"I will rephrase. Did the police investigate your report?" the defense continues.

"I assume so."

"Did they find any wrongdoing?"

"No, but that is because he moved out before I found out. When I came in the house, it smelled horrible, like marijuana, and there was tons of damage, including dirt all over carpets and holes all in the walls. I researched it. The holes are for heating lamps. He covered up vents too, which is another sign."

"You have quite an imagination don't you, Ms. Fontana?"

"I know what I saw."

"Did you see marijuana?"

"I found seeds."

"Did you turn those over to the authorities?"

"No."

"Why not?"

"They already blew me off."

"Sounds like you need a lot of attention, Ms. Fontana."

"Objection, counsel is testifying." ADA Kemp looks frustrated.

This goes back and forth for some time until ADA Kemp has his turn. The ADA's questions are brief and easy to answer. He seems to be tying up loose ends.

When the questions finally stop, I quickly get up to leave. I feel like a failure, a liar, and a fraud. I don't want to make eye contact with anyone.

Ms. Henry takes me to another room to decompress. I immediately fall into tears. The humiliation is just too much. I don't want her to speak. I don't want her to tell me how clearly they can see that I am a liar. Thinking of my stupid, fraudulent testimony is mortifying. The defense lawyer is right on the money. After a time, Ms. Henry informs me, "There is a chance you will be called to testify."

More news I don't want. Greg is waiting when I walk out. He has a big smile on his face, until he sees the weariness on mine. "Are you okay?" His protective instinct is in play. He is angry for me. I don't like to see him angry. I reach out and bury my face in his shoulder. He does not ask anything further and walks me defensively to the car. I see Detective Haas across the parking lot. I hide my head in shame. He has worked so hard and I can't even perform this small task.

Chapter 18

I am disheartened. Greg instinctively knows how to handle me. He drives without speaking until he pulls up to the drive thru. He orders me a number five Whataburger. That means he orders me the best burger in town with bacon and cheese. I had not realized how hungry I am, until this moment.

We wait to eat until we get to the apartment. The food nourishes my broken soul, but I still can't get out of my own pessimistic head. I know I have done nothing right. Not that day at The Swap Center. Not today. Greg doesn't know I lied about John trying to sell me marijuana. What will he think of me if I tell him what a liar I am? I have no intention of telling him. Greg attempts to console me. "You are so brave and strong."

Part of me resents him for not understanding that I am neither brave nor strong. I am a coward.

"I'm sure you did fine." Greg offers.

I can't explain what happened and not explain why it is so confusing. Greg assumes that I am overwhelmed. I wish I could explain that I am officially a criminal who just committed perjury. I can't even commit perjury satisfactorily.

"It's not over. Ms. Henry said they could call me to testify in court. I really wanted this to end today."

I turn down Greg's offer of a massage. I am unworthy. I don't deserve Greg. I guess I deserve, what, prison? Heaviness hangs in the air until it is the time for me to go into work.

Greg is also working tonight, but he is going in a little later. "I'm going over to my parents' house before heading into work." Such a good son. I wish I had a family to visit. Greg invites me to a family dinner later in the week. I, in typical fashion, decline though in the back of my mind I am starting to feel the inevitable meeting needs to be set. Not today.

I give Greg a kiss and make my way to work. The evening is going by pretty much like any other day. While straightening shelves, I observe a woman who had obviously been shopping for some time abandon her basket after a phone call. I wait a time to see if she will return, but alas, I start putting away the returns.

During my reflection on the rudeness of this woman's actions, Craig and Jake walk up. "What a job? Reverse shopping." While they have the stupidest sense of humor, their conspiratorial laughter sells the show to onlookers. I am sure anyone walking by thinks this is the joke of the century.

I give a half smile. "What's up?"

"Dad asked that we check up on you."

Heat rises in my belly and makes its way to my cheeks. "Really? How often does he have you two check up on me?"

"Weird, but lately more and more. Good thing we need to pick up some beer and you work here." The conspiratorial laughter again, this time including some playful arm punches.

My co-worker Audra comes over to interrupt, "Need any help, Ella?" Audra obviously wants to meet my cousins. She has that extra skip in her step and flirty eyes blinking extra fast. I wish I had her easy mannerisms. She is probably a good match for one of my cousins.

Jake takes the lead and responds, "You can help me pinpoint the beer."

Audra laughs a little too loud and eagerly places her hands on his bicep, "Follow me."

Craig looks annoyed that Jake took the opportunity. He holds back with me while the two wander off. Craig loses his bright sunny disposition and becomes more serious. "Dad says you're in trouble. He hasn't told us anything, but I don't like it. We're here if you need us. Let me give you my number."

Something about his serious manner and expression make me feel that he is truly being protective. "I am not allowed to carry my cell on the floor. I can give you my number and you can text me." I rattle off my phone number.

After typing into his cell and hitting send, Craig gives me a genuine hug. I don't know why but I almost start crying. Neither of the boys ever hug me. Punch me, push me, laugh at me, yes, but never a hug. Not even at the funeral. Craig strolls off with a brief waive of hIs hand.

Greg starts working a few hours after me. I walk to the front of the store to say "Hi." Greg is happy to see me. "I can't stay and talk but I'll hold off to take my break with you."

While watching us interact, some co-workers smile a little too broad and some roll their eyes. We must be the new talk of the front end. Dating at work is quite common and this is pretty typical of new couples. I guess that is what we are, a new couple.

Returning to my solitary job, I consider how much my life has changed. Up until a few weeks ago I had only had one awkward kiss and now I feel like I have been with Greg for a lifetime. I always thought that coupling would be hard, but with Greg everything happens so easily. Like we are meant to be. Maybe Greg was sent to me to by my parents to be my family.

My mind then wanders to my neglected school work. I need to start a paper for English literature this evening after work. Luckily college classes don't have daily homework, just required reading. I never do the required reading. I just skim over everything and generally I do okay. School is pretty easy for me. I also have a project that I have to do for my physics class but that can wait until next week. I've been considering some ideas on perpetual motion using magnets, but that may be outside of my abilities. Luckily YouTube has plenty of videos to follow. I can't imagine what college students did in the past.

Lost in thought, I jump and yell when Greg taps me on the shoulder. "What?!"

"Sorry, I didn't mean to startle you. Are you ready to grab a bite?" Greg looks contrite.

"No, I'm sorry. I am just preoccupied. Let me get my purse from my locker."

"No need, lunch is on me. Well, dinner really." We clock out and head over to the Sandwich Shop.

We cross the parking lot without paying much attention. Initially, I don't see her. At least not until Greg opens the door to the Sandwich Shop. Anna is standing on the other side of the glass door. She looks bad. Concerned, I tell Greg, "Order for me. I'll be right in."

I immediately walk up to Anna while Greg watches from the doorway. Anna has been beaten. Her hair covers her eye but the shiner is large, swollen and unmistakable. She needs to see a doctor. She can't stand upright. "What happened?" I ask, afraid to touch her bruised arms.

"I can't go back. I'll die if I go back." Anna looks broken, physically broken.

I already missed work for the deposition. I can't ask to leave early. I decide to drive Anna to my apartment. She can wait for me. I will be home in an hour and half. What can happen in an hour and a half? My gun is in my car. At least there will not be a weapon in the house available to her.

Greg walks over with a concerned look on his face. "I'll take her to the ER," he offers.

"I'm not going to the hospital nor am I leaving with you." Anna asserts while holding her side.

To Greg I say, "I'll drop her at the apartment. I get off soon. I'll grab a sandwich after my shift." Greg doesn't appear to like the idea, but I give him my strong eye contact to indicate that this is not a discussion. Greg hands me his keys. I leave before he has a chance to argue.

Anna is quite on the drive to the apartment. "Look, I need to go back to work for a short time. Are you sure you won't go to the hospital?"

"No. They will call the police. No police. I'll be fine."

At the apartment, I have to assist Anna up the stair. I can tell she is in quite a bit of pain. "Take a shower. I have hydrogen peroxide under the counter for your cuts and Neosporin. I am sorry but I have to clock back in in a few minutes." I leave without taking any more time to look over her injuries.

Driving away, I am tense. Should I call the police? Is this a good idea? I look around to see if anyone is following me. I don't see anything unusual. I park and rush to clock in on time.

The last hour and a half of my shift lasts forever. Images of Anna's injuries scroll through my mind. When my shift ends, I clock out and rush back to the apartment. Upon entering I know something is wrong. My apartment is torn through. There is no sign of Anna. My apartment looks like the rental house without the smell. Cabinet doors hang open, drawers lay sideways on the floor, cushions are thrown about. Someone went through my dresser and closets.

I haven't even been gone that long. I wish Mr. Ed were here to stop them. He had always been my watchdog. Fear overtakes me. What if they come back? Did Anna do this? Or was this done to her? I should have taken her to the ER. I run back to my car to retrieve my gun and call 911.

As usual the police do not rush. After almost an hour a police cruiser pulls up beside me making a short "whoop" sound with his siren. I am not lost in thought this time. I am vigilant. I exit my car and meet the officer at the hood of my car.

The officer is young but built like a body builder. He stands over me in a hostile stance. I back up to give myself room he doesn't allow. "Evening, you reported a breaking and entering?"

"My cousin came by my work a few hours ago. She was beat up. I dropped her off here at the apartment. When I came home, she was gone and someone ransacked my apartment."

The officer takes down my statement. He asks questions. I am sick of questions. When he asks for Anna's address or last known whereabouts, I am ashamed. "Sorry, officer. I don't have any information. Not her phone number, address, or anything." I am the worst person in the world. I let Anna down again.

I give the officer my uncle's address but tell him she hasn't lived there in some time. The officer knows my uncle. I am sure not for good reasons. His attitude toward me becomes more dismissive. I am embarrassed of my family, but more importantly I am scared for Anna. She never had a chance in this world. I should have protected her. This was the second time I let her down. She wouldn't tear up my apartment. Not without someone twisting her arm, which obviously had occurred prior to her coming to me.

The officer walks through my apartment. He seldom speaks but when he does, I wish he hadn't. "Nice," he says while opening my undergarments drawer. I don't feel protected or served. I decide that I dislike police officers. Whether male or female I have generally come to the conclusion that rather than a calling, they have jobs they think of as droll and unimportant. I long for a good television cop with a chip on his shoulder and a desire to right wrongs. As with other nights, the officer calls in the crime scene crew that takes pictures and looks for prints.

The officer is packing up with the crime lab crew when Greg walks in. The officer brusquely approaches Greg, "What is your purpose here?"

"I am Ella's boyfriend and kind of live here." As his whereabouts at the time of the intrusion are clear, the officer blows him off as unimportant. I am happy to see the officer leave.

Chapter 19

I can't stay at the house. I feel unsafe. Greg offers, "I can rent us another hotel room."

"That is ridiculous. I'll go to Tiffany's house tonight. Why don't you go to your parents' house?" I am not really listening to Greg's response. I pack a quick bag, give Greg a kiss on the cheek, and leave ignoring Greg's protests.

Once in the car, I drive around looking for Anna. I let her down once again. Even if she let in whomever had ransacked my apartment, I am sure she did so against her will. She needs to be at a hospital. I should have taken her to the hospital.

My cell dings. Tiffany sends a text, "Where are you? I thought you were coming over?"

I feel bad that I didn't go straight over or give her a head's up. I have been driving around for an hour. I give up my search for Anna and head to Tiffany's house. I respond through my Bluetooth, "Be there in five."

Tiffany lives in her father's house with several roommates. I generally do not like coming over as her roommates are slobs, but Tiffany's room is immaculate and private.

Tiffany left the front door open so I enter without waking her roommates. I lock the door behind me. The house smells like a litter box and her home has scattered paraphernalia from her roommates last all-nighter. I cannot understand how Tiffany is okay with the living situation. She remains a very obsessive-compulsive neat nick in her own space. I am not a fan of this part of her life.

I knock quietly on her bedroom door. Tiffany opens the door. She obviously just woke up. Her hair is disheveled and her eyes look like slits. Tiffany gives me a big hug and yanks me toward her bed, shoving the door closed with her foot. We lay wrapped around each other without talking. There is nothing sexual for either of us in the gesture, but rather it feels like being with my parents when I was a young. Comfortable, safe. These are feelings I need to feel. Tiffany falls asleep before me. I long to have a mind that lets me just relax into sleep. My mind swims chaotically through memories. Memories mixed with horrible images solely from my imagination. How has my life gotten so messed up?

At some point in the night I fall asleep. I awake feeling restless and my eyes burn. I have to go to work. I brought my uniform in my overnight bag. I shower and change. I can smell breakfast when I leave Tiffany's room. Tiffany made blueberry pancakes. "Hungry?" She smiles.

"I can't eat. My stomach is in knots." After a pause I add, "I appreciate your efforts. You are the best friend a girl could have." I start to get choked up.

"I love you. I'll make dinner for us tonight." Tiffany is always steadfast. She understands not to push me to talk.

When she kisses me on my forehead, I respond, "Thanks, Mom." Tiffany makes me feel like a little kid. I would never admit it, but I like it. This moment is an escape from the truth of my life and gives me the boost I need to go to work. Before I leave, I hug Tiff hard. She is my rock. I love Tiff because she loves me, like family.

Work passes without any surprises or upsets. Just a boring day straightening shelves, showing customers where to find merchandise, and putting away items disposed of by shoppers. I skip lunch. Sitting and thinking while unable to act is just torture.

When clocking out, Greg approaches me looking upset. He was off today unlike myself. "When are you coming home?" He asks impertinently.

I react. What does he mean? He sounds like my parents admonishing me for staying out too late. "I have no idea when I'll sleep at my place again. Certainly, I have no plan to stay there tonight." I stubbornly goad him with my stern glare to push me.

"What about our first big date I planned for tonight?" Greg looks miserable, not patronizing. I realize that I abandoned him last night. I sent him home without considering his feelings.

"I'm sorry. I was so upset last night; I didn't really consider you." I relax my stance and lean towards him.

Greg leans in too. We stand forehead to forehead. Dean interrupts our moment, "Really guys, take it outside. This is a place of business." I am embarrassed for a second, then I choose to steal a quick kiss. Greg glows and Dean rolls his eyes and walks away.

"I think we can get in trouble for that," Greg says.

"Worth it." I laugh and grab Greg by the arm, leaving the store.

Outside of the store Greg explains, "I stayed at your place last night and cleaned everything up. I want you to come home and be with me. I don't like being there without you."

"I'm sorry. I was out of my mind last night. I drove around looking for Anna then went to Tiffany's house."

"I would have driven around with you. I was scared something would happen to you. I wanted to be with you." I should have given Greg the chance to support me.

The air is heavy. I decide to change the subject. "Did you actually plan a date for tonight?" I ask.

"An amazing date, but nothing that we can't do another night. I'd like to take you out, but tonight isn't the right night for my plan. I want you to be in a good mood."

My interest is piqued. "What was the plan?"

"Nope, not until we have the right mood. For tonight, let's just grab dinner and take a walk on the Bayfront."

"Tiff is expecting me. I need to call her." I dial Tiff.

Tiff answers, "When should I expect you?"

I feel guilty. Tiff probably moved her schedule around to take care of me. Greg is listening to every word. I try to think of the best way to make everyone happy.

"Greg planned a special evening for us. I think I'm going to stay at the apartment."

The long pause alerts me that Tiffany is not happy. "Fine."

I consider saying more but that will upset Greg. "Let's get together tomorrow for lunch."

Greg rolls his eyes. I hold in my urge to cuss both of them out.

"Whatever. You guys be safe." Tiff exits the conversation.

As we drive to dinner, I think about letting Tiffany down. I decide to send her a text. "I can't come over. Greg is upset. I'll explain everything tomorrow." While this betrays Greg, I feel better. I need to feel better. These are the two most important people in my world.

We end up at Harris Bluff which is a restaurant on the Bayfront t-head. This old series of barges floats along the t-head tethered together with ropes. The view is great with the added sweet sounds of sailboat ropes lopping in the wind. Something about the atmosphere is very calming. We sit in the back section behind the bar. A solo guitarist is singing the classic, *Brown Eyed Girl* by Van Morrison. Greg smiles, "Hey, you are my brown eyed girl."

I love this song. I was my daddy's brown eyed girl. I am not sure I am willing to give this to Greg. I don't feel like explaining this thought process, so I just smile and sing along. The guitarist sings easy listening music dating back to the seventies. We both enjoy this moment.

We order nachos with beef fajitas and a cranberry salad with walnuts and feta cheese to share. The rhythmic movement from the barge is relaxing. Swaying to the rhythm of the bay, listening to soft warm music, and eating comfort food turns out to be a delightful distraction.

Towards the end of the meal my mind wanders back to my apartment. The now all too typical feeling of anxiety returns in my chest. Maybe I need medication. My mother was strongly against medication for psychiatric issues. She believed that feelings serve a purpose of self-protection. She would tell me to wallow in my feelings and really figure them out. Right now, that is my preoccupation, wallowing aimlessly in my feelings. I am beginning to feel a little crazy.

"What are you thinking about?" Greg asks.

"What?" I reply coming out of my internal dialogue.

"You have the strangest look on your face. I don't think I've seen that expression before."

"This is my self-judging, you're a mess face."

"Good to know. I was starting to worry you were thinking of a way to escape from our evening."

I try to think of how my face must have looked, then realize I am probably looking even crazier. I respond, "I don't want to go home." The desperation in my voice is real.

"Do you want to take a walk?" Greg asks then offers, "If you don't want to stay in your apartment, we can look for a new place together. I can put some money in and we can even upgrade."

Greg just changed my real-life fear of reprisal into fear of commitment. "Ah. No."

"Too much, too soon?" Greg jokes.

"Let's take that walk." We pay the bill and walk up the t-head toward the boardwalk. Once we are on the street, familiar feelings of being watched overtake me. I see eerily unfriendly faces looking at me. My imagination plays all sorts of tricks on me. My breathing quickens. I start pay attention to my breathing.

Greg recognized my distress. "Let's just drive around." We walk back to his Jeep. As we are pulling out of the t-head, I see him.

Chapter 20

At first, I second guess myself, then I drill my eyes into him. He stares back unabashed. Fear runs through me. I thought he was still in jail. When was he released? Did he break into my apartment? Anna looks so much like me. Did he hurt her? Does he have her? How long has he been watching me?

I dial my cell.

"Who are you calling?" Greg queries.

I don't bother to answer. Greg will know soon enough. "When did he get out?" I yell into my cell.

Detective Haas is slow to respond. "Yesterday."

"You didn't think that was something I should know?" I cannot hide the rage and betrayal in my voice.

"Legally, I have no recourse. He has not threatened you. Actually, the case has been dropped." Silence hangs in the air.

I am immediately aware that my testimony is the problem. My lying. My perjury. My FAULT. Anger is replaced with regret and shame. "Why would he be following me if he was released?" I sputter.

"What makes you think he is following you?" Detective Haas's voice becomes higher. I assume this means he is interested.

"I just saw him 20 yards away staring at me. I stared back. He didn't even look away." Greg pulls over. His face is red.

"Strange. Look all charges have been dropped. He is a free man. You can attempt to put in a restraining order, but without pending charges and no threat. Has he threatened you?"

Incredulously I respond, "Someone has been watching me. Sending me pictures. Someone broke into my apartment."

"Yes, but Big John only got out yesterday. I'm not saying a protective order won't be granted, but it's not a sure thing." Detective Haas is dismissive. Obviously, he has no immediate plan to remedy my situation.

"Thanks. Thanks a lot." I hang up the cell without giving the courtesy of a response.

Greg demands, "What are you talking about?"

I ignore him and call Craig. I don't have my uncle's number so Craig is the closest I am going to get. No answer. I decide to leave a message. "You said to call if I needed you. I need you."

Greg pulls off onto a wide portion of the shoulder on Crosstown and turns on the emergency lights. "Who the hell are you calling now?" Greg's voice spews over me as I finish my call.

I appreciate the location of our stop. No one can sneak up on us without obvious detection. Somehow sitting on the side of a freeway with cars zooming by each pushing the Jeep to the left qualifies as the safest spot in the world. I put my cell down and gather my emotions and thoughts.

"My uncle knows what is happening here. I don't. So, I need to see my uncle."

Greg looks perplexed. I realize he only knows half the story. I consider filling him in, but I do not even know where to start.

After a pause I tell Greg, "Big John was released and all the charges have been dropped. No one notified me, but he was outside Harris Bluff. He was watching us."

"Why would your uncle know what is happening?" Greg tries to connect the few pieces of the puzzle he has at his disposal. I realize this is futile as I have many more puzzle pieces and have no clue.

"He urged me to be forgetful at the deposition. He wouldn't have done that if he didn't know something." Greg accepts this as a reasonable conclusion.

"Okay, so what is his address?" Greg continues.

"No. I can't just go to his house at night. He is kind of mixed up in some bad stuff. I don't go over there at night." We both take a minute to digest our thoughts.

The quiet is disturbed when my cell goes off. Craig is calling me back. "Answer it." Greg bullies.

I am annoyed at his goading, but hit answer just the same. "Hello."

Craig sounds nervous, "Where are you? What happened?"

I answer him. "I'm sitting on the side of the freeway. I'm fine. I need you to be honest. What do you know about my situation?"

"Shit. I don't know shit. You are the one leaving me weird messages." I can't tell if Craig is clueless or misleading.

"Where is your dad?"

"At home I'm sure. I'm out. I'm not planning to go home tonight."

"Do you have his number?"

"Yeah."

"Can I have it?" I start to wonder if Craig is being evasive. He certainly is not being helpful.

"Why?"

Really. That angers me. Why shouldn't I have my uncle's number? Asshole. "Can I have it?" I demand.

"I'll text him your number and tell him to call you. He'll get mad if I give you his number."

This infuriates me. My scumbag uncle doesn't want me to have his number. "Fine. If he can call me back sooner as opposed to later that would be great."

"Got it." Craig hangs up. So much for my hug. I guess his worrying about me is over.

Greg hears the entire conversation in real time as my cell was on speaker. For a short time, we sit in silence. I break the silence, "Let's go home. Too many accidents happen on this stretch of the Crosstown Freeway."

Greg drives us home. I assume he doesn't know what to say and we remain silent.

When we pull up to the apartment, Uncle Billy is sitting on the front stoop. I exaggeratedly waive my hand towards my uncle and comment to Greg, "Can I introduce you to Uncle Billy?" I would have preferred he called. I don't want his stopping by to become the new normal.

Greg retorts, "Next time I ask you to go to dinner with my family, you'd better say yes." While I know Greg is joking, his demeanor does not support this premise.

Before getting out of the car, I grab my gun from the glove compartment and slide it in the back of my jeans. Greg gives me a disapproving look. I do not care.

Chapter 21

"Craig said you needed me to come by." Uncle Billy is disheveled as usual and holds his typical convenience store cup in his hand. I know I will be in for a turned stomach. Just as the thought crosses my mind, he spits into his cup.

"Yeah. What do you know about my situation?" I ask.

"Am I going to be arrested too?" He challenges.

He knows that I had made a charge against Big John. "Do you know Big John?"

"I know of Big John. My circle is wide." The thought of his wide circle makes me think of all that is wrong in Flour Bluff. So many junkies and meth heads. I'd never met a friend of Uncle Billy's that I would want to stand next to alone in an elevator. I don't know the extent of my uncle's interactions with the underworld, The Syndicate, or whoever runs in his circle.

Greg stands behind me listening without interrupting. Uncle Billy looks him up and down with a disapproving face. "Who's the schmuck?" He nods his head toward Greg.

I am immediately protective. I wish Greg wasn't here. Greg does not respond. I am sure he wants to get the hell out of here. "This is Greg." I don't turn but give a small gesture towards Greg. I am not being dismissive, but I also want the conversation to stay about Big John. I immediately ask, "Why did you come see me the other day? I mean, what did you hear or know that made you come see me?"

"Girl, you just don't know nothing. You go blustering around disrespecting everyone. You need to know your place."

Uncle Billy overdramatically spits into his cup. I am sure he is well aware of my distaste for his chewing tobacco habits.

Greg moves in front of me. "Are you here to help her? I'm confused." I panic momentarily as I do not want Greg in this conversation. Before I react, I can tell that Greg's interference diffuses the power struggle and Uncle Billy relaxes.

"I know Big John's connections. People have taken an interest in you." Uncle Billy is at least responding to my question now.

Greg yields his stance and moves back to sit in his Jeep. I continue, "Big John was let out of jail yesterday, my apartment was ransacked last night, and tonight I saw him outside of dinner following me." I do not mention Anna. I am afraid to mention Anna. "I'm scared."

Uncle Billy's shoulders fall. He walks down the stairs towards me. When he is within arm's reach he stops. "I think there is more to the story then you are telling me," Uncle Billy sneers through his gnarly teeth while staring intensely with knowing eyes.

"What? I really want to know. What? I need this to stop. The charges against Big John have been dropped. How do I fix this?" I lose my composure and tears run down my face. I am heaving rather than breathing.

Greg comes to my side and protectively puts his hands on my arms defensively.

Uncle Billy thinks for a minute in silence, then says, "I have to go. Have you seen Anna?"

This feels like a trick question. I haven't mentioned her coming by last night and now Uncle Billy is playing my game, asking a question I do not want to answer.

"No." This is the truth; I haven't seen Anna since I abandoned her broken in my apartment before someone ransacked the place. 'Oh Anna, where are you?' I think to myself while averting my imagination from images of her bruised body. Guilt overwhelms me.

Uncle Billy appears to pick up on my aura. "Yeah. I'm going to be getting back to you after I check a few things out." And with that Uncle Billy walks off. No car that I can see.

Greg and I head into the apartment and lock the door. Greg takes the time to look around the apartment. Checking in the closets and under the beds for bad guys. We are both spooked. I walk aimlessly around hoping Greg won't ask any questions.

This is the first time I am in the apartment since it was ransacked. I was violated. Someone went through all my worldly possessions. Greg has cleaned up without me. The mirror on my armoire has a large crack along the upper right corner. Among many other missing items, my small crystal jewelry box that once held my mother's wedding ring when she would wash her face is missing. I'm not concerned because the crystal box has any value, just it is not where it should be. Who was Greg to do this without my permission? Was it broken or stolen? I have an urge to charge Greg with this injury, but upon looking at his face the urge abates.

Greg looks distraught like never before. Worry lines his young face. He does not deserve this. He didn't lie. He didn't perjure himself. He didn't bring this on himself. He is experiencing this because of me. All of this is my fault.

I sit back on the couch and pat the seat next to me. Greg is too distracted to notice. Lost in his own thoughts. I move towards him. Greg instinctively puts his arm out to embrace me. I stop short. I need to stand alone for what I am about to say. "I think we should take things back a step. This is all too much."

Greg looks despondent. I feel so guilty, but I have a strong desire to release him. Greg does not respond. Ignoring me, he walks into the bedroom and gets undressed. He climbs into bed and lays there like I have said nothing. Part of me is mad and the other part curious. I follow and sit beside him. After a long time, Greg finally speaks, "I'm not going anywhere. I'm still waiting for you to fill me in on the details I'm missing."

I place my gun on the side table. Greg gives me his disapproving look but says nothing. "I'm scared. I'm afraid that I went after the wrong guy and I'm afraid I'll pay with my life or worse, your life. I was hoping my uncle knew something that might help me find a way out of this, but if he does, he didn't share that information with me."

Greg corrects me, "You didn't go after the wrong guy. He came after you."

I want to tell Greg about my lies but the words get stuck. I am so tired. "Where is the crystal box that was on my dresser?"

"It's gone. Shattered."

The word 'shattered' reverberates in my brain. Shattered is the word that describes my life. Nothing in my life is solid, whole. Everything is in pieces and I can't put the pieces back together. The more I try, the more broken everything becomes. My life is shattered. I fall asleep contemplating the shards of my life that lay before me.

✑✑✑✑✑✑

I awake with a busy day planned. My potential renter, Joe Magnum, is meeting me this morning at the rental house. Step one in picking up the pieces of my shattered life.

I feel like I am letting my parents down. They set me up with everything I needed to make it. I am squandering my life advantages. Not that losing your parents is an advantage, but my life is an advantage over, let's say, Anna. I cannot think of Anna right now, though I cannot not think of Anna. On some level I believe having a good renter will make me the responsible adult my parents raised me to be. I can't wallow in all that is before me. Instead I will get this one thing done.

Greg starts moving around when I get out of bed but he is not fully awake. I jump in the shower. When I come out, Greg is smiling. "Any chance I can get you out of that towel and back in here with me?" He pats the bed enticingly.

I start to put him off, but realize I am really tense. Maybe a quick roll in the hay is a good idea. I pretend to ignore him, then playfully throw my towel into the air and jump on top of him in the straddle position. Greg is caught off guard but not for long. In one quick motion he rotates me beneath him. The spontaneity of the moment increases the intensity and power of our interlude, but shortens the duration. In all truth, I am happy that it is good and happy it is over. I don't have the time or emotional energy for in-depth love making.

While Greg jumps in the shower, I throw on a nice pair of pants and a dress shirt. I want to look professional. This morning I am basically a realtor. At least that is how I see myself. My goal is to get a contract signed. I open my laptop and print the pages I need. I read over the contract noting a few errors, ugh. I correct and reprint. By the time Greg is dressed, I am ready to head to the house.

Greg insists on coming with me. We both work later this afternoon.

When we drive up to the house, I take note that the lawn is getting a bit high. I make a silent prayer that I will have a deposit in an hour which will go a long way towards the final touches like getting a lawn mow and move in cleaning. Repairs are done and the house looks good. The marijuana smell is less abrasive, but still present. I light candles in several rooms after opening the windows. This will have to do. Thank goodness this morning is not too humid. Later this afternoon the place will be sweltering.

Joe Magnum is late. My excitement and energy fade. I don't want to have to put in for additional advertising. I haven't even had a call in the last week with any real interest. What will I do if no one rents this place? I decide to send a quick text to Mr. Magnum. Within minutes he texts back, "Not far off. Held up. Be there in five." My excitement returns.

Greg occupies himself looking over the work of the contractor he found for me. Considering Greg isn't reporting anything back, I assume he is happy with the work. I don't see any obvious issues and the place is ready to rent. Remembering back to how the place looked just a few short weeks ago, the difference in the house is startling. My parents would still be furious, but I am proud of my quick turnover and control over costs.

I hear Joe Magnum drive up. The engine in his pickup truck is loud. I peer out the front window to see a huge black jacked up Ford pickup truck with shiny silver running boards and bars across the back windows for fishing rods. I can't understand how anyone would think that is a reasonable vehicle. What a waste of fuel.

Greg joins me. "I'm totally getting one of those."

Men. The idea annoys me to my core. I judge him silently.

Joe Magnum is a tall man who looks no older than myself though based on his application I know he is 28. He has a nice smile. "Hi. I'm Ella." I present my hand out to shake his.

"Joe. Nice to meet you." Joe shakes my hand while taking in Greg.

"This is Greg. He is helping me today." I do not want to explain anything else. My function today is realtor not girlfriend. All of a sudden, I feel like a child playing make believe. I hope Joe takes me seriously.

Greg offers his hand and stays quiet letting me continue.

"Are you ready to sign or do you want to take a minute to look around?" I waive my hand around as an invitation.

Joe walks around. I see him trying to figure out the smell. I internally debate whether to let him in on my last tenant. I decide to give him the G rated version. "My last tenant violated the lease and there is a slight smell of marijuana, though when you move in that will dissipate."

Joe laughs, "I was trying to figure it out. It didn't smell like cigarettes."

"I hope it is not an issue for you. The property is a non-smoking property and will remain a non-smoking property." I clarify.

Theresa Kuhl-Babcock   Not Quite Broken

"We don't smoke. We actually have a new baby. I'm concerned about the smell a little and the carpets look not so good, especially in this room." We landed in my old bedroom. This is the room with the most soot on the carpet.

"I could agree to re-carpet this room." I suggest.

"How about the rest of the rooms? They don't look so good either."

I don't have the money to put into re-carpeting three bedrooms. I decide to offer a compromise. "I am not planning to re-carpet all the rooms, but I could either give a $500 rent credit and you could use it to re-carpet which rooms you desire. Or I could have this room re-carpeted."

Joe looks disappointed. "I'd rather all rooms be re-carpeted."

"That isn't an option at this time." I hold my ground while increasing my silent prayers that he won't simply walk away. "I will be having the lawn mowed and a move in deep cleaning prior to the next tenant moving in, though." I hope that shows good faith that I will be a fair landlord.

"Can I have a day or so to think about it?" Joe is backing out.

"Of course, keep in mind that the property will remain on the market. Hopefully, we can work something out." I am so disappointed. I put my hand out and offer a big warm smile despite my desire to have a meltdown.

Joe courteously shakes my hand and with a nod of his head Joe is gone.

Greg waits until the loud sound of Joe's engine fades then says, "Maybe you should have re-carpeted?"

157

For a man who has proven he can read a situation in the past, I am seriously disappointed. "Not now." I go around locking up the house and blowing out the candles.

My thoughts spin out of control. What do I need to do to get a renter? I needed this to work out. Nothing is working out. Shattered. I am shattered. I continue beating myself up emotionally. I should have spent the money for new carpet. I should have realized Big John was not a good renter. I never should have made that accusation. Shoulda coulda wouldas are driving me crazy, but I cannot stop my ruminations.

Chapter 22

"Let's get lunch," Greg offers.

We turn on the radio for background music, only to hear a public service announcement. "Corpus Christi, we are under a hurricane watch for the next 24 hours."

"Yesterday they said it was a tropical storm," Greg comments.

"Corpus Christi hasn't been hit by a hurricane in like 40 years. Hurricane Celia, right." I pull up the weather report on my cell. Hurricane Isabella is expected to be a category one hurricane and is projected to hit just north of Corpus Christi in two days. "The storm will turn to Houston. Houston always gets hit."

"I'm not worried if it is just a category one." Greg responds.

Greg pulls up to George's for lunch. George's is a nice Greek restaurant, but the chicken fried steak here is excellent. The big screen hanging above our table continues to provide news coverage on the storm progression.

To distract Greg I tell him, "We evacuated with every storm when I was a kid. Miserable. The last time I remember rushing to leave only to sit in traffic all day. My dad was sure we were going to run out of gas. We took our cat, Teddie with us to a hotel in Austin. Teddie, was the cutest cat with orange spots. She had the best personality. Teddie was usually really playful, but on that trip, she had a panic attack the entire drive to Austin. She held her mouth open, fangs showing, panting like a dog. Totally freaked me out. I remember begging my parents

159

to let her out of the cat kennel. Then she pooped. Oh my gosh, that was the stinkiest drive in history."

"Gross." Greg laughs.

"She didn't like being in the hotel either. She hid behind the headboard of the bed and would not come out. My parents were so frustrated. We didn't even leave the hotel room because they were sure Teddie would get out. I was so mad at them for holding me hostage in that stupid hotel room."

"Sounds horrible. Luckily we don't have any pets yet." Greg says.

I think to myself that with my recent luck, the storm will probably hit Corpus and my rental house will flood. "This says we are probably going to get a lot of rain because the storm is moving really slow." I let the flood and windstorm insurance go on the rental house. I am regretting that choice. Too late to get insurance now. "Either way, the storm is going to go north." I refuse to give the storm any more of my attention.

My evening shift starts out fairly typical, but with a major storm headed our way panic set in. Everyone is coming in tonight with poor attitudes, looking to fill up on fresh foods, canned foods, water and batteries. Within a few hours, Taylors is sold out of water. On my break I check out how the storm is doing. Isabella has strengthened to a category two and is expected to be a category three by morning. Corpus Christi is not under a mandatory order of evacuation as the path of the storm is expected to hit 60 miles north of us. Port Aransas and surrounding areas are under a mandatory evacuation order.

I clock out and wait for Greg. He gets out in an hour. I have four messages from Tiffany. She is already on her way to San Antonio with Bob. I call her back, "Hey Tiff. You decided to leave?"

Tiffany sounds alarmed, "Aren't you leaving? That thing will be a category four hurricane by the time it hits."

"It still sounds like it is hitting north of here. I don't have money to evacuate either." I explain.

"You are so full of it. You have money put away from that rental house. You work, go to school and barely spend any money. Don't be stupid. Use your savings and be safe." Tiffany isn't one to mince words and she is correct. I actually have money in savings. I never use it though. The money is their money, my parents that is, not mine.

"Greg gets off soon. I'll ask him what he thinks. I'm still thinking of staying."

"In that apartment? If the storm hits, your apartment will be gone." She is probably right. The old building isn't particularly sturdy. Tiffany sounds exasperated. "Call me when you decide. If you stay, you need to be in a house. Promise me you won't ride the storm out in your apartment."

I do not make any promises. I am more resolute that Corpus will be just fine. While waiting for Greg I think about seven-mile island and the research that showed that the closer you live to danger the less likely you fear the consequences of a mishap. I hope I am not being stupid.

I return to reading the weather updates. According to the local forecasters the storm is intensifying because it is moving so slowly. "The problem with this type of intensification is that wind will now be high, but even more problematic, the storm will likely sit, not moving for a few days causing catastrophic flooding."

My anxiety about flooding increases. Not because I fear being stuck, but because I don't want to lose the rental house. My rental house tethers me to my old life. The house provides for me, takes care of me, and is a path to realizing my future. I am sure this line of thinking is disturbed. I've been dealing with so much. I can't imagine nature coming in and finishing off my rental house. Maybe I should ride out the storm in the rental. There is no electricity, but if the storm hits then the electricity will be out everywhere.

Greg comes into the breakroom with a frustrated look on his face. "What's wrong?" I ask.

"My parents came in earlier. They want me to evacuate with them. I didn't say yes or no. My mom started crying. I am very annoyed. Do you think you would be willing to evacuate with them?" Greg looks nervous.

"Go with them. I'm going to say here." I casually respond.

Greg's eyes harden, "You really are infuriating. I am not leaving without you. I was thinking that you could come with me and my family. They are staying at my older sister's apartment in Austin. We could stay there in the living room or get a hotel if you don't want to go with my family."

"I'm not going to Austin. I've been watching the weather and most likely the storm is not going to even hit here. It is going to hit Port Aransas or Rockport then head inland to San Antonio and Austin with massive flooding. Austin and San Antonio are just as likely to flood. I'm staying here." I decide not to mention my awesome idea of staying at my rental house.

Greg is annoyed. "We need to evacuate. We are both off work tomorrow and classes at Del Mar are cancelled until after the storm. Why not leave?'"

"You know what. Let's just wait. The city only has a mandatory evacuation order for the island. If the city issues a mandatory evacuation order, I'll leave."

Greg gives up. "Alright."

Taylors set aside water for employees. We pick up our allotment, some basic necessities, fill up the gas tank, and head home.

The apartment complex is full. "See everyone is staying." I comment.

"No, in the morning all these people will be stuck in bumper to bumper traffic trying to get out of the city. Leaving tonight would mean avoiding the traffic."

Once home, we make a batch of popcorn and watch the local weather. "For those of you waiting until the last minute to decide on evacuation, you need to make the decision by noon tomorrow. After noon, you will need to stay and weather the storm as roads will not be safe."

We spend the evening watching local weathermen having their moment. Dave Howell has been the top local forecaster since I was a child. "He is having a good time tonight." I tease. "Look at the lines on his face. How old is he now?"

Greg ignores me and listens attentively to the forecasters. Tears come to Dave Howell's eyes as he dramatically pleas to the community, "An elderly man asked me today if he should evacuate. I asked him if he had any family. This man lives alone. I urged him to take the city evacuation bus out of town. Anyone alone will be at greatest risk if this storm turns and we get a direct hit."

Dave Howell's young protégé dramatically follows the lead of his mentor. "I urge the public to leave despite their being no mandatory evacuation order. Your life is more important than your possessions. Tomorrow will be too late. The time to make this critical decision is now."

Greg looks increasingly distressed, "We should leave. Let's just go."

"This is ridiculous. The storm is going to hit north of us. The weather stations confirm that being south of a direct hit is our best-case scenario. This storm is going to hit north. I am sure of it. The rain, tornados, and eye are not going to hit here. We are going to get high winds, but as long as we are in good shelter there is no real concern."

Greg points out, "In every other hurricane I can remember, the eye always turns at the last minute. We should leave. The current predicted path runs 60 miles from here. Why are we staying?"

"I'm going to bed." I am not so much tired, but I am ready to move time forward and see what the light of day tells us. "We will see if the path changes over night. We have until noon to decide."

Chapter 23

Greg and I awake to sounds of strong winds hitting the back window of the apartment. I reach for my remote and turn on the television. Regular programming. No forecast. Last night the coverage was all about the pending storm and this morning nothing. How can the *Morning Show* be on when a storm is bearing down on us?

Finally, Channel 6 brakes through with an update. "Hurricane Isabella's winds have increased to 115 mph. We now have a category three hurricane headed this way. We expect Hurricane Isabella to be a category four by the time it touches landfall tonight at around eight pm. The path of the storm is still projected to hit somewhere between Port Aransas and Rockport, 60 miles north of us." I am sure we made the right decision in staying put.

Greg calls his parents. I can only hear his side of the conversation, "We are staying put...No. We are going to be fine... We have water and food... Alright. We'll stay at your house."

I am annoyed Greg is agreeing to anything without speaking to me first. When he hangs up, he explains, "My parents left last night. We can stay at their house. Just us."

I am relieved and call Tiffany. "Hey girl. We are staying here, but in Greg's parents' house."

"Why are you so stubborn? Just get in your car and come up here." Tiffany is being a bit of a bully.

"Nope. I'm staying. I'll check on your house and make sure everything is okay after the storm hits. Don't worry about us."

Tiffany finally concedes. "At least you won't be in that stupid apartment. Be safe and call me. I'll be worried about you."

We pack up and head over to Greg's childhood home. I have only previously been in the driveway. I have never gone into the house. I am excited to see Greg's room without having to do the parent meet. I am about to see how he lives without me and get a feel for the place without any actual human interaction other than with Greg. I give a small thank you to Hurricane Isabella. The calm before the storm.

The house is a brick ranch style home in a cul-de-sac. The exterior of the home is better maintained than many of the neighboring houses with shutters and fresh paint on the siding. Inside, each wall has a different subdued color. The floor has many transitions between tile and hardwood. The furniture is plentiful and of a small scale.

"What a beautiful quilt." I comment on the wall hanging. The quilt features a small-town landscape set in winter. In the foyer is an antique hutch adorned with knick-knacks, mostly Hummel figurines. The house gives the impression of an antique shop that, while nice, simply doesn't belong in South Texas.

Greg explains, "My parents moved to Texas from Massachusetts when I was 11. I drove across the country with my dad and the rest of my family came a month or so later. I hated it here. I didn't make any friends. My mom hated the weather. She had never lived anywhere so hot and humid. She

complained all the time that my dad had stolen her from her
family. I thought we would move back, but we have been here
ever since."

"Do you still miss up north?" I ask.

"I miss having four seasons, big trees, and all my family,
especially my grandparents. We went back a few times. Things
are different now. I don't have friends there anymore. This is
my home now. I'd miss being able to go to the beach in
winter." Greg smiles.

"When do I get to see your room?"

Greg eagerly leads the way to the back of the house. His
room is just past his parents' room. I smile at the fairly empty
room with clusters of collectibles. There is a book shelf filled
with some books, childhood trophies and various awards. On
the floor beside his twin sized bed with Star Wars sheets is a
pile of comic books haphazardly strewn about. A dirty glass top
desk holds Greg's computer, papers, and a pile of video games.
I hadn't really thought of Greg as a gamer. I imagine young
Greg sitting in this relatively dark room eating junk food playing
music in the background while being obsessed with video
games. This room doesn't look like the Greg I live with.

Greg stands next to me, waiting for my thoughts as I
take in his room. I don't rush to comment. I am fully aware that
my response might be perceived as judgement. Greg is older
than me, but his personal space still reflects his younger self. I
hope that is the case and this is not the real Greg.

"I have to say; this is not what I expected." I give a
playful half-smile.

Greg smiles broadly, "Come on, this is a great room!"

"For a 12-year-old. Do you even fit on that tiny bed?" I state without filtering.

"You don't want me to bring my décor to your place?" Greg spreads his arms to encourage me to really take it all in. "I mean this artwork featuring my future Challenger RT with a V8 engine, including an embedded clock. This will look great in the bedroom."

The idea disturbs me. "I don't think it will look right. You can hang it in the closet."

Greg looks around with a nostalgic look on his face. Obviously, each of the items that repulse me hold a happy memory or a dream of the future. Even though I am not impressed with his personal items, I love the look on his face.

Inspiration hits me. "Doesn't matter, for the next 24-hours or so this is our space. You have been living in my space and now I get to live in yours." I mean it. This is an exciting adventure. "I have never slept at a boy's house before. Do you think that bed is big enough for two?"

An ornery look comes across Greg's face. "I've always dreamed of getting a girl in here."

"Well, I'm here now. What will you do with me?"

By the time Greg and I finish, the winds had really picked up which made our interlude that much more exciting. I start to think, if we get a two-bedroom apartment Greg should bring this little bed just for the memory. I laugh at myself for this silly thought, especially since the springs are very uncomfortable.

Since going out in the middle of a hurricane is not an option, we decide to make cookies. Greg has on his boxers and I have on his button up shirt. Our naughty afternoon at his parents' house is turning into the best of days. We gather the ingredients and preheat the oven. While mixing in the chocolate chips the electricity goes out. "The hurricane is not going to hit for another eight hours. This doesn't make sense." I complain.

"Maybe it will come back on." Greg responds.

I am disappointed. "Considering the dire circumstances, we can always eat the cookie dough raw and risk salmonella poisoning." I suggest.

Greg quickly puts a handful of cookie dough in his mouth.

"I was kidding." I chastise while moving the bowl outside of his reach.

"I'm not afraid of cookie dough." Greg bellows loudly while giving a loud obnoxious evil villain chortle.

I run around the room protecting Greg from this inevitable danger, until he catches me by pushing me into the couch. I am laughing so hard my side hurts. Greg takes a finger-full of dough and attempts to feed it to me. I finally give in and take a bite. "I guess we are doomed together."

Greg kisses me gently. The silliness passes and the tone of the conversation becomes more serious. "We better not eat too much." Greg concedes.

"Now you say that." I smile. I love this youthful Greg in his childhood home. I will cherish this moment forever. This is the first moment I really think about that word, love. I am not ready to declare anything, but I am sure in this moment that we have something real. Something different from ordinary. "I like it here. You are more yourself. I like it."

Greg beams, "I like having you here. I'd love for you to come over one day and meet my parents. I know I'll never have to face that moment with you, but I did get to meet your uncle and cousins. I think the time has come." He pauses then continues, "This is the next step. Right?"

"I think I'm ready. I already feel at home here. I didn't think it would feel like this. I want to meet your parents." I do. I trust Greg. With everything I have experienced since we started seeing each other, he is the one thing I trust. At this point, I don't even think I trust myself. I keep making stupid decisions. Greg is my safe bet, my safe haven.

The evening progresses slowly without electricity. Greg has an old radio that takes batteries. We listen to reports of the progression of the storm. We check Facebook constantly. Channel 6 news continues to post short updates. Friends comment on whether they stayed or evacuated. It appears most of those who stayed are also without power. Distant friends and relatives send well wishes that we stay safe.

The electricity remains off and we assume that we will be without electricity for the remainder of the storm. The storm's path has not changed but has escalated to a category four with expected sustained winds of 150 miles per hour. Our winds shouldn't be quite that high since we are south of a direct hit. I worry for the small coastal towns under mandatory evacuation orders. I hope everyone evacuated.

The wind is hitting directly against the back of the house. We decide to open the front door out of curiosity. In the shelter of the foyer, there is no wind and a strange sense of calm. Greg wanders out with his cell to capture the scene of trees bent nearly to the ground with no letup of intense winds.

My mind wanders to the Native American Prayer, 'May you be as strong as an oak and as flexible as a birch.' I feel like a wounded tree with weakened roots without my parents. Not full grown but strong enough to handle some wind, but fragile enough to falter in a hurricane. This storm, these trees, are a metaphor for my reality. I am figuratively and literally in a hurricane.

I hear it first. The snap. My head swings to the left just behind Greg. A 30-foot palm swings across the front of the lawn where Greg stands. I scream and run towards Greg. The tree lands just inches from Greg then rolls rapidly towards him. Greg falls.

Luckily Greg is not seriously injured, only bruised and shocked. His cell falls on the grass next to him. I pick up the cell and help Greg to his feet. "Go back in. I don't want you hurt." Greg barks.

I hold my tongue and focus on getting Greg back into the house. For the first time the winds feel forceful and impede our progress towards the house. I know this must partially be my imagination, or possibly Greg is more injured then I realize.

Once in the house, I look Greg over to make sure he is okay. The gash to his thigh is pretty big with some bleeding. He holds a hand towel firmly over the gash while I head to the medicine cabinet to find something to clean the wound. Inside the medicine cabinet I find hydrogen peroxide and Neosporin. As a child that was the cure for all cuts in my family.

Greg is sitting innocently enough on the couch holding the hand towel over his injury. He looks like a little boy ready to be scolded. I have no intention of scolding him. I pour the hydrogen peroxide onto a napkin and dab at his wound. Greg makes a sound of discomfort and wrinkles his lip slightly as the medicine cleans his wound. "Please, you could have injured yourself much more seriously." I scold despite my first thought.

Greg gives a big 'I am appreciative and sorry' smile.

I feel bad. I smooth a big glob of soothing Neosporin on the wound. Lifting my shoulders slightly I say, "I couldn't find any Band-Aids."

"I think I'll be fine. The bleeding has mostly stopped. The pain is less thanks to my awesome and sexy nurse." Greg smiles suggestively.

What a flirt. I can't help but smile at his poor choice of moments. "Really. You know going out in that wind during a hurricane wasn't very bright, but I suppose sitting in the doorway wasn't either."

"I guess we'll have to stay in for the rest of the storm and hold each other."

There really isn't anything to do other than hang out and talk while munching on everything in the house. I enjoy the sound of Greg's voice when he is talking, regardless of the subject. The storm outside makes a dramatic howling noise that is comforting from within the quiet dark house lit only by a few candles. At 8:18 the storm directly hits Port Aransas 45 miles to the north. This is the worst of it. We survive. Knowing we aren't going to die; we fall asleep on his parents' king size bed.

Chapter 24

While we awake in general comfort and the happy haze of embracing each other, outside the house a very different picture is before us. Leaves, branches, fences and roof tiles are strewn about. The electricity is still off and the quiet is befitting of the wreckage.

Greg takes pictures with his almost dead cell phone and sends them to his parents. Greg's parents text back, "Not too bad. Glad you are safe. This is why we have insurance."

With nothing else to do, Greg and I decide to drive around and assess the damage. This also allows us to charge our cell phones through the car battery. No major damage is observed. Sections of fencing are down as well as a few of the tall business signs. The "A" in Taylors is missing across the front of the building. For the most part, we drive through a ghost town. Tiffany's house is intact with similar minor damage. I take pictures and send them through Facebook messenger.

We then drive to the apartment. The complex does not appear to have suffered much in damage that a rake cannot remedy. The old complex has no fencing and no trees. The pool was removed some years ago. We halt our progression up the stairs when Greg notices the door slightly ajar.

We immediately call the police. "911, what is your emergency?" As had become customary I explain the situation, giving my name and address.

The operator clarifies, "Due to the storm, the city is under a strict triage policy. Only emergencies will be receiving immediate help. I will dispatch an officer, but there is no guarantee how long that response could take."

I return to my car to retrieve my gun. Greg objects, "Give me the gun."

"Nope, get your own gun."

Greg rolls his eyes. "Fine, but I'm going in first." He hurries up the stairs.

His actions infuriate me and cause me to rush more than I had previously planned. We make it to the door at the same time. I grab his arm, careful not to move in front of him, but with the intention of slowing him down. I call out, "I have a gun. I am entering."

Upon hearing these words, Greg concedes slightly allowing me to enter with him. He obviously prefers the idea of holding the gun, but recognizes that the gun should not enter behind him.

The apartment is small so we see her immediately. My heart pounds in my ears. I am disoriented. Anna lays on the floor in the hallway. I don't trust running to her. Instead we carefully check every corner of the apartment. Once the apartment is cleared, we return to Anna. Her lifeless body is slumped over in a heap. She is thin and frail. Her body has bruising patches all over in many different shades but nothing that looks new. There is no blood. She looks unkempt and sickly.

I quiver as I think how she looks like an alternative universe me. Dead in my apartment. Did she die because someone thought she was me? Why was she here? How did she die?

While I stay kneeling beside her, in a stupor, Greg is already calling 911. "911, what is your emergency?"

"This is Greg Sparsky. I called a few minutes ago. We entered the apartment and my girlfriend's cousin is here. She's... dead."

The conversation continues but the word dead just reverberates in my mind, over and over again like a stuck record player.

I am frozen holding Anna. Greg reaches down attempting to pull me up. I push him away. "Leave me alone." Huge tears roll out of my eyes and a guttural noise exits my throat. Time isn't moving. How can Anna be gone? Why did I stop looking for her? Why was she here?

An officer arrives and instructs me to move away from Anna's body. His cold direction is like a dagger to my heart. "No. No. No. Get out!" The officer does not ask again. He grabs ahold of me firmly by my trunk and pulls me into my bedroom, dropping me on the bed. I spill out in a heap on the bed. Agony. I feel agony. The officer stands over me. I cannot speak normally; my throat is sore, like a ball is obstructing my airway. I frantically take long deep drags of air. The officer is speaking but my vision blurs from the outside in. I have tunnel vision. I cannot breathe.

When I awake, I am confused. Everything has changed. For a moment I think I had a nightmare, but where am I? My vision returns through a fog. Initially, I see very bright lights and white. Am I dead? Was the alternate universe body I had seen in my apartment my own, as I passed to the other side? I hear voices and imagine they are my parents. A sense of calm passes fleetingly replaced with bewilderment. The voices are not my parents but strangers. A woman in unattractive green scrubs and a clipboard stands over me. "She is coming around," the stranger comments.

I realize I am in a hospital. I have no memory of leaving my apartment. Where is Greg? "Greg? Greg?" I anxiously scan the small space surrounded by a curtain. An emergency room. I am in an emergency room.

"Can you tell me your name?" The nurse questions.

"Of course, Ella Fontana. Where is Greg?"

"What day is today?"

"I have no idea."

"Who is the president of the United States of America?"

"Lincoln. Leave me alone. Where is Greg?" I am completely frustrated with this nurse.

The nurse is equally annoyed. "I'll answer your questions once you've answered mine. Who is the president of the United States of America?"

"Donald Trump." I respond. "Now where is Greg?"

"One more question, what year is it?"

"2018."

The nurse smiles halfheartedly, "I'll check to see if anyone is waiting for you." She leaves without further conversation. Fortunately, she returns relatively quickly, "There is a Greg Sparsky in the waiting room. He was not allowed in the room while you were unconscious."

"Unconscious. How did I become unconscious?"

"You hyperventilated and passed out. You were given a sedative in the ambulance and have been sleeping for several hours. Your pulse has returned to normal and your color has returned."

The idea that I had passed out bothers me. I am becoming quite a piece of work. "Can Greg come back now?"

"Yes, with your permission. We will need you to fill out papers now that you are feeling better. I will return in a few minutes."

As the nurse leaves, Greg enters and immediately sits at my side. "Hey, I have been worried about you. They wouldn't let me ride in the ambulance and barely told me which hospital they were taking you to." Greg picks up my hand and kisses it gently despite his obvious agitation.

The nurse returns with a stack of papers. "I need you to fill these out. Do you have insurance?"

"No insurance."

"You will have to meet with one of our account managers before checking out, but we can worry about that a little later." She leaves.

I avoid thinking about the cost of this trip to the hospital. I didn't consent to coming to the hospital or an ambulance. This just isn't fair. I work through the forms. I have no next of kin, at least no one I consider a next of kin. Uncle Billy? Oh gosh, I will need to call Uncle Billy and tell him about Anna. How will I do that? My chest tightens.

Greg notices immediately, "Are you okay?"

"I have to call my uncle. How am I going to do that?"

"You don't have to call anyone. The police will do that."

"No. I can't wait until they call him. Do you know where my cell phone is?" Greg walks to the corner of the stall looking for my cell. Images of Anna float through my mind. Young Anna, strung out Anna, Anna asking to stay with me, Anna slumped lifeless on the floor. I will never see her overcome her poor life choices. I will never see her grow old. Our dreams of the future together are no longer unlikely, but impossible.

Greg finally returns with my cell. I still don't have my uncle's number. I have to call Craig. Should I tell Craig? That is like a cop out, but significantly safer. I decide to call and figure out what to say after, yank the band aid off quickly. No answer. I decide to leave a message. "Craig, this is Ella. I need to speak with Uncle Billy immediately. This is an emergency. It's about Anna." I hang up.

Within 5 minutes I get a text response. "Don't bother to call us. We know."

A flood of emotions overwhelms me. *Don't bother to call us. We know.* Anger, confusion, sadness, fury. I immediately dial the cell again, but this time I realize I am blocked.

Chapter 25

I never want to enter my apartment again. Greg's parents are not home yet so we decide to stay at their house. I am exhausted, emotionally and physically. My muscles hurt like I have been doing hard labor. My head pulsates. My skin is in flames. My mind hurls ugly, hurtful thoughts and images. Anna is dead. My family dismissed me. I am a pathetic mess. I can no longer hold everything in.

As I sit on the couch, I feel my muscles simply give out. My limp body bounces slightly as I weep quietly, then loudly, then quietly.

Greg tries to comfort me. "I am so sorry, Ella."

I push him away and bury myself into the couch.

Eventually Greg makes himself busy in the backyard, working on the sections of the fence that fell. He is a good son. Part of a good family. I have no business being with Greg. We do not match. I consider walking out, but I have nowhere to go. I realize that while I do not deserve Greg, he does not deserve to be abandoned. I know his feelings are as strong as mine.

By the time Greg comes in, I am spent. I have no emotional energy. No tears to cry. No thoughts worthy of processing. He sits beside me. "I wish I could do something to make things better," he comments.

"You do make things better. By being here." After a pause I confess, "I considered leaving earlier."

Greg looks hurt, "Leaving. Leaving me?"

I thought for a second before answering, "I am so hurt and confused. I don't know how to feel. You don't deserve any of this. You can do better than me."

Greg rolls his eyes then says, "Every time something bad happens you just give up on us. How do you think that makes me feel? You don't let me comfort you. You pull away. You have to start trusting me, trusting us. I don't know how many times I can deal with the rejection."

I do not respond. Part of me really wants to walk out. Be on my own. Screw this idea of us. I hold in these thoughts. I close my eyes and pretend to sleep. Before long I fall asleep. A restless ugly sleep. Anna walks into my apartment, "Why didn't you let me stay with you?" I awake startled and shaking.

Greg is still sitting beside me. "Are you okay?" He holds me and I hold him back. His strong arms embrace me.

I squeeze him a little tighter. I hope he reads into the gesture what I mean. *I need you. I want you.* For now, this will have to do. Greg strokes my hair and accepts my unspoken communication.

Greg's cell rings. "Hello." After a pause, "I can come in tomorrow. Ella is not going to be ready. She had a death in the family."

"I can go in. Tell them I will come in." Getting back to work sounds perfect. Everything is closed today due to the storm. I cannot just stay home with my thoughts. Working will be a nice distraction.

Greg hangs up. "Are you sure? I think you should take a day off."

"No, I don't want to. The distraction will be good for me."

Greg finishes the call then looks at me. "When do you think the funeral will be?" Greg asks.

My aunt and uncle will be making those decisions, and they aren't talking to me. I don't know if they will even do the typical obituary. They thought all of the pomp and circumstance of my parents' funerals was a waste of money. Maybe I should offer to pay for the funeral. Would they even take my call? I give up on these thoughts.

"I don't know. Did the police say how she died?" I ask.

"No. They asked me a bunch of questions about how she got into the apartment and where we were. Then you needed me." Greg squeezes my hand.

The electricity remains out which sucks because there are no distractions from my horrible thoughts.

"My parents are coming home tomorrow," Greg tells me.

"I do not want to be here. I don't want to be in the apartment. Maybe I can go to Tiffany's house."

Greg looks upset. "Where can we go?"

I realize that I am not considering Greg, again. "My apartment lease is up in two months. I doubt they will release me early, but I am going to ask. I can't go back there again."

"What if we ask to be moved into a different apartment?" Greg asks, then changes direction, "You have a house. Have you considered us living there? What is the mortgage?"

I hadn't considered moving back into my house, but the rental is just sitting there empty. "I own it free and clear. No mortgage, just insurance, taxes, and upkeep."

"How much were you getting in rent?" Greg asks.

"Sixteen hundred a month." Part of me is cautious about giving Greg so much information. Disclosing finances is not such a good idea. Greg is adding up my expenses in his head. "Look this is making me very uncomfortable."

"Sorry. We can look for something else, or I could start paying rent. My half would be $800 month which is a little steep but apartments are that much, so yeah it is an option." Greg lifts his eyebrow as if asking me a question.

"You would pay $800 plus half of the bills and do all the lawn work?" I follow up. I will not actually be paying any rent. But I also will not be getting any rent. Big picture, my costs will not be significantly higher. Add that I never touch the rent money.

Greg responds, "I can do that. I like the idea of us moving into a new place together. A real house."

"Keep in mind this isn't a new place for me. I grew up in this house, and it will be my house. You will be my renter. A tenant. Will you be okay with that?"

Greg pauses, "I guess I didn't think that through. Seems weird that it would be your house not our house. If we rented any other house it would be ours."

Feeling guilty I reply, "Well, it will be our house 50/50 split cost, but I will still own the house. I will still have final say on anything that an owner has say over. You will have to sign a lease with me. I am a stickler for the legal stuff. I have to protect my interests."

"How romantic." Greg says sarcastically.

"Then we shouldn't live there, but it is the quickest and easiest solution to our problem. You don't have money laying around. Where does your money go now?" I ask.

Now Greg looks uneasy, "I pay $200 rent to my parents and I spend the rest. I own my Jeep but have car insurance and my cell phone bill. I have a few credit cards. I don't really pay attention to my spending, but, at some point, I'm going to have adult bills. I have an adult job. I guess I just need to start paying attention."

"What can you afford in rent with your other bills? And how much credit card debt do you have?" I question.

"I get why you got uncomfortable earlier. This sucks. I guess if we want to really live together then we need to share this kind of information. This grown up stuff is not so fun." Greg concedes. "I should be able to do $800 month. I work 40 hours a week and have a steady income. I just need to sit down and figure out where my money is going."

I compromise, "Let's move into my house, tomorrow. No lease and give it two months. If it doesn't work out, you can go home and I can find a new apartment. I don't want to be in my apartment anymore. I can't get Anna out of my mind. I don't even want to go back for my things."

Greg takes charge, "Well you work in the morning. I will go to the apartment and start packing. I will try to rent a truck. I'm not sure if anything will be open with the storm. Tell me what you want from the apartment and I'll bring it to the house. I can arrange to have anything left donated to Goodwill. I don't really have any furniture to bring. Everything belongs to my parents. Are you okay with that?"

"I have everything we need. Remember I have everything that belonged to my parents. I actually have a storage unit with the rest of the furniture. I kept almost everything." I start to think of the storage items. "We can use the stuff in storage for now. I really don't want to go back to the apartment."

I am so tired. We go to bed. My sleep is restless. Every noise makes me bolt upright. My thoughts vacillate between pictures of Anna, my parents, and moving into my old house with Greg. My anxiety is grossly out of balance.

Chapter 26

I start my day early. Greg is still in bed and I do my best not to rouse him. I straighten up the house so Greg's parents will come home to a clean house.

When I get to Taylors, the electricity is still out and the store is closed. I have a message on my cell informing me that I will not be needed today. With multiple transformers down throughout the city, Taylors is at the mercy of the system.

Usually I welcome a day off, but not today. Time passes slowly when there is no electricity or businesses open. I sit in my car considering my options. I can go to my apartment and start packing, but the thought of my apartment makes my stomach hurt. I can call about a rental truck to get my furniture out of storage, but my anxiety keeps me from doing anything related to moving.

I decide to visit Mr. Ed. The drive is different today. The streets are barren. Fences are knocked down. Tree limbs are strung about. Roof tiles clutter yards. My city is intact but tattered. I unsuccessfully try to stop myself before I compare my life to the aftermath. I wish my personal storm was over, but I feel like the storm is still brewing behind the scenes without any forecast as to the possible impact. Nothing is resolved. A sense of unease pervades.

Mr. Ed's convalescent home is unaltered. The building is a fairly new structure. No significant damage. The place remains stale and quiet, too quiet without electricity. The same clerk checks me in though she does not appear to remember me. As I walk to Room 286, I decide I will pay a visit to Ms.

Berth. I ask an orderly while in route. "What room is Ms. Berth in?"

"Sorry, but she is no longer with us."

I start to ask what *no longer with us* means then decide that I cannot take any bad news. I continue to Mr. Ed's room.

Mr. Ed is in his bed, staring off when I enter. He does not immediately notice me. I sit at his bedside. He finally notices my movement. I await his generously kind eyes, but today something else shines through.

Mr. Ed's hand trembles as he grabs my arm roughly. Though still difficult to understand, he irately asks, "Ella. Why Ella? Why?"

"Mr. Ed, I've missed you." I lean in to hug him, but his hand halts my progression.

He holds my arm firmly and repeats, "Why Ella? Why?" His face looks distorted and sad.

I do not understand his question. "What do you mean?"

Mr. Ed furrows his brow and choppily says, "You were there." He is angry and struggles to find the words to say more.

I cannot comprehend what is happening. Mr. Ed immediately becomes cold and withdraws his hand. A nurse enters the room, "I think you should leave."

"Mr. Ed, I love you. You are like family to me." I reach for Mr. Ed but he turns his head and does not respond. After a minute processing, I realize Mr. Ed believes something about the night he was assaulted that he cannot explain to me. "I swear on my life I wasn't there that night. It wasn't me. I'm sorry, so sorry." I walk out of the room choking down tears as the nurse tends to Mr. Ed.

Walking away, I know this will be my last visit with Mr. Ed. It feels unfair that Mr. Ed is angry with me. I don't blame Mr. Ed, but the loss is more than I can take. I wasn't there during his assault, but I am sure the assault is my fault. Mr. Ed is safer without me.

I sit in my car feeling sorry for myself, mourning my losses, discouraged and broken. My cell brings me out of my trance.

"Where are you? Taylors is closed." Greg sounds concerned.

"Sorry. I went to see Mr. Ed. I didn't think to call you."

"Are you alright? You don't sound like typical you." Greg is attuned to my moods.

"I'm fine, just tired, really tired." I don't want to give Greg any more of my burdens. I will hold this guilt alone.

"Well, I'm off work and you're off work. Do you want to meet at my parents' house? They are on their way home today. I think they get in around five."

"I want to meet them and tell them thank you, but why don't we see if we can get a trailer to bring the furniture to the house. I don't think I'll feel comfortable sleeping at your parents' house tonight with them home. That would just be too weird."

I imagine Greg rolling his eyes. "I'd love for you to meet them. I mean, they'd love to meet you."

I choose to ignore him and we agree to each call around to see if any rental truck places are open. I am not having any success when Greg calls, "I found a trailer that belongs to my friend's dad. I can pick it up right away."

We meet up an hour later at my storage unit. Greg eagerly looks through the unit, opening boxes and commenting on the furniture. I guess to him the furniture is new, but for me each item brings about memories of a time that I had all the support I needed in this world. My heart hurts.

We decide to transport my parents' old king-sized bed and frame, their dresser, their couch, a 60-inch television, and their tall dining table set as well as a few boxes of kitchen supplies and necessities. We will have all the basics.

We grab some burgers on the way to the house. Greg is obnoxiously excited. I try not to ruin his day, though no part of me is enjoying any part of this. I can't get Mr. Ed or Anna out of my mind. I have very few people that I am close to in my life and they are dwindling down. I work very hard not to show my true feelings to Greg and focus on the job at hand.

We work hard moving everything into the house. While Greg is imagining a new home, I am experiencing flashbacks of a much happier time. I know where each item belongs.

"How about putting the couch over here?" Greg offers.

"No. The couch goes over here and the T.V. hangs in that corner." Everything fits naturally back into its place. I wish I fit as easily back into this life. I am no longer that young girl with big eyes excited about growing up. I am a twisted, sad version of that girl but no longer that girl.

Chapter 27

Greg wants to take full advantage of the trailer as he told his friend he would return it tonight. "I'm going to the apartment."

We make a list of everything that he needs to pack up and bring over: clothes, personal items, cleaning supplies. "Let me call to see if I can find someone to help me get the washer and dryer."

While Greg makes his call, I continue setting up the house. I don't want to go to the apartment. Plus, I am not strong enough to help move the appliances down stairs. I plan to leave that to the guys.

"All right. I'll be back in a few hours." Greg pecks my cheek and heads out.

After about an hour, I have everything generally in place. The house looks empty and lacks character. I head over to Value-Mart. I find a soft set of grey sheets along with a fluffy Duvet with a modern interweave of stripes in various shades of grey and blue. I add in two mismatched side tables and a sleek lamp. A simple teal shower curtain with matching rugs for the guest bathroom will work well. The master bath has a standing shower and garden tub so I pick out dark brown rugs and a few matching towels. The walls are barren so I choose a few wall hangings for each the rooms. When going to the checkout, I see a wall mount for the television. Greg will want that. I am happy with my purchases and return to the house.

Distracted, I enter the house with a handful of items that I throw onto the sofa. I hear the front door. I turn expecting to see Greg, but instead Big John stands in my entry way shutting the front door. My heart immediately races with fear, until another emotion takes over. "You, this is all your fault. Anna, Mr. Ed. You have taken everything from me." I run at him with the intention to scratch out his eyes.

Big John easily subdues my attack by grabbing my hands and twisting me around. He holds me with one arm across my chest while firmly holding his other arm that he has wedged behind my head.

My dad taught me some self-defense and told me to think about what I would do if attacked. I fight, kick my feet at his knees, thrust my head back, and wail with all my might, but to no avail. My actions are futile. Tears roll down my cheeks as I start to understand that I will soon meet the same fate as Anna.

To my surprise, as my fight leaves me, Big John releases me. Rather than anger, I see a different emotion on his face. I struggle to understand what is happening. Big John stares at me for a long moment then he says, "I still can't believe how much you look like her."

My mind swims. He can only mean Anna. He did kill her. My rage returns, "You killed her. It was you." I run at him once more wishing I had my gun. Stupidly, I left it in my car. I use my fists to pound on his chest.

I brace myself for the counterattack but Big John is not defending himself. Big John slinks to the ground. I kick him as hard as I can. "You coward. How could you kill her?"

Big John responds in a hoarse voice, "I didn't kill her. I couldn't kill her. I loved her. We lived here. Together. Before all of this happened."

"Liar! Liar!" I continue my assault but slowly the energy from my anger dissipates replaced by a need for answers. I sink to my knees in front of him. "What are you talking about, you piece of shit?"

"We lived here, together. It was the best year of my life. I think it was the best year of her life too. She hated you. She would laugh that we were living in your house while you lived in that shithole apartment."

"Screw you. You don't know anything. Liar." I stand and pace. Pieces of the puzzle begin to fit together. He moved out and Anna showed up. My aunt and uncle hadn't seen her because she was living here. Why was she living here? They were growing marijuana in my house. Anna trashed my house. I never realized how angry she was with me. The watches. He is after the watches. "Why are you here? You haven't killed me, yet. So why are you here?"

"I shouldn't be here. I miss her. She was my world. You look so much like her." He sits listless on my floor.

"Are you going to kill me?" I ask.

"She made me promise not to hurt you. She was so angry with you, but in the end she was different. She was mad at all of us. She started defending you. She was trying to save you. She wished she was like you."

Lying piece of shit. I do not believe anything he is saying. "Who was she saving me from? What was she saving me from? Who has been following me?"

"Did you find the watches? I need the watches. All of this can go away if I can get the watches back. Anna tried to get the watches."

"Were you with her in my apartment? Did you beat her?" I can feel the anger coming back. Someone beat her.

191

"I fought with her. I hit her, but I didn't beat her. She was strung out and not thinking straight. She told me to go away and she never wanted to see me again. That is when she made me promise not to hurt you, to leave you alone. She was trying to fix things. She said this was all her fault."

"I don't have any watches." I say flatly.

"Well, then I don't know what to do to make this better. They will come for the watches." He stands, looks around nostalgically, and says, "Thanks for screwing up the deposition. Even though you were lying to begin with." Without another word, he walks out the door.

I sit and try to process what just happened. He could have killed me but he didn't. Was he really in love with Anna? I can see him being her type. Could they really have lived in my house and me not have known? I start to imagine Anna living in my house, feeling good about one upping me. We hadn't left things on a very good note, but deep down I know we still loved each other.

I play back my visit with Mr. Ed. I didn't come to his apartment that night, but he could have mistaken Anna for me. Anna must have knocked on Mr. Ed's door. Had she hit Mr. Ed? I can't imagine Anna assaulting him. How deep had Anna been into this underworld? Maybe I should have given Big John the watches. Would he have killed me if he had gotten what he wanted? What if he finds out I have the watches?

My heart jumps as the door opens. Greg and a friend struggle to bring in my washing machine.

Chapter 28

I haven't met Greg's friend before. Javi introduces himself on the way in. He is grimacing due to his being over-exerted carrying my washing machine. "Hi, I'm Javi. I am in Greg's computer science class."

"Hey! Thanks for the help." I respond feeling guilty.

Greg adds, "Javi and I have been partners on a few projects over the years. I tricked him into helping me out."

"No problem. With the storm, I just want to be helpful. This is a nice house," he comments to me directly.

"Thanks. This was my parents' home. I've been renting it out, but we decided to move in." The fewer details the better.

I give the guys a hand negotiating the washer into the closet. Over the next hour, we bring in all the big items Greg brought from the apartment. Javi even helps Greg install the appliances. Without electric or water though, no telling if they did it correctly.

"Thanks. Can I get you a drink?" I ask Javi.

"Actually, I have to go. My girlfriend wants me to help her parents. Maybe we can go on a double date sometime?"

I silently hope that double dates are on my horizon instead of drug dealers coming to retrieve hot watches. I don't explain my dark thoughts and just nod sure.

The electricity still isn't on across most areas of town, but aside from my house, my neighborhood is lights on. Greg calls to arrange electric and utilities. I am pleasantly surprised when he tells me there is a chance we will have power and water tomorrow despite city crews working to get services online.

After incorporating my new purchases, the restrooms and master bedroom have a little color and style rather than the blank slate from which we started. The minor changes in décor on my parents' old furniture make the place feel new and old at the same time. My mother didn't really appreciate change. She was happy with the same bedding and wall hangings. I am relieved that not everything brings back strong memories.

Greg spends the bulk of his time hanging the large television in the living room. While there is no electricity yet, he is looking forward to a little Netflix and chill when the power is turned on. When he finishes, he turns and says, "Ready to meet my parents?" Greg smiles apprehensively, his trepidation shows through.

I consider telling Greg about all that has happened today and cancelling with his parents, but decide that avoiding reality and pretending to be a normal young couple for one night is preferable. We throw some empty boxes into the Jeep so that we can pick up some of Greg's things after dinner.

Greg is excited about our progress and can't wait to sleep in the house tonight. His ability to live in the moment is impressive. All the while, I keep reliving the past, grieving my losses, and fearing my future internally. I am working hard to get out of my head before we make it to his parents' house, but I am getting concerned that my mental resources are too depleted.

Upon pulling into his parents' driveway, I feel a pang of anticipation in my chest. I enjoyed the last few days at this very house, though tonight is different. This time his parents are home. Greg reaches across, pulls my hand to his lips, and gives me a gentle kiss. "They picked up dinner. Still no electricity, but they are really excited to meet my girl."

My girl, I love Greg's sweet nature. I hope his parents are like him. I smile, squeeze his hand, and pull open the door. We approach the house slowly.

Before walking in, Greg hugs me and kisses my forehead.

"Compared to reality lately, this will actually be easy." I smile at Greg, letting him know I am ready.

We walk into the dining room and Greg's mom immediately comes around the corner from the kitchen. She is tall with stark blonde hair. She shares many of Greg's facial features including a warm and welcoming smile. She has on shorts and a tank top which is unexpected considering she is at least 45. "Ella? I have been waiting to meet you. I must admit I've seen you at Taylors. Greg said I wasn't allowed to approach you." I can imagine her being friends with my mom. I like that there is no standing on ceremony. She has an easy way about her.

"Hi. You can always come up to me, customer service." I am concerned that my response is dismissive. I continue, "Sorry it has been so long. Things have been a little crazy in my life lately. Greg was just trying to give me some space while I worked a few things out."

"Greg mentioned that you have been having a hard time. I'm sorry to hear about your cousin and your parents. I can't imagine so much loss at your age. If there is anything we can do to help." Rather than hover, she withdraws into the kitchen and starts getting things ready for dinner. I greatly appreciate her disengagement as it releases me from needing to respond. Dusk falls and the room darkens. Greg lights candles and the lanterns we set out the other day. Greg's mom is preparing the take-out barbeque. Barbeque is a favorite of mine. I sit at a barstool nearby.

Within a few minutes, Greg's dad enters from one of the back rooms. "Sorry. Finishing up some important business. I was on the phone with FEMA. Looks like we don't qualify for any help and my deductible is so high that I won't be making a claim on my homeowner's policy. Basically, all damage will come out of my pocketbook." After a short awkward pause, he moves his attention to me. "Hi. Ella? Why have you not come by sooner?"

Greg's dad sits next to me and holds eye contact a little longer than my comfort. I am less happy with the direct nature of Greg's dad. Greg steps in, "Dad, we're lucky she came by tonight. She just lost her cousin."

Greg's dad rethinks his response, "Sorry. I think my head is full of all this hurricane nonsense. Glad you made it by tonight." Greg's mother interrupts and moves us all to the dinner table.

Greg's mother serves dinner. I didn't eat anything all day so I'm famished. I happily engage myself with eating while Greg and his father discuss fixing the remaining items on the house. Greg already started on the fence, but they need to cut the large palm that fell in the front yard into smaller pieces so that the city can pick it up with brush pick up. I don't think Greg told them that he was almost smashed to death by that tree. I hold my tongue as that might not be the best dinner conversation.

Greg's mom asks, "So Greg has been staying at your apartment often?"

"Yeah. I like having him with me." I reply while making eye contact with Greg.

"We miss him around here." Greg's mom is communicating something to Greg not meant for my understanding.

Greg responds, "Actually, we are officially moving in together into Ella's house tonight! Her parents left her the house. She was renting it out before. No one is living there now. We've decided not to stay at the apartment... after..." Greg doesn't go into the details about Anna. Thank God for small favors, but I feel the change in the tension in the room.

"When did you decide this? You barely make the $200 a month rent living here. You have no idea how much all this will cost. Don't you think you should have discussed this with us first?" Greg's dad is clearly not happy.

Greg's parents are ignoring my presence. I try to diffuse the situation and speak up, "The house is off Flour Bluff Drive not too far from here. The area has some amazing walking trails. We may end up somewhere else in the long run, but for now the house is move in ready. I don't want to go back to the apartment."

Greg's mother tries to get her emotions in check, "I can imagine not wanting to go back to the apartment. You don't have a friend to stay with in the meantime?" She moves her eyes to Greg, "I think too much is going on and the two of you need to slow things down."

I am unsure what Greg has told his parents, but I am getting very defensive. They have no idea. I don't totally disagree that Greg doesn't need a complicated girlfriend like me, but he is also a grown man with a job. "I think I need to get back to moving. Dinner was nice, thank you." I get up to leave.

Greg stands, "We have been moving all day and can't stay long." He tries his best to transition based on my move toward the door. He stops and says to his mother, "I know you have your opinions, but I've made my decision. I need to get some things from my room. Do you mind if I pack up a few things now or should I come back tomorrow?"

I am angry that Greg mentions staying and packing. I want to leave and leave now. At the Jeep I que Greg in. "I'm not going back in there. I had a bad day. I probably need to tell you about it, but I can't add this to my plate. I need you to take me home."

Greg looks conflicted but hops into the Jeep. He picks up his cell and calls his mom. "Hey, we forgot that a friend is meeting us at the house to help us move a few items. I'll be by tomorrow." After a short pause he responds, "Love you too."

While I am frustrated with Greg and his parents, I am also envious. I miss my overprotective parents who didn't want to let me grow up. I am alone and have no choice except to be a grown up. Well, I guess I am not alone. I have Greg. I reach over and squeeze his hand. Greg holds my hand then pulls it to his mouth and kisses it. This is enough for the moment.

At the house, I fill Greg in on everything that has happened. "I should have told you earlier. After I went to the store, Big John came to the house."

Greg is furious. He demands details. I tell him everything, including Big John asking for the watches. I also tell him about my visit to Mr. Ed and my belief that Anna went to Mr. Ed's door that night. "I think Anna is the key to all of this."

Greg is speechless.

I go ahead and come clean to Greg about making the false allegation against Big John and committing perjury. The verbal vomiting of all that I know relieves long held tension.

Greg sits silent for a time. "Big John never tried to sell you marijuana? You just made that up? Why?"

"I was mad, impulsive. I regret it now."

"He never threatened you?"

"Showing up here while I was alone was threatening!" I get a little heated.

Greg changes his approach, "No. I just don't understand. Did you believe him when he said that he could make it all go away if he got the watches?"

I consider the question. Truth is in the moment I believed him. Something about the way he spoke of Anna and how he didn't fight back when I attacked him. "He could have hurt me, but he didn't."

"You know I'm kind of mad at you. You didn't even call me after he left. He could have come back." Greg pulls back and avoids eye contact.

I understand how he must feel. "I think that I've been on my own for so long, I feel like I have to fix things on my own. Plus, you probably shouldn't even be here. Your mom is right."

"Not this again. I love my mom, but she is not right." Greg's face is red and his voice level increases. I have never seen him this angry. "I'm not a child. I don't need her permission. Sometimes I feel like I see us as a couple, and you think I'm just some guy hanging around. Do you love me?"

I don't hesitate. "I love you."

Greg softens immediately and tears well in his eyes, "Well, that is what matters. I love you too. I want to spend my life with you."

I wonder how long the rest of our lives will be. This should be a time of great joy. Instead, anxiety looms over our heads as an imperceptible future threatens us.

Chapter 21

Greg and I sleep in late. We both have evening shifts tonight so no rush. School is still cancelled, but otherwise Corpus Christi is ready to start anew. We are excited that our electricity and water are flowing. A sense of ease overtakes me. Our first night in the house was nice with no incidents. Today is like a fresh start.

We put our few cold items from the cooler into the refrigerator. Greg makes us cream cheese bagels. He gets himself a glass of orange juice and a cup of hot tea for me. There are still boxes to unpack but neither of us has any desire to dive in. The place is functional for our purposes, except we never thought to arrange for cable and internet. Greg makes it a priority to call for both. Strange that in the middle of disaster recovery businesses are making appointments. People are going to work. Today is a new day and I will move forward with the rest of the world.

I call my old apartment complex and leave a message. Greg is willing to pack up the remaining items and put them into storage. Part of me just wants to donate everything, though I do not trust myself to make any permanent decisions in my current state of mind. We lay in bed watching Netflix with my cell data. Not the large screen Greg wants but functional. Yes, functional is the bar for today.

My cell's ring automatically pausing the movie. Greg is annoyed but Tiffany is a must answer. I am so distracted by my thoughts I am not really watching anyway. While I leave the room, Greg reads the news feed on his cell.

"Did you just get home?" I ask.

"Yes. Things are okay. I need to get the gate fixed and a roofer over to see about the missing roof tiles, but no damage inside the house." After a pause, "How are you? I can't believe... Anna..." They were never friends but Tiffany knew Anna most of her life. We all attended from grade school to high school together.

I fill her in on all the details. Tiffany is shocked to hear that Anna had been living in my house and more so to hear that Greg and I had moved in my rental house while she evacuated from the hurricane.

"Can I help clean out the apartment?" Like a protective mother she says, "You don't need to go back again."

"Greg has it covered. I really appreciate the support from both of you."

Tiffany asks, "When is the funeral for Anna?"

"My family is not speaking to me. I have no idea." Intense sadness overwhelms me at the realization. I choke up a little.

"Bullshit! I am calling Jake. Give me the number and I'll call you back." Tiff and Jake dated briefly in high school but hadn't maintained contact as far as I knew. I give her the number I have for Craig as my cousins are always together. There is no point arguing with Tiffany when she is angry and has made up her mind.

The afternoon flies by quickly and before I know it, I have to start getting ready to go to work. I am no longer living across the street and now have a ten-minute commute which, while not too bad, means I need to hurry. I want to be on time. Work has been really easy on me considering the last year. I really am a mess.

Taking a shower in my parents' bathroom reminds me of old times. I prefer the stand-up shower to my tub-shower. As a teenager, I almost exclusively used my parents' bathroom. My parents never minded my intrusion. They would pound on the double-doors yelling at me to finish up already to ensure they had enough hot water for their showers. I made sure to get out before I used up all the hot water for Greg.

I visualize all my mother's products on the counter around her sink and the pills my father had on his side of the sink. I carefully use and return my items to their designated spots while getting ready just like my mom had done. My mom would approve.

I laugh out loud when I think about the idea of my mother catching Greg in her shower. We never had any awkward boyfriend moments because I did not date back then. So many things I will never experience with my parents. This idea makes me a little sad. I hope Anna is with them and they are treating her with all the love they used to give me. This idea is a little more pleasant but tears still come to my eyes. Work will be a nice distraction from all this downtime.

After making Greg and I a sandwich with some chips, I give Greg a kiss and leave for work. Opening the door, I see my neighbor across the street, Rene, mowing the lawn. He notices me immediately, "Are you staying here, Ella?"

I walk over and give him a hug. "For now. I've decided to move in with my boyfriend, Greg. We moved in yesterday. We're not sure we will stay but are going to see how it goes."

"How exciting! I'll be keeping an eye out for this Greg guy. He better treat you right."

I smile despite my annoyance. "He's a great guy. No need to worry. I'll see you later. I have to get to work."

I stop before leaving, "Hey, was there a girl living with Big John, my tenant?"

Rene looks uncomfortable, "There were many people going in and out. In all truth, I wasn't even sure who was renting the place."

"Thanks." I withdraw. Rene waves and continues mowing.

I guess I have officially notified the neighbors that Greg and I have moved in. My thoughts drift back to Mr. Ed. He had been my neighbor and look what happened to him. I hope I won't bring any more drama to the neighborhood. I am already embarrassed about calling the cops last time.

The evening has a steady stream of customers which is far less busy than I imagined. The store has already replaced the A in the Taylors sign and is fully functional. Two days and back in business. The shelves are not fully stocked. The hurricane is slowing or stopping deliveries of certain impacted foods and brands. Customers are not complaining but are certainly noticing the many missing items, especially fresh meats which are in short supply. People had to throw away food items due to the long power outage and are coming in to restock when their electricity comes back on. High need items are plentiful including water bottles, mosquito spray, and wipes. For the most part, people can get what they need, but not necessarily everything they want.

During my break, I walk next door to the Sandwich Shop. Greg is working. We won't be sharing a break tonight. I am on my own. I order a turkey, bacon, guacamole sub. While sitting and eating my sandwich, I realize someone is approaching me through my peripheral vision. I look up and Jake is now standing over me with red, sad eyes. Immediately my eyes well and I join him in a hard cry. I wrap my arms around him, burying my head in his chest. He holds me tight. No words are necessary. After a time, he loosens his grip and we both slide into the booth. I am afraid to say anything and wait for him to start the conversation.

"I'm sorry." He keeps his eyes down.

"I know. I'm sorry too. I don't know when she came to my apartment. I wasn't there." I explain.

Jake does not respond right away. "Tiffany called me. She's a good friend to you." I can only imagine what Tiff said to him. I hope she wasn't too hard on him. "We are having a graveside service Tuesday at noon at the Shoreline Cemetery. Immediate family only. I think mom and dad are embarrassed they can't do a proper service. They don't want you there."

"Do you want me there?" Jake tears up and doesn't respond. I am okay with that, realizing he is in a difficult situation. "Well, I'm coming. I promise I won't start any trouble. I really appreciate you telling me, but I won't say how I found out if anyone asks."

"I don't give a fuck about that. Anna deserved better. I know it wasn't your fault." Anguish enters his eyes. I want to comfort him, but he is increasingly rigid and I can tell that our moment has passed. I wonder how much he knows about my situation, but I am afraid to ask. I need this connection more then I need answers.

I change the subject, "I moved back into my old house yesterday with Greg."

Jake rolls his eyes. I struck a nerve. "Good for you. I have to go." Jake leaves abruptly.

On my way back to Taylors, I see Greg's mother enter the store. I make sure to avoid her.

Chapter 30

The next few days are busy between work, moving in, and appointments to set up services at the house, but by Tuesday everything is squared away. The big news is that my old complex is as happy to be rid of me as I am to be rid of them. They release me from the lease a month early so I have until the end of the month to move out. Other tenants complained regarding the police coming to my apartment and, well, a murder.

Anna's death has been ruled undetermined, though speculation abounds. Officially, Anna died of an overdose. Her body showed signs of violence (bruising and cuts that appeared to be both old and new) but not severe enough to cause death. They could not determine whether the overdose was accidental or inflicted by someone else. No fingerprints were found in the apartment other than mine, Greg, Tiffany, and Anna. The investigation has stalled. Anna was basically a vagrant, so the chance of a comprehensive investigation is unlikely.

College classes resume today, the day of Anna's funeral. I am going to miss my last morning class. I sent an email last night to my professor explaining and he excused me. Since I am going to the funeral directly from my second class, I wear black dress pants and a nice shirt. I am overdressed for my usual attire to school, but not so much so as to draw attention. Greg is also wearing black dress pants and a white button up shirt. We look like a power couple on this very relaxed campus.

We drive together to the Shoreline Cemetery. My parents are buried here. I plan to visit them after the funeral.

Shoreline drive is always beautiful, overlooking the bay, which I appreciate when heading to visit my parents. I am not sure where the actual site is for the graveside services but the cemetery isn't that big. We enter through a side entrance closest to my parents' gravesite. I am shocked to see a tent set up in the very area adjacent to my parents' plots. While unexpected for my family, I like the idea of family plots.

We park and walk to the site. We are 20 minutes early. Only a few people are present: my uncle, aunt, cousins, a few friends of my uncle, the two goons I saw with Anna at the Mediterranean restaurant, and a handful of people I don't recognize. I feel very uncomfortable and uninvited as I approach.

The two goons closely watch me as I walk up with Greg. My aunt is wearing a long oversized dark floral print, sitting closest to the casket. She has definitely made an effort today. She does not see me right away. My uncle is the first to see me and touches her arm while nodding his head in my direction. Aunt Donna looks up and the look of disgust is unmistakable. She barrels towards me. "What are you doing here?"

While I am not surprised, I did promise Jake to avoid a scene. I choose my words carefully as all eyes are on me. "I just need to be here. I am sorry. I have to say goodbye." I keep my eyes downcast and wait for a response.

Aunt Donna makes a huffing noise and walks off. Once she turns away from me, I hear her say, "She has no business here. This is for family." As she didn't explicitly demand I leave, I stay without socializing or joining *the family* in the designated seats. My uncle and cousins ignore me. I assume for my own good so as to placate my aunt's anger.

The service is simple and short. From a distance I see Big John standing outside of a dark blue Ford F150. At first, I am the only one to notice, but then the goons stop watching me and walk towards him. I watch intensely to discover if the interaction will be friendly or combative. Big John told me he was in love with Anna and they had lived together. I have no way of knowing if that is true. My curiosity grows. I consider walking over but then think better of it. These are dangerous people. I am sure of that.

I can't hear the conversation. I rely on interpreting the body language. Big John stands firm. He does not move away as they approach. The three of them are having a deep conversation but not yelling or displaying any angry gestures. From a distance the interchange appears to be tenuous rather than friendly. The goons finally withdraw. Big John remains.

The funeral director finishes. The family places flowers on the closed casket. The funeral director announces that the services have ended. Guests are welcome to stay or leave. Everyone stands and moves about.

Uncle Billy looks distraught. His eyes are red and puffy. He has obviously been crying during the service but his facial expression changes when he sees Big John. Much like Aunt Donna with me, Uncle Billy makes a b-line for Big John. This time body language is clear. Uncle Billy is angry. Angrier then I have ever seen him before. Big John sees him coming and opens the door to his truck. By the time Uncle Billy makes it over, Big John is inside his truck with the engine running. Uncle Billy yells and kicks the truck tires. I cannot make out the words but there is no mistaking the words are full of fury, blind fury.

My cousins follow and pull my uncle away from the truck. Big John drives off.

Uncle Billy and my cousins do not return immediately but have an argument. The rage is gone, but obviously strong words are nevertheless being said. I assume Uncle Billy is upset Craig and Jake intervened. Then again, funerals bring out the worst in many people so who knows.

Aunt Donna has not moved at all. She sits slumped next to the grave. Her face is hidden. I do not dare approach. A part of me desires to comfort her, though I realize am not the right person. My heart sinks for her loss. I remember back to a year ago when I was that person at my parents' funeral. My heart was broken and people were just noise and chaos. Words of comfort weren't received as comfort, rather most of the time I was angry that I was having to comfort others. I decide my gift is to fade into the distance.

I intend to visit my parents' gravesite, but as it is nearly adjacent to Anna's burial site I decide to come back later when I can spend private time with both of them. While not acknowledged by my family, this truth is proof that we are family. Regardless, I am only barely tolerated at this funeral. I leave without further interrupting my family's mourning.

In the Jeep Greg is quiet. He squeezes my hand and waits for me to say something. I imagine all of this is mindboggling to Greg who has a normal loving family.

"Well that went as well as could be expected." I finally offer.

"I could not believe your aunt." Greg looks mortified.

I give a small uncomfortable grumble, "She's never been much of an aunt or even much of mother for that matter. I can only imagine she has a lot of regrets. I forgive her."

"I'm sorry for all of this." Greg consoles me.

"It's not your fault. This is just the reality of the situation. I'm glad she didn't make me leave." After a pause, I say, "What did you think of Big John being there?"

"Was that Big John in the truck? I've never seen him. He is a really big guy. I figure he could have taken your tiny uncle easily, but maybe he didn't want a scene."

"Yeah, Big John was also talking with the goons before that. Did you see that?"

"The goons?" Apparently, Greg hadn't noticed.

"The two rough looking guys. They had been with Anna when she first approached me when we were eating dinner." Greg does not remember that day either. "We were dropping off the watches."

"I remember the day and even Anna, but not those guys. They were certainly looking at you. I thought maybe you knew them."

Greg has been a constant support through all of this craziness, but I realize Greg is not up on all the players. I am going to have to put these puzzle pieces together on my own. "I want to go back this afternoon. I didn't get to visit my parents."

"Sure. Why don't we get lunch, pick up some flowers, then I can meet your parents?" Steadfast and unwavering as always. I never imagined there were men on this planet as wonderful as Greg.

Chapter 31

Since we are close to Shoreline Boulevard, we decide to eat on the Bayfront. The day is gorgeous. The Shrimp Shack is on the t-head overlooking the bay with a relaxed atmosphere. Greg isn't big on shrimp and orders chicken fried steak. In Corpus Christi every restaurant serves chicken fried steak, a staple of this community. I order the shrimp platter with shrimp brochette, grilled shrimp, and coconut shrimp along with a loaded baked potato and corn on the cob. We sit on the patio. The breeze is a little strong, but watching the waves in the harbor relaxes my over active mind. While looking at the view, I imagine Anna floating by on one of the sailboats unencumbered by the burdens of this world. She is free. We eat slowly, finishing our drinks while letting time pass, taking in the vast horizon.

After lunch we stop at a small flower shop to pick up two bundles of fresh flowers, one with white roses and one with red roses then return to the cemetery. Thankfully the cemetery is abandoned. The tent remains along with a few men working on filling the grave site. We visit my parents' site first. My parents' site is a mature site. The first time I visited after the funeral my parents' spot had fresh earth, then the next time it was sunken it. I had asked them to add additional dirt. Now there is no indention. I chose the brass headstone with the inscription, "Gone but forever in my heart." Each time I visit I read this inscription and feel a renewed sense that my parents are still very much with me. I place the fresh red roses in the vase.

Greg stands behind me ceremoniously while I have a silent moment alone. After a short time, I introduce him formally. "Hi mom and dad. I want you to meet Greg."

Greg smiles awkwardly while he moves forward. "Hi." I appreciate that he addresses them aloud. He understands how much this means to me. Even though the response is emptiness, I feel a warm sense of them smiling and welcoming Greg into my life.

I kneel and pick weeds from around the site. I play images of them in my head. Memories fly by easily. I remember being annoyed at my dad who kept asking me if I had a boyfriend and threatening to get out his pistol for introductions if I ever brought a boy home. My mom would slap him on the shoulder and tell him to stop. Then both would laugh at my expense. I left many a room at that very moment. I try to imagine what my parents would have done if I had brought Greg home. After all my imaginations I decide they would have been jokingly mean, then accepted him with open arms. Greg would have liked them too.

I stand dusting off my knees. With tears in my eyes, I fall into Greg's arms. "Thank you," I whisper. I dread my next step so I just stall.

I cannot avoid saying goodbye to Anna forever, so I walk the 20 yards to the tent which has not yet been taken down. The grave is already covered, but the dirt rests dry and loose in the sad little rectangle. Flowers from the casket lay atop. There is no headstone. I am unsure if a headstone has been ordered. I decide to call and give an anonymous donation tomorrow. I figure my family will accept an anonymous donation even if they assume the donation is from me. Such a sad state of things in this family.

Tears flow in a torrent as I sink back to my knees. This time the sadness is deeper and darker. The vision of Anna laying lifeless in my apartment overwhelms me. I loved her. Some part of me knows she knew I loved her, but another, larger part, shoulders the boulder-sized weight of guilt. I did not take care of her in her time of need. If Big John was telling the truth, Anna was trying to make things right and protect me. Sure, she had been a big part of setting all of this chaos into motion, but in the end, she was doing the right thing. I was able to see that I had tried to do the right thing the last time I saw her alive by taking her to my apartment and even looking for her but my efforts were too little too late. Anna hadn't saved me either. I know that trouble still lurks in the shadows. I look around as I have become distrustful of the world.

Greg kneels beside me and puts his arm around me. I squeeze his hand briefly but my energy fades. As quickly as I reach towards him, I drop his hand. I sit flat on my butt Indian style as my knees hurt. I am not ready to leave.

I talk incessantly. "When we were kids, she liked to steal my clothes. I hated when she looked better in them than me. She was gorgeous. She took all sorts of chances that I just couldn't. I remember her fully embracing the Goth look in 7th grade. She came to school in all black. I mean she had black finger nails, black eye liner, and pitch-black hair with a weird blue tint. Who went and just dyed their hair without any thought? She looked good though. I asked my parents if I could dye my hair and, of course, they said no. They convinced me that I would regret it. I'm sure they were right. I could never have pulled it off. Just as quickly as she had dyed her hair blue, she dyed it platinum blonde and showed up in daisy dukes and a half top. People noticed her; boys noticed her. She was brazen. Nobody ever messed with her. You could just tell that she could and would kick your ass. She actually got into several fights. She wouldn't back down. I think her brothers being so hard on her made her strong. But she was also fragile. I could tell when we stopped hanging out that she was different. She walked different, talked different, totally different."

"I bet it was hard watching her change," Greg comments.

"I missed her. I missed the old her. The new her did not appeal to me. I didn't want to try drugs and thought she was being stupid. I told her she was making big mistakes. She would say the meanest things to me about being a goody-goody, being judgmental, and a stick in the mud in front of her new friends. Pretty quickly we just avoided each other. We no longer had anything in common. Our families only interacted on the holidays." I pause.

Greg tries to be supportive, "It happens. You don't need to over think it. Hindsight is 20/20."

Before I can respond, I see the goons driving up. "Let's get out of here." I hop up quickly and grab Greg's arm to pull him up. We quickly walk to the Jeep while keeping an eye on the oncoming car. The goons are pursuing us, but we noticed them with enough time to get into the Jeep. The goon in the driver's seat rolls down his window and they both hold up their hands. Greg turns on the engine and puts the car into drive. I hold my hand up to signal Greg to wait a second. I roll down the window cautiously and wait for them to speak.

"We're going to be needing the watches." The goon has an ugly expression that is very disturbing.

I respond, "I don't know what you are talking about."

The goon glares at me with a malicious smile, ignoring Greg, "Time is running out. Either we get the watches or we take payment in some other way. Consider Anna to be a warning. See you soon." He winks, rolls up his window and drives out of the cemetery slowly.

I look toward Greg, hoping he knows what to do. Greg says nothing, puts his foot on the gas, and drives off while rolling up my window.

I sit for a time wondering what I should do. I lied to Big John and the goons, denying having the watches. Only Greg and I know I have the watches for sure; and, well, the police who did a search for them on some database for stolen items, and Mr. Kirby, the consignment store owner who is looking to sell the watches. All of a sudden, I realize my possessing the watches is not such a secret.

Chapter 32

Fear. This is what true fear feels like. I am already used to feeling anxiety, but I am sure the goon just admitted to killing Anna over the watches. *Anna is a warning.* These thoughts turn in my mind over and over again.

Anger. Anger takes over next. I am infuriated that these goons threatened me at the cemetery. Every time I visit my parents in the future, I will remember this moment.

Sadness. Tears roll down my cheeks. How can this be my life? How can all this not just end? I am emotionally spent by the time we return to the house.

Greg pulls directly into the garage and shuts the overhead door. The garage is fairly empty. Greg leans over and pulls my gun out of the glove compartment. I have never allowed him to touch my gun, but in this moment, I do not have the energy to take care of myself. I am experiencing the death wish Freud theorized about. The unconscious desire to die. Maybe I want to die. I would no longer have these problems that I cannot fix and can barely comprehend. I would return to my mom and dad's loving arms. I would walk arm and arm with sweet Anna.

Consumed in my negative thoughts, I follow Greg into the house. The alarm system goes off indicating no one has entered without the code. Greg resets the alarm so that we will know if any doors or windows are to open, though we have not paid for a monitoring company.

We both collapse into the bed. Strangely we do not talk. Greg sits my gun atop the bedside table. Greg turns on soft music and wraps his arms around me. I melt into his warmth. The smell of Greg is comforting and I draw him in. Tears return. I sob in his arms until I fall asleep.

Usually I awaken if anyone touches me in my sleep, but I awake two hours later still wrapped in Greg's arms. My neck aches due to the angle I had slept in. Greg is awake scrolling through his cell. I stretch then return to him but in a more comfortable position. Greg sets his cell down. He leans over and kisses me. I return his kiss and move my hips toward him. Greg responds by moving his hand down my back to caress by lower back and bottom. I need this moment. Our bodies move together like the ocean. The tides raging through all the emotions overwhelming me under the surface. Feelings of urgency, comfort, fear, anger, and passion find expression until I am spent once more. I lay still, not feelings, not thinking, and more relaxed then I have been for some time.

The bliss of a quieted mind does not last long. Thoughts of all that has happened return. The goons, Anna, Big John, the funeral, finding Anna in my apartment, and moving into my childhood home. So much has happened. "Should we call the police?" I ask Greg.

"I don't know. You still have Detective Haas's number? Maybe you should call him." I consider Greg's idea. No part of me wants to talk to Detective Haas after the charges were dropped against Big John. I imagine he is quite frustrated with me for wasting his time.

"I don't know."

"I do. We need to call Detective Haas. He is a police officer and the only officer who answers any of our questions."

Greg insists. Atypically, I concede. I no longer trust my judgment. I certainly have no other, better ideas.

I call right away. Contrary to what I secretly wish, Detective Haas answers immediately, "Detective Haas."

"Uh. Hi. This is Ella Fontana. Do you remember me?"

"Of course, Ella. What can I do for you?" Detective Haas is being affable which is really kind considering my perjury and wasting his time.

"Um. You know how my cousin, Anna, was found dead in my apartment after the hurricane?"

"Yes. I am aware."

"Well, her funeral was today. I went back to the cemetery after everyone left, with Greg, and two scary guys drove up to us asking for the watches we turned in to you. I told them I didn't know what they were talking about. They then told me that they needed the watches or else. Then added that Anna was a warning." I pause to hear what he might have to say.

"Did they threaten you?" Detective Haas probes.

"I feel like they did. Anna just died in my apartment of unknown causes. Isn't that a threat?" I am defensive now.

Detective Haas clears his throat and answers after a pause, "I get that it felt like a threat, and it may have been a vague threat, but to take a report, a clear threat would have to be made." Detective Haas hesitates, then adds, "Where are the watches?"

Greg shakes his head. I immediately understand. I ignore his question and ask, "I guess I'm asking what I should do?"

Detective Haas offers, "You should call the investigating officer for Anna's case. Detective Peters, right? Her death is still on his caseload."

"Thanks. I'll do that. Sorry to have bothered you." I end the conversation.

I think Greg is as disappointed as I am. "Why did you not want me to tell him where the watches are?" I ask.

"I don't know. I just started thinking that the more people who know the bigger problem we have."

I agree, but either way Detective Haas already knows we have the watches. We have resolved nothing. No part of me wants to call the other detective. That will just be another person aware of the watches. We decide to sleep on it.

The next day, Greg and I attend our classes at Del Mar following our typical routine. I meet up with Tiffany in the Student Center and fill her in on all that is happening. This time Tiffany has a little information of her own to share.

"When I talked to Jake about the funeral, he confirmed that Anna was living in the house with Big John."

I stare, shocked. Tiffany continues, "He told me Big John and Anna were in charge of the house and product, but your aunt and uncle run the business side of things. Craig and Jake are also involved, superficially." She looks nervous but continues, "Apparently, Big John and Anna decided they no longer wanted any part of all of this. Your aunt and uncle didn't trust Craig and Jake to oversee the operations at the house. They sold the marijuana they were growing and converted the money into the watches for laundering purposes. They need the watches to pay back the original debt to the Syndicate."

I am truly dumbfounded, "Jake told you all of this?"

Tiffany again looks nervous, "I feel bad for him. He doesn't know what to do. No one expected you to get Big John arrested. Big John was the last person in possession of the watches. Big John swears the watches were left in the house."

"Did you tell Jake that I have the watches?" I ask, scared.

"Do you have the watches?" Tiffany questions.

"No. But Big John asked for them the other day and two goons asked for them yesterday. They threatened me, sort of." I feel both guilty that I am lying about the watches and pleased that Tiffany won't need to lie to Jake. I wonder why Jake is being so forthcoming with Tiff while not telling me anything, although once upon a time they had been close. He is not the brightest bulb in the box and may just have more knowledge then he knows what to do with. I grasp the idea of not trusting Jake and Craig with anything of material value, but no doubt they are loyal to their parents.

Tiffany pleads, "Ella. I am scared for you. I don't want to get involved. Have you called the police?"

I understand Tiffany not wanting to get involved. I wish I wasn't involved in all of this. "I called the police. A lot of good that has done me." I am afraid to say too much. "I have to go. Love you." I give Tiffany a hug and head to my next class.

Right now, only Mr. Kirby, Greg and I know where the watches are located. I am happy Mr. Kirby has not called although he should have called by now. Other than the three of us only Detective Haas and, I guess, the police know I am in possession of the watches. Everyone else is assuming. I could have thrown the watches out with the pile of trash in the garage that day. I hope that all interested parties assume that.

After classes are over Greg and I head home to get caught up on some school work. With everything that has been happening we are both falling behind in our assignments. I have to keep my grades up to maintain my scholarship. I make every effort to focus my thoughts on my physics project but fail miserably. I welcome the interruption when my cell goes off.

"Detective Haas?" I answer.

"Ella, I need you and Greg to come to the station. I will explain when you get here."

Greg drives me downtown.

At the station Detective Haas takes us to an interview room and leaves us alone for too long. "Wait here, please."

I joke with Greg, "This room reminds me of interrogation rooms in *Law and Order* episodes." While funny, this does feel eerily like an interrogation room. Every other time I had come into the station Detective Haas and I spoke openly at or near his cubical. Greg and I sit silently, afraid to speak.

Detective Haas enters with the man he introduces as Sergeant Peters, lead investigator for Anna's death. Both men sit across from Greg and me. They offer us a drink, which we decline.

Detective Haas starts, "Did you contact Sergeant Peter's after calling me yesterday?"

I answer flatly, "No," then add, "Is this an interrogation?"

Detective Haas opens a manila folder with several pictures inside. "We want to see if you can identify the two men who confronted you both yesterday."

Detective Haas presents a sheet of paper with eight images of Hispanic men of similar age, four on the top four on the bottom. I easily point to the two goons. Greg agrees. "That is definitely them."

Detective Haas documents that we picked out Carlos Monri and Robert Cantu. I have never heard their names before. Sergeant Peters then speaks for the first time, "Both of these men were found dead this morning. Both men are known associates of your cousin, Anna. Do you have any other information that you wish to share with us?"

Greg interrupts, "We've been together since we ran into these men yesterday after the funeral. We called Detective Haas because they threatened us. We have not seen them since. Do we need lawyers? Should you be reading us our rights?"

Detective Haas replies, "We are not interrogating you. That said, at this point, we are investigating a string of murders. You have the right to a lawyer, but we do not suspect either of you as being involved in either homicide. These two men were gunned down on the West side late last night. No witnesses. We are trying to figure out what is going on? Both men are members of the Syndicate."

"I have no idea what is going on. I called you because they scared me." I defend.

After a pause, Detective Haas adds, "We found pictures of you both, but mostly of you, Ella, on one of the cell phones. The evidence supports that these are the men who were stalking you."

Sergeant Peters hands me hundreds of pictures: me on my stoop giving them the finger, at work, with Greg, at school.

My blood pressure elevates and I start to sweat. "Some of these were sent to me." I am overwhelmed by the sheer number of pictures.

"They never sent the pictures to anyone besides you. There is no evidence that they forwarded the pictures to anyone else. We are at a dead end." Sergeant Peters looks exasperated. "This could be the end of the harassment, but my instinct is that more is going on here. Do you have any ideas to share with us?"

I consider offering up Tiffany's information regarding my aunt and uncle, but I have not even told Greg. I do not feel safe at this time. My trust issues explode and I can feel panic setting in. I don't trust my family, the police, strangers. I just want to escape. "Are we free to go?"

"Yes, but I want you to call me if anything else comes to mind. We don't regularly investigate multiple homicides in Corpus Christi. This case is unusual as is the complicated pattern of stalking we now have evidence of. Are you sure there is nothing else you can tell us?" Sergeant Peters is carefully watching us and scratching notes on his pad.

With nothing else to add at this time, we leave quickly. In the car, Greg loses his composure. "Ella, I'm scared."

"Me too." Silence drives us home.

Chapter 33

Coming into the house our class assignments still sit where we left them, but neither of us are going to accomplish any scholastic achievement tonight. My chest tightens. I am far too young to have a heart attack. Greg has been silent since telling me he is scared. I have no one to call. There is nothing I can do to help our situation.

I talk aloud, "Anna was looking for the watches for someone, someone who likely beat her. The goons make sense. They all but admitted to killing Anna. Big John was in love with Anna and could have killed me but didn't. He seemed sincere although he wants the watches. At the funeral, the goons looked to be in good standing with my aunt and uncle as well as Big John. My uncle was furious with Big John. Why would he be furious with Big John?"

Greg responds, "Who killed the goons? The Syndicate?" After a pause he answers my first question, "Didn't you say that Big John was the last person to have the watches? Maybe your uncle blames him for Anna being killed by the Syndicate because Big John lost the watches."

"Makes sense. Since everyone thinks I have the watches, am I next?" The question hangs in the air with neither of us daring to answer.

Greg and I sit for a long time. We are in way over our heads.

We turn on the television as white noise. I assume neither of us are really digesting. Early evening, we decide to go to sleep. Greg has already turned off the lights and laid in bed when he says, "I signed us up for the license to carry course for this Saturday morning."

I guess that is something. We have a plan. We both pretend to sleep, though breathing and movement are giveaways that we are both having a restless night. At some point I must have fallen asleep because I awake early morning with a jolt when Greg is getting up. I am unsure if he slept.

"Where are you going?" I ask.

"Bathroom." His answer is short and sweet.

All of this has to be more than he bargained for. "Have you told your parents what is going on?"

Greg does not answer until he returns. "No. They would demand that I break up with you. They already think I'm not thinking this through. They don't need to know that we are actually in the middle of a string of homicides."

"Have you considered breaking up with me?" I ask earnestly.

Greg reaches over and pinches me on the butt.

I laugh without thinking, "What was that for?"

"Telling you that I am not leaving does not sink in with you, so from now on every time you ask me that question, I plan to pinch your ass." He reaches for me again and I playfully jump to my knees.

"Oh really. Well that will result in retaliation." We wrestle. I have him pinned, but he shifts his weight and quickly turns the tables. I buck, surprising him with my strength and he nearly falls of the bed. While he is off balance, I push him slightly and he falls to the floor. "Give up?" I ask.

"Never." Greg jumps on the bed and pins me. I can't move so I bend my head forward and go in for a kiss. Greg loosens his grip and I again buck him off his balance. "No fair. I thought you were conceding to me."

"Never." Our wrestling match continues until we both decide we need to release some real steam. We each undress ourselves and enjoy the moment. When we finish, we lie next to each other with a slight separation. "So, you haven't considered leaving?"

Greg reaches over and pinches me again. I laugh. He keeps his word and I have never needed any gesture more.

Eventually we have to get up and start the day. We both are scheduled to work full shifts. I think we both like the idea that we have a schedule to stick to. Greg will go to work a few hours earlier than me. He suggests, "Why don't you hang with Tiffany?"

"Tiffany is already overwhelmed by everything Jake told her. I don't want to put her through anymore."

Greg then suggests, "Do you want to drive in with me so that at least you are not home alone." Part of me likes the idea, but then I am a prisoner.

"I'll be fine. My car is parked in the garage. The house has an alarm. I am safe."

Greg looks conflicted but he does not push further. "Keep your gun on you." Regardless of his concerns, Greg leaves for work.

I guess he had a change of heart about my carrying the gun. I am glad he now sees things as I see them. I get dressed. I make sure to put the gun on my hip in my holster. I have become quite accustomed to the feel of the gun, though I have never actually drawn the gun during a confrontation. The idea that I could actually find myself in a situation where I would need to draw the gun makes me feel anxious.

With two hours to fill, I decide to go shopping. I don't need anything, but I am stir crazy in the house. A public area is safer than sitting here. I wander the mall but nothing catches my attention. Regardless, time passes and I head to work.

I am disappointed with myself for being afraid to stay home alone. Is this my new thing? Afraid to be alone. Hiding in public places while Greg works. How long can I cling to him before he is done? I imagine Greg pinching me which helps for a millisecond, then the reality of the situation plays out in my head once more. This relationship is doomed.

Work is a happy distraction. My nine-hour shift slowly passes. I realize that my life has flipped. Opposite from the life I had lived in my protected childhood when I was blissfully unaware and happy. Now, with all this change and chaos, I dread every moment and simply tolerate time passing. This is no way to live. Guilt overwhelms me. Greg deserves better. I deserve better too, but this is my mess. Greg just happened upon me at the wrong time.

I clock out. Greg is standing at the front of the store with ice cream cones. He really is the sweetest guy in the world. Mine is strawberry. We sit in the deli eating our cones. "What did you do with the last two hours?"

"I just hung out waiting for you." Greg smiles.

My heart sinks. Much the way my life has been hijacked, so has Greg's. I have no idea how, but I have to release him. Not today. I can't do it today.

We drive to school together the next morning. Things move forward much the way they always have. We attend classes and even play cards in the Student Center with Tiffany and another friend. Bob isn't around today. We have fun, but I constantly scan the area.

At lunch, Greg tells me, "I am going to buy my gun today."

"Great. Now we both feel like we need to carry a gun." I sympathize.

"No. I always wanted a gun of my own. I need one for the concealed carry class. I've been researching them all week."

I am saddened that I brought all of this into Greg's life, though I will feel safer with him having his own gun. I have a few hours before I have to be at work. "Have you ever shot a gun before?" I ask.

"No. Will that matter for the class?" He asks.

"You can pay at the range to try different guns. There is an indoor range on Saratoga Boulevard." I recommend.

The range is upscale and decorated Texan style with blue bonnets and the state flag. Deer heads on plaques hang from lacquered wood on the walls. The clerk explains, "For $15 dollars you can shoot any of the guns in this case. You only need to pay for the bullets."

Greg and I try six different guns before I start coughing from the gun smoke and abandon the indoor range. We sit in the overstuffed leather chairs, relaxing while Greg considers his options, "I like the colt 45. It has a nice kick."

"How about the semiautomatic nine-millimeter, like mine?"

"Nope. That is a girl gun." I roll my eyes. Greg continues, "My favorite shot was the Glock."

Time is up. I have to head into work. Greg is off for the evening. "I think I'm going to get the Smith and Wesson 1911 45 caliber. The force is strong enough to take someone down."

Part of me is concerned with this machismo talk. If two goons could be gunned down, then what chance do we have if someone comes for us.

Chapter 34

I drive straight home after work. Greg is working on math when I come in. He is more relaxed than the night before. I guess as time passes you have no choice but to accept the new level of alert and just move on. His new gun sits on his laptop. Some part of me thinks our circumstances are quite funny. Two mild mannered Texans and their guns in the modern day Wild West.

"Howdy, Partner." I laugh.

"Hey," Greg gives me a little side eye.

"Nice piece." I nod towards his new gun.

Greg gives a knowing smile, "I'm packing." He puts his hand on his new gun.

"You have the safety on, right?" I check.

Greg looks a little more serious, "Definitely. Made sure I understood all the basic features and took it for a spin at the range. It's a nice piece. I actually think I want to join the Corpus Christi Pistol and Rifle Club. I was looking into it online. This could be something we do together. There are even competitions."

"Sure. Might be fun." I wonder if Greg is as worried as myself or thinks of this more as a game. I decide I like the idea that he thinks this is a game more than I like the idea of asking another heavy question about this dangerous situation that would not arise with a typical girlfriend.

All relationships have problems. I just wish we had normal relationship problems. I decide to join Greg and sit at the table, pulling out my homework. A conventional evening, generally relaxed, being college students. I decide to not overthink things tonight; or at least to not vocalize my over thinking.

✎✎✎✎✎✎✎

The next few days go by. Tiffany is coming over tonight for dinner and game night. The doorbell rings. I am surprised to see Jake, not Bob.

"Sorry I didn't tell you before, but Jake is my date tonight. Bob and I broke up." Tiffany is avoiding eye contact.

"Great." I respond while feeling absolutely on edge. I do not feel comfortable being around my family right now. "I wasn't expecting you tonight, cousin." I offer Jake a hug.

Jake teases, "An upgrade from Bob, I'm sure."

I look to Tiffany, annoyed that she gave me no heads up in regards the change. I like Bob. Tiffany, though, has always followed her gut and moves quickly in and out of relationships.

Tiffany playfully redirects Jake, "No Bob bashing. We're still friends." She looks at me, "I'll fill you in later."

Jake holds a six pack of beer which he offers to all of us. Tiffany enjoys one, but Greg and I pass. "More for me then." Jake comments while opening his third beer.

Game night is quite different with Jake then previous game nights with Bob. Bob is juvenile, but Jake has an attitude which ignites my competitive side.

Tiffany and I are skilled Spades players, while Jake and Greg are still learning. The teams are evenly matched.

Greg and I are on target to reach our bid of seven, when Greg throws out the King of Spades pulling my Ace of Spades and moving us from a position of strength to a position of

232

chance. My face flushes and I point out a little too tartly, "Really, you are supposed to throw low."

Greg looks embarrassed and Tiffany redirects me, "No talking across the table."

"Whatever. The guys don't even know how to play," I rebut insolently.

"Speak for your man. Beating you has never been much of a challenge." Jake laughs and looks like the smug asshole I remember from my youth.

My eyes go hard and my voice goes flat, "Yeah. I remember how Anna hated you when we were kids." I regret my words as soon as they fly out of my mouth.

The happy leaves Jake's eyes and is replaced with hard steel, "What would you know about how Anna felt? You abandoned her time and again. You are the one who broke her heart."

I bolt from my chair in a fury. Tiffany maneuvers to stand between us with her arms outstretched. "Stop this. You are both just hurting each other."

"Isn't that the truth? All this family does is hurt each other." Jake turns and walks out of the house without another word.

While trying to restrain my anger, my heart aches for Jake. He summed up a truth I had not previously put into words. I had never considered Jake as insightful. I push Tiffany's hand down. "I'm sorry. Stay here. I need to talk to him."

Tiffany looks protective. "Don't hurt him. He is very upset about his sister. I know you are hurting, but you were out of line first."

I reach for Tiffany's hand and squeeze it while making my way to Jake.

Jake is standing by his truck. I assume he is waiting for Tiffany. He is no longer angry. I can tell he has been crying by his red swollen face. "I'm sorry. I shouldn't have brought up our stupid childhood." I hope he can hear that I truly regret my words.

"I've always been a shit brother. Hell, she was a shit sister. We all came from a shit family, but at least we stuck together. You were just too good for us."

There is truth in what Jake is saying. "Do you know she came to my work a few days before the hurricane? Someone had beaten her pretty badly. I took her to my house, but by the time I got home she was gone. That was the last time I saw her. I abandoned her."

Jake's silence speaks volumes.

I continue, "Before that she asked to stay with me so she could start over. I never said no, but saying nothing wasn't really any different. I have so many regrets. I loved her. I did. We had plans to live our lives together, but none of that worked out. I miss her so much."

Jake sobs silently. I reach for his shoulder, but he brushes me away. He walks to the back of his truck and puts down the tailgate. We sit for a long time without talking. "You really did beat us at everything when we were kids. I think your comment triggered me." I admit. "We were the little dorks who followed you guys around incessantly."

Jake half smiles at my reminiscing. I go on, "Remember when we use to run through the woods..."

234

Jake cuts me off, "Did you know what was happening to us?" His voice sounds different, despondent.

I shake my head and wait, knowing he is going to tell me a hard truth.

"Life was different when you were around. Mom and Dad, believe it or not, put on a show when you all would come over, but when no one was there they didn't give a shit. They didn't make meals. Half the time we didn't have any food. We would go to school with dirty clothes. We didn't have school supplies. Kids would make fun of us, well, until we beat the shit out of them. As teenagers we started selling drugs for mom and dad to the kids at school and things changed. We were important, had a little money, plus my great looks kicked in." Jake wasn't smiling. Not even a little.

I don't know what to say, so I stay quiet. I reach towards him, but again he pulls away. My feelings are not hurt and I respect his space. "Anna got it the worst. One of the kids she sold to raped her, sort of. We beat the shit out of him, but she never got over losing the baby."

My heart thumps in my ears and I feel like I am going to throw up. "Sort of?"

"She was at a party and was drinking. Maybe it just went too far. Anna said he raped her. I don't know. You went with her but left early."

Knife to my heart. "That was the last time we spent together as friends. I thought we had just grown apart and changed our choice in friends. I had no idea. I left her alone." I sob. Uncontrollable distress takes over. Guilt and despair overwhelm me.

Jake reaches for me this time. I start to pull away instinctively, but stop myself. Instead I lean on his shoulder. We cry together. At some point, Greg and Tiffany join us. Jake and I shift from each other to our partners. Jake is first to stand, alerting me he is ready to go. I hug both him and Tiffany. "Thank you both for coming tonight." I say to them. Then separately to Jake, "I needed to understand better and I'm sorry."

Chapter 35

Greg and I fall into bed. Once again, I am emotionally and physically depleted. I need rest. The firearms handling class is in the morning. Greg is asleep almost as soon as his head hits the pillow. My thoughts are of Anna. If I had taken Anna with me the night of that party, she wouldn't have gotten raped, wouldn't have gotten pregnant, and wouldn't have lost a baby. I should have taken her with me. Our drifting apart was my fault. Sleep used to be such a happy time, but now my mind torments me with images, both real and imagined, relating to all the chaos of my life. Greg is sleeping soundly.

In the morning, we drive to Calallen, a suburb of Corpus Christi about 20 minutes from the center of town. Our handgun class is being held at the Superior Inn. The hotel is your average dilapidated hotel with a strange smell, tile floors, and modern furniture that would only be chosen for a space station.

The class is held in a meeting room, not big enough to be called a hall. The far wall has floor to ceiling windows with cheap blinds. The florescent lights are a little bright. In the front of the room a rectangular table is set up with a laptop sending a power point to a large screen hanging from the wall across from the windows. A dozen banquet chairs have been placed in front of the table. A fairly basic set up for a presentation.

The instructor is a stocky man who looks suited for law enforcement. "Hello everyone. I am Terry Bradley, Border Patrol Agent. I'm originally from Sandia, Texas. I still have a ranch out there with a shooting range. I built it myself with some fellow officers. My retirement. In the meantime, I am stationed near Kingsville and do these trainings on the weekends." Terry asks us all to introduce ourselves.

"I am Frank. Me and my two friends here, Ben and Steve, work in the refineries. We are hunters and are here to make it legal to carry our guns on our hunting trips." Ben and Steve don't bother to give separate introductions.

"Hi. I'm Sid and this is my brother-in-law, Mark." Mark waves. "We like to shoot recreationally. We believe in our constitutional right to carry arms and decided this would be fun." These guys are definitely white-collar Republicans.

After two older couples introduce themselves, Greg and I make our introduction, "Greg and I are here to start a hobby. We've gone to the shooting range a few times and had a great time. We figure getting the open carry would be fun." I leave out that I am being threatened by the Syndicate and have taken to illegally carrying my gun.

Terry is a great instructor. He is comfortable with public speaking. He is knowledgeable in firearms and takes gun safety and the legality of firearms seriously. For the most part, the presentation follows the booklet provided by the State. "There are limitations for carrying firearms in public especially government agencies, schools, and bars. These entities are required to post signage limiting your right to carry in easily visible locations."

None of us have noticed the signs previously, but have now officially been informed of our responsibility as open carry persons to look for signage. All these rules are very disconcerting as I've been carrying my gun on campus for some time now, and will continue with or without a license despite the sign.

Terry goes on, "If you are pulled over in a traffic situation. Be aware the officer has already looked you up, seen your open carry, and is fully aware that you are likely to have a gun on your person. You should expect and be prepared to be asked where your gun is. Not providing this information could escalate the situation."

Again, this is disconcerting as I have multiple interactions with police officers when I had the gun on my person or in my glove compartment. Luckily, I didn't have a license to carry alerting them, and they never asked.

Terry continues, "Scarier is that officers don't always know your rights and might violate your rights. If this happens, don't argue with the police officer as this, again, could escalate the situation. After the situation resolves, call a lawyer." Terry has information on insurance for open carry. Greg is interested.

Terry spends the remaining time, telling his stories and those of his colleagues regarding times they had to protect the safety of bystanders and confront an aggressor. "If your life is in danger you have the right to defend yourself. Keep in mind, when given the opportunity, participants are encouraged to walk away from dangerous situations." Flashbacks hit me of the night I pulled my gun on the intruders in my backyard.

At the end of the presentation, we each take a comprehensive test. There are no surprises as Terry covered all subjects thoroughly. Both Greg and I pass easily.

My anxiety is quite high. I am glad when we transition to the second part of the class and move from the hotel to the range. The drive to the range is about ten minutes.

We wait together for Terry to open the gate. We caravan to the range through a metal grate with a long dirt drive, maybe a mile. At the end, we see about ten rows of paper targets clipped onto metal frames.

Terry gathers materials from his trunk then meets up with us, "I am part owner of this range. We have a membership with unlimited use." He goes on to give the details, but as Greg and I live in Flour Bluff the 30-minute drive is prohibitive. We will have to find something closer to the house.

Terry details how the shooting test will progress. "Each of you will have to show proficiency in different positions and distances. Please put on your personal ear muffs and safety glasses." Greg and I pull out the muffs and glasses we brought for this purpose. After a lengthy and detailed safety rules and procedures speech, we are ready to start proficiency testing.

On the first set, the first six of us, Greg and I included, stand in ready position pointing our guns at the targets. Every ten seconds we are required to aim, shoot one round, then get back into ready position and repeat ten times. When we break, I am pleased to have done better than all the others in our round. Greg did pretty well too. After three rounds, we move ten feet closer. On some rounds we are required to shoot three times successively. My anxiety reduces as this is the fun part of this experience. I am feeling quite comfortable and confident in my skills.

At some point we are required to reload. Greg has some minor difficulty with a bullet that is lodged in the chamber. Terry assists him, "Anyone who cannot dislodge their bullets needs to increase their practice until this is an easy task." He emphasizes, "Anyone with a concealed carry should be very comfortable reloading and unloading his/her gun."

After completing each of the tasks, we receive our points. All participants who met the percentage cutoff receive credit for the course. Greg and I are proud to hear that we more then met the cutoff.

I am frustrated to learn that this class is only the first step in obtaining the license to open carry permit. Terry finishes the class, "You will have to get fingerprints then go online and submit proof of fingerprinting. The results of the class should be sent to the Department of Public Safety along with $135. The soonest you can expect to legally carry your firearms will be in a month." I had hoped that the process would be faster.

On the ride home, I offer, "I will pay for both of us. You only need the license because of me."

Greg, of course, argues, "No, I always wanted to learn to shoot. I'll pay for my own permit."

I point out, "Rent is due."

Greg concedes, "I guess this is my first month's rent. Alright, Sugar Momma."

With my usual issue of over thinking everything I mention, "We haven't really discussed the details of breaking down the bills. I want to ensure that the division is fair."

"Let's go over the bills when they come in. We would be guessing right now. Let's each put aside $200 in the meantime." This seems sensible. I drop the issue for the time being.

Greg then states, "I have to admit I am far more worried about illegally carrying this gun now that I have had the class. I can't pretend to be ignorant of the law."

I had thought of this too. "I agree. I can really get in trouble. I don't feel safe without it though. I don't know. So much has been happening. I wouldn't feel safe living my life without it."

"Those goons aren't around anymore. Nothing has happened lately. Maybe we are okay." Greg remarks.

I want to see things the way Greg sees things, but the reality is that I am still waiting for the hammer to fall.

Chapter 36

Sunday is not a fun day. Back to work for me. Greg stays at the house. He really is enjoying living in his new home. He has taken full ownership of the lawn and is all about landscaping. Today he plans to recreate some flower beds in the front yard. My mother would be pleased. I did not inherit her green thumb but I found a partner who has one of his own. I figure he likes that I am giving him complete control of the yard. I mostly set up and designed the inside of the house which includes over-ruling some of his boyhood décor which is now hung in the garage. Greg understands that I want to live in an adult space. I am pleased that he compliments and likes our final style in the house. The house is comfy and simple.

The lawn will represent and present his tastes. "I'm thinking of renting a rototiller and putting down new fertilizer. I'm going to redo the three beds." There is a large bed at the front of the house framing the front windows and two flowerbeds around the trees. They are overgrown and full of weeds. Greg continues, "I want to get some stone pavers to help frame the edges. I'm going to ask about the plants at the home store. I like the look of the red mulch." Greg has a good idea of what he wants.

"Sounds good. Value-mart probably has better deals on the mulch," I suggest.

Greg is easy going, "I'll check both out." I give the now distracted Greg a kiss. I like him relaxed and excited about his project.

Driving into Taylors, I see Tiffany and Jake. I have not heard from them since game night. Only a few days have gone by but Tiff has not called me at all. I expected to hear from her to tell me what happened with Bob. My feelings are a hurt. I don't like the idea of Tiff and Jake as a couple. Tiff is mine or at least she was.

Oh well, I have to get to work. The day drags along unbearably. Knowing Greg is happily landscaping and Tiff and Jake are having a couple's day while I move tiny bottles of aspirin to the front of the shelf for eight hours is intolerable. For the first time I really want a new job. When I had been working outside, I could at least see the sky. The florescent lighting is making my head throb. My mood just falls lower and lower and lower.

My uncle's friend with the tattoo on his head runs into me while I am putting away returns. I am positive he did so on purpose. He does not apologize, but rather gives me an ugly look. I keep my composure since I am at work, but every part of me wants to go crazy on this guy. I spend my last 45 minutes playing in my head what I should have said to the jerk. I come up with some real hateful stuff.

Just before my shift is over, I am interrupted by Dean. "What did Greg do to put you in this mood?"

I am so not in the mood. No part of me is simpatico with this guy. "What are you talking about?" I say with disdain.

"You look like you are ready to rip someone a new one." Dean answers while backing up a bit.

I hadn't realized that I was projecting my feelings so far outside of my head. Strong emotions are pushing to the surface. I try to calm my inner tantrum, but when I start to

244

speak, tears embarrassingly roll down my cheeks. "It's not Greg. It's me. I just…" no words come.

Dean leans in and gives me a hug. He is not being oogie. This time he is being a friend. I really appreciate him not judging me in my current vulnerable state.

I pull back to thank him when I see Greg walking away in the corner of my eye. "Thanks. I have to go." I run towards Greg.

Greg is hightailing it out of the store. I yell after him, "Greg. Wait up." He does not turn or acknowledge me. I am certain he hears me. The rage restarts within me. I have done nothing wrong. After a really shitty day, I do not deserve this shit.

I catch up to Greg as he is getting into his Jeep. "Are you freaking kidding me?" I yell when I am too close for him to pretend not to hear me.

"No need to leave Dean's embrace, I was just here to take you to dinner." Greg is being such a condescending asshole.

I turn without another word and head into the store to clock out. I am hurt, angry, and, dang it, my day has already been awful. Negative thoughts swirl through my brain. My parents are dead. Greg is an asshole. Maybe Dean wasn't being a friend. Tiffany doesn't care about me. I know that I am being irrational but no part of me wants to abandon my inner tantrum. Fuck it, fuck it all. After clocking out, I drive out to the beach.

Once on the beach, my anger abates and transforms to feeling sorry for my pathetic self. I walk for about half a mile with my feet in the warm salty water. Heron dive bomb into the water trying to catch dinner. A large grey pelican spreads his broad wingspan just over my head then crashes into the water, coming up with what looks like a nice sized amberjack. He swings his head back and swallows the large fish whole. I envy these beautiful birds; the peace they must have in their lives. Soaring above the chaotic world and enjoying a nice plunge into the ocean for a perfect dinner. No cooking, no job, no incessant talking. Of course, I would miss everyone. I am not a loner. I would probably even miss working and taking care of things. Every time I have time to sit with my thoughts alone lately, they turn negative.

I decide I need to drive home. Greg will be worried.

When I pull up to the house, I immediately notice the lawn. Greg did an excellent job. The flower beds really pop with the red mulch. There are beautiful bright yellow and red flowers in front of small bushes that I assume will grow to almost reach the window sill. Greg has even cleaned up after himself. I do not see his Jeep.

I pull into the garage and head into the house. Greg is nowhere to be found. I decide to call him. No answer. I leave a message. "Hey, it's Ella. Sorry you got your feelings hurt. Believe me it wasn't what it looked like. Call me back."

I sit around and wait for quite a while and nothing. I decide to call his parents' house. His mother answers on the first ring, "Hello."

"Hey, it's Ella. Is Greg there?"

His mother immediately overreacts. "No, I haven't seen him in some time. You can't locate him?"

I do not want to explain so I minimize the issue, "He was working on the lawn while I was at work. I'm guessing his cell battery died and he is at the store picking up a few more things to finish the job. Sorry to bother you." I hang up before having to have any further conversation. We have not visited Greg's parents since the original meet-the-parents dinner that went horrible. I feel a little guilty. That said, I am not up for a visit.

I turn on the television to pass time. Nothing is on in the late afternoon. I check the DVR. I peruse but most of the recorded shows I watch with Greg. I turn to live television; the Home and Garden channel will do. The couple in this show appear to have an amazing relationship. They joke with one another and keep it playful. I like their interactions. The final home make-over presentation is amazing. The couple incorporates lots of metal and antiques that I would think were trash, but the way it all comes together is really impressive. I cannot imagine living in the house though. So perfect that you can't just relax. A nice fantasy though. Greg and I have done well enough putting this house together.

I look around the house. I did a pretty good job. Our place looks really nice. There are still elements that remind me of my parents but overall the place looks like Greg and I despite having much of my parents' furniture.

While lost in my thoughts, I hear a car door outside. I decide to turn off the television and just wait for Greg. I do not want to fight or makeup in the front yard. I wait, practicing my calm face.

Jake walks in without ringing the doorbell. He has a distressed look on his face. I look for Tiff behind him, but no. I brace myself for whatever would make him violate the social rule of knocking. I remain silent, confused. Jake moves to within a few feet of me before he speaks, "You have to come with me."

"Where?" I am dumbfounded.

Jake rocks back and forth on his feet. He is uncomfortable. "Where is Craig?" Most of my life I have only seen the two together. Lately, I had been seeing Jake with Tiffany.

"He's in the car. I can't explain, but I need you to come with me." Jake is not being his usual self. Jake's usual jocular nature is replaced with a pensive and anxious persona. The difference is disconcerting. I step away from him.

"This is not okay. I'm going to need you to tell me what's going on." I am now worried. I left my gun in my room. I assumed Greg would be here when I got home from work. My false sense of security has left and I am at a heightened sense of awareness.

Jake's demeanor does not change. He struggles to find the right words. Too much time is passing. My nerves are starting to make me feel sick to my stomach. "I need to go to the restroom." I am not asking permission. I turn and head into my bedroom. I lock the door. I grab my gun from the drawer then resolve my now urgent need to go to the restroom. When done, I sit on the bed avoiding joining Jake. I hope Jake leaves.

I pick up my cell to call Greg. No answer, but then I get a text message from Greg in return. "Go with Jake!" My heart sinks. Nothing about this situation is right. I call again but no answer. I text back. "Call me, now. I'm not going anywhere with Jake."

My cell dings immediately. "This isn't Greg. If you want to retrieve Greg, go with Jake." I decide to look in Greg's gun safe. His gun is sitting inside. Once again, my heart drops to my aching stomach.

Panic starts to take over. My breathing increases. I realize that I am having another panic attack. I cannot pass out. Last time I landed in the hospital. Someone took Greg. I have to get my shit together. I put my shirt over my mouth and nose while concentrating on my breathing. I visualize running into Greg's arms. Tears threaten. The idea that his last thought about me was that I had betrayed him in some way with Dean hurts. Nothing could be further from the truth. I ready myself and open the door.

Fury takes over and I lunge at Jake. Jake looks upset. He does not fight back. I consider pulling my gun on him, but think better of it. I need to wait until I locate Greg. I step back, "So I guess I have to go with you."

Jake nods his head in agreement while remaining silent. I am not sure if his silence angers me or calms me. I follow him to the truck. Craig is sitting in the driver's seat. "Any chance I get to drive myself?" I ask.

Jake shakes his head letting me know that nothing is in my control. Craig does not even acknowledge me and remains silent. Good soldiers. Bad cousins. After we are on the freeway, Craig asks Jake, "Did you get her cell phone?"

Disbelief that my cousins would actually do this hit me, then outrage. I hand Jake my cell. I wish I had thought to use it to text someone, do anything, but alas I am now headed to who knows where under duress. We drive away from Flour Bluff, turning on the Crosstown Freeway towards the west side of town. Other than Del Mar college, I am never in these neighborhoods. The area looks foreign to me. I did not even know areas of the city looked so desolate and industrial in town. We drive up behind a large warehouse that looks abandoned. Boards cover large broken windows. Bay doors are shut for what looks like a loading dock. The building is surrounded by an eight-foot fence with barbwire on the top.

Big John opens the gate that rolls on four wheels. A large intimidating dog halts at his side. I expect to see my uncle but only Big John is visible. I am increasingly alarmed.

Craig drives to a private area that cannot be seen from the street. There are no houses close by. A few small businesses scatter the mostly abandoned area, but nothing is open. I see no point in screaming for help. Plus, Greg is my priority. I scan the parking lot for Greg's Jeep. Part of me hopes he isn't here. If he is here, they could easily shoot us both with no witnesses.

Chapter 37

Craig and Jake exit the car and walk toward Big John. "What is the plan from here?" Craig asks.

Big John looks uncomfortable and shrugs his shoulders. Craig hands Big John my cell.

Big John walks over and opens my door. He holds out his hand like a gentleman.

Fury replaces my fear. I slap his hand away and step out of the car independently. We are not going to pretend like I came here of my own free will. "Where is Greg? What do you want?" I hold eye contact to let him know that I am not backing down. I am leaving with Greg, come hell or high water.

Big John laughs condescendingly. His veil of gentlemanly behavior has fallen.

"I guess no more sob stories about how you were sent by Anna to protect me this time." I look directly at Big John, then to Jake, "...or about your sad childhood." Craig looks at Jake questionably. I care less about what he understands. I don't understand what is happening but I know Greg should not be involved in any of this.

Big John looks more serious this time, "You definitely know how to push my buttons. Not such a good idea if you want to see your boyfriend again."

Jake remains silent.

"So, what are we doing, boys? I'm here against my will. This is your show." I try to look like I have enough moxie to be a threat. I might be able to pull it off better if I wasn't still in my Taylors uniform.

251

From inside a door to the large warehouse I hear her, "Oh this ain't no boy's show, for sure." Aunt Donna walks out with a large caliber gun in her hand. "Your uncle is with Greg. You are going to give me the watches."

All my moxie is gone. My aunt is truly a scary woman. "I don't have any watches."

"That is not what your sweet little boyfriend said." I do not know Aunt Donna well enough to read her.

I cannot be sure if Greg said anything. I do not have the watches regardless so I decide to stick with my story. "I've never had any watches."

I hear the loud boom before I feel anything. A blinding flash of light hurdles towards me. Something grazes my thigh and pain pulsates like a full force cleat kick from an opponent in a soccer game. A small stream of blood flows from my leg. In disbelief that my aunt shot me, I fold over applying pressure to my wound. Craig and Jake start to move toward me to assist, but one look from Aunt Donna and they stay still.

I consider pulling my gun, but I am surrounded and Aunt Donna is too far away to be able to do anything about her.

Hurt, I sink to the ground. Aunt Donna moves closer and puts the gun to my head. Uncle Billy runs out of the door. "What the hell?"

Craig and Jake look eager for their dad to intervene.

"Stupid little bitch thinks I'm stupid." She turns her attention back to me. "Greedier than I pegged you for." Aunt Donna wants to pull the trigger. I reconsider pulling out my gun but she has the upper hand and would kill me. I sit defeated.

Uncle Billy comes closer. "We don't know she has the watches."

Relief comes to me. Maybe if she genuinely thinks I do not have the watches then she won't kill me. She has no reason to kill me.

Evidently, I am wrong about that too. "I don't care anymore," says Aunt Donna. She glares at me with the hate filled eyes I have seen so many times in the past, "It's your fault Anna is dead. She didn't want to hurt poor Ella. Poor Ella who never gave two shits about us. She felt guilty and wanted to walk a different path. We'd still be running product out of the house if she wasn't worried about you. Then you go and get Big John arrested. You don't even know the shit storm that you brought down on all of us."

Big John steps in. "That isn't Ella's fault. I'm at fault. I should have taken Anna away from this life."

Aunt Donna objects to being interrupted. Another loud burst. Big John falls to the ground. He is silent. I am unsure if he is alive or dead. The large dog runs to his side whining and nudging him with his snout. Big John is not responding.

From the corner of my eye, I notice Craig nudge Big John without a response. Jake backs away from the now huddled group and is texting on his cell. Who he is texting?

Uncle Billy moves closer to Aunt Donna, "Honey, you have to stop. What is the end game here?"

Aunt Donna closes the short distance between us, holding the gun out in my direction. "If we can't pay them back, we are all dead. If I'm going to die, so is she." I slowly stand to face my fate, maintaining eye contact with Aunt Donna. She wiggles the gun to show me she is in charge.

253

I realize that my function here is no longer to save Greg but to escape my own fate. I hope Greg is not in that building. She could have already killed him for all I know.

Uncle Billy is on my side; at least, he does not want her to kill me. "She doesn't need to die. We can just leave town."

Aunt Donna diverts her attention from me to Uncle Billy. "Fuck that. Where would we go? The Syndicate will hunt us down or we will spend the rest of our lives running. What would we do to make money? This is the only life we know."

Recognizing my only chance, I reach behind my back, swipe the safety, put my hand on the trigger, and whip the gun around my side pointing my barrel directly at Aunt Donna's forehead. Caught off guard for only a second, Aunt Donna laser focuses back on me, aiming her gun at my forehead. We stand arms outstretched in a stalemate, facing each other's weapon. Aunt Donna is my greatest threat. Any one of them can take me down, but my greatest chance is to put down Aunt Donna.

Aunt Donna's cruel sneer is matched by my strong will to survive. I watch for even the slightest movement, but if Aunt Donna is anything, she is selfish. She wants to live as much as I do.

I can't pull the trigger unless she makes some sort of gesture showing me that she intends to act but I am ready, willing, and able to take action. No one moves or speaks for what seems like forever.

From behind me, I hear a loud crash through the gate we entered. We both turn with a start, breaking our stalemate. Four police cars flood in and surround us. The officers quickly exit their vehicles standing behind the doors of their respective squad cars. Aunt Donna turns the gun away from me to focus on her new threat. In the commotion, I dash toward the warehouse, while listening for the sound of her shot that never comes. My leg throbs but I can't focus on that for now.

Inside the building I frantically yell, "Greg. Greg, where are you?" No response. The entry is a large three-story open storage area relatively empty except for a few hundred crates in the corner. I run to the far side of the room looking in the large window into what looks like an empty office. I run to the next door and swing it open. This door leads to a long hallway with several doors on each side. I run opening every unlocked door yelling, "Greg?" Behind the fourth door, I hear something. "Greg. Greg. I'm here."

The door is locked. I thrust my hip into the door, but the pain from the bullet graze sends inconceivable pain throughout my body. I point my gun at the lock and shoot. The noise reverberates throughout the hall.

Within a few seconds, officers enter through the far end of the hall, "Put down your gun or we will shoot."

The door I desperately want opened remains shut. I hold the gun above my head and yell back, "I have no intention of shooting. I am going to place the gun on the ground." I slowly lower my body to the ground, ignoring the intense pain pulsing from my leg. I lay the gun on the ground and scoot away from the gun. "I think my boyfriend is locked in this room. I have no idea if he is hurt or not."

Officers quickly come to my side yelling commands. I comply instinctively. I hear sirens outside. I have no idea what happened outside with my family. The officers place me in handcuffs and brusquely yank me to a standing position. I hear an officer radio for a battering ram. My mind imagines a battering ram used for storming a castle, but shortly after two officers enter the hall carrying a heavy large black cylinder. They swing the device at the dense steel door. I startle when I hear the loud bang of a gun at impact. The battering ram has a large caliber pistol attached to the end of the cylinder which fires automatically upon impact. Unlike my attempt to shoot the door, the door opens with the momentum.

Moments later, Greg staggers past the threshold being supported by two officers. Greg is massaging his wrists which appear to have been bound. Regardless, he is here. He is alive.

Greg is downcast initially, but the moment he sees me he shakes himself free of the officers and runs to me. "Her leg is bleeding. Why is she in handcuffs?"

Greg is ignored and redirected. The officers escort Greg and I to the parking lot. A body bag lay next to the spot where Big John had fallen. My family members are nowhere to be seen, but all the same cars are in the parking lot. I presume they have all been arrested.

Detective Haas moves swiftly to my side. "Take off the cuffs," he demands.

The young officer weighs in, "She had an illegal weapon pointed at one of the suspects when we entered, Sir."

"Take the cuffs off now! That is an order." Detective Haas is not joking around. The young officer complies.

Once the cuffs are removed, Greg weaves through the officers and embraces me. We cling to each other. "I was so scared. I love you." I whisper through tears.

A paramedic touches my shoulder gently, "Can I take a look at your leg?"

Greg immediately releases me, "Yes, she is bleeding."

In the ambulance, I lay on the gurney. My leg is elevated. The paramedic adds pressure to my leg which hurts, but necessary to stop the bleeding. He gives me a shot of something. After the bleeding ceases, he pours a liquid over the wound. The substance burns. While applying a bandage the paramedic explains, "The good news is the wound is superficial. I cleaned it with an antiseptic wash and gave you a shot for pain and swelling. The bullet grazed your leg and did not hit any critical areas."

"And the bad news?" I ask.

The paramedic looks confused, then turns his attention to Detective Haas, "Not a bad idea to go to the hospital. Your call."

Detective Haas orders, "She needs to be cleared by a physician."

"I don't want to go to the hospital." I respond.

Detective Haas rolls his eyes, "No one is going to force you, but you have been shot and have certainly experienced trauma. I recommend you take a ride. We will need to interview you, but I'd rather wait until you have been seen by a physician."

I decide to listen to Detective Haas and take the short ride to the downtown hospital.

After about an hour Greg shows up with Detective Haas. I have been medically cleared and am awaiting discharge.

"Hey," I hug Greg.

"Detective Haas gave me a ride to my Jeep which was left at Taylors. After you stormed off, I was waiting to apologize for overreacting. I was distracted. Your cousins parked between me and the building, then Craig pulled a gun on me. I didn't want them to wait for you, so I didn't put up a struggle. They brought me to that warehouse where I had the nicest time meeting your aunt."

Sarcastically I respond, "Can't be nicer than the time I met your parents." I reflect on how all this happened while I was having a breakdown at the beach. I add, "I'm so sorry. I had no idea. Obviously, you should have taken your parents' advice and dumped me some time ago."

Greg reaches out to pinch me. I slap his hand away almost laughing.

Detective Haas is confused with this inside joke and changes the subject. "Your cousin, Jake, probably saved your life. Jake was arrested not long ago for being in possession of a large amount of marijuana with intent to sell. Sergeant Peters, the officer you met investigating Anna's death, was using him as a snitch. Your Aunt Donna is the local lieutenant in the Syndicate, a high rank for this community. The crates in the warehouse included thousands of pounds of marijuana and some weapons. This was a big sting operation you ended up drawn into."

I respond, "She said they were going to kill her if she didn't give them the watches."

Sergeant Peters enters, "Speaking of which, those watches are now evidence of laundering and a powerful motivator in the string of murders we intend to prosecute. Where are the watches?"

I give them Mr. Kirby's information. "What about Jake?"

"We arrested him for his own protection. If the Syndicate had any idea that he turned State's evidence his life would be in danger. You are unlikely to see him again."

258

I am having a hard time processing all this information.

Detective Haas informs us, "You will both need to testify as to the events of today and how you came to be in possession of the watches. As the Syndicate has a vested interest in protecting their power and structure, you and Greg are being placed under witness protection." Furthermore, Detective Haas explains, "Only married couples are placed together in witness protection."

My heart breaks in two. Like losing my parents all over again. I will be alone once again. I try to keep my composure but my hands start to shake and my eyes are wet.

"The official story is that you and Greg are both found murdered after you are released from the hospital." Detective Haas gives me a moment to process. My life as I know it is over.

Detective Haas continues, "For the cover story to work you will not be allowed to make any plans for your assets. You have to agree to leave everything and everyone behind." The idea that once again nothing remains in my control is devastating.

Chapter 38

Marshal Paul Severa, a tall serious looking man, with witness protection commands the room when he enters. After introducing himself, he quickly explains our rights and the rules of the witness protection program. Greg interjects, "Can you give us five minutes?"

Marshal Severa gives limited consent, "I know you've both just started your lives and aren't ready to start anew. Five minutes." He holds up five fingers and walks brusquely out of the room.

As soon as he leaves, I start in, "I am so sorry. I have ruined your life."

Greg reaches into his pocket and falls onto one knee.

Initially, I am perplexed until a single tear rolls down my cheek.

"Will you marry me?" Greg holds a black box which he tilts open. The gorgeous vintage ring with a steepled effect leads to a large diamond that glistens exquisitely.

"Where did you get a ring?" I ask stunned.

"That was not the response I was expecting." Greg says disappointed. "I bought it right after we decided to move in together. I was waiting for things to calm down so we could go on that romantic date I had planned."

"What was the plan?"

"Again, not the response I am waiting for. We have limited time. Will you marry me?" he asks again.

"Sorry." I immerse myself in this moment. "I can't imagine ever meeting anyone as wonderful as you." Greg grins eagerly waiting for my answer. "But I've ruined your life. You don't have to go forward with your plan to propose. Too much has changed."

Greg stands, "You really are a pain in the ass. If none of this had happened, we could have chosen to finish school somewhere else together. The only way this doesn't work out is if you say no. I can't imagine living without you." After a short pause, he adds, "Unless you now have feelings for Dean?"

"You idiot."

"Wow, three strikes."

"No. I have no feelings for Dean. Yes. I will marry you. I love you with all my heart." In the middle of our passionate kiss sealing the deal Marshal Severa enters the room.

"What did I miss?" Marshal Severa asks. I hold out my hand to show him my new ring. "Nice." After a pause, he continues, "Where did you get a ring?"

Greg and I laugh wholeheartedly. "Detective Haas took me to my Jeep. I was storing it in my glove compartment waiting for the right time. I was already planning to propose."

"This changes things." Marshal Severa contemplates then addresses us, "Look this isn't a game. If you are getting married, we can keep you together, but our plan will be binding. Are you both sure this is the decision you are ready to make?"

"Yes." I state with confidence while holding Greg's hand.

"See there is the answer I was expecting." I smile and kiss Greg again.

We are discharged from the hospital and leave in Greg's Jeep. We are instructed to go home and wait for Marshal Severa.

We do as we are instructed. Upon entering the house, three marshals greet us. We are given 15 minutes to pack a small bag of necessities only. Nothing of a personal nature is to be taken. No pictures, not my mother's jewelry, nothing. Greg's engagement ring is truly my most precious possession. I stare at it for hours as we drive away from the only home I have ever known. Greg takes pride in me being distracted by his token of love.

We drive for most of the following day until we arrive at a safe compound where we are assigned a room. Each day for two weeks, we meet with our counselor, Sam. We learn about our new home, Fort Collins, Colorado. We are from here forward to be known as Gregory and Ellen Still. We were allowed to choose our new names and encouraged to keep the same first name. We memorize and practice our cover story. We are newlyweds from upstate New York. We practice our signatures repeatedly.

Marshal Severa arranges a special outing the day before we are placed into our new lives. We are driven out to a beautiful clearing just north of the bridge at Butterfly Woods. Wild flowers are abundant and the world looks natural and peaceful from this vantage point. The only building in sight is a small rustic wooden cabin with a deck. The place is charming with two idyllic rocking chairs adorned with oversized floral pattern cushions sitting on an open porch overlooking the vista.

"Detective Haas sent a gift for each of you." Marshal Severa hands us each a large box.

Inside is a simple lace wedding dress with a long dip in the back and a small train. "Is this a wedding dress?"

Greg opens his tuxedo.

Marshal Severa performs our simple wedding ceremony and a photographer documents the occasion. As a parting gift on our last day in the compound, Sam gives us a photo album of the wedding and a copy of our marriage certificate signed by a judge we never met.

Fort Collins, Colorado is beautiful. We enroll in Colorado State University. We live a simple life accepted by the college community as out of town newlyweds.

While we build a happy new life, both Greg and I have moments of weakness where our hearts ache for those we lost. The news reported that we were found dead in a field. Our funerals have been held. We aren't allowed to use social media. Mainstream articles are our only window into our friends and family. Our deaths were not reported with the exception of one brief story in the local paper with a picture of Greg's mother devastated. We lost so much, but at least we have each other as partners in our grief.

Occasionally, when alone, we speculate on how Jake came to be our hero and how he is doing. Greg swears he got a glimpse of Jake at the trial. We testified in a closed court room before the judge under heavy guard. I guess we will never know for sure, but we hope Jake made it to a new and better future.

263

Epilogue

I wonder what happened with Greg and Ella. Jake's mind wanders. Ten years have passed since I saw Ella run into that warehouse leaving a trail of blood from her leg. I was arrested and taken away before she came out again. The news said they were killed, but I am sure I saw a glimpse of her at the trial with Greg. My mind might be playing tricks on me, but believing they made it out together makes me happy and softens my guilt about turning on my family.

Today, I am sitting on my very own couch, in my very own house. This is the only home that has ever felt like home. My mucky boots rest heavily on my coffee table. My wife, Sally, would yell at me if she saw me. She is in the kitchen cooking while Anna and Craig, my tweens, wrestle in front of the television making sure I can't follow this most recent episode of Fix my Ride.

"Settle down." I command.

The redirection backfires as both of the kids decide to bring me in on the fun. Anna jumps on my legs, while Craig puts me in a headlock. I playfully pull Craig over my head and plop him beside me on the couch.

Anna yells, "Dog Pile!" She jumps on top of Craig.

I slump over them heavily yet protectively.

"Dad, I can't breathe." Craig yells out.

I sit up laughing so hard my stomach hurts. I am getting too old for this. "Stop! I'm done."

Young Anna and Craig continue wrestling but leave me out of it. Big picture, my kids are soft compared to their Uncle Craig and me when we were kids. The kids would have liked their Uncle Craig, well if he had made it out. The guilt I feel is a heavy burden. Craig has been sitting in jail for the last ten years. Sally thinks our kids were named after foster siblings lost years ago. At least I can still tell her my stories, just tweak the details.

I still remember that day in our childhood when my brother Craig stole my sister Anna's journal.

Mom and Dad were sitting at the table talking with Ella's parents. Anna and Ella had taken over the XBOX playing Minecraft.

"Get off. We want to play." Craig goaded.

"No. We were here first." Anna was being stubborn.

"Get off now or you will regret it." Craig threatened.

"Go outside. Now! All of you." When Mom gave an order, we listened.

Craig was mad. He looked at me conspiratorially, "It is hot outside. Watch this!" Craig grabbed Anna's journal and ran outside. I followed as always. Craig was my idol and the coolest guy I have ever known.

"Give it back!" Anna didn't have a chance. Our bikes were parked out front. We hoped on with the skill of trick bikers.

I did a revert on an incline across the street. I yelled to Anna knowing she didn't even have a bike, "Try and keep up, losers!" Messing with Anna always made for a little action on a boring day.

"Evil Knievel, let's go." Craig called to me then told the girls, "Let's see who finds your diary at the flats."

I did an endo 180 by breaking hard then whipped my bike around following Craig along the path. Bike tricks are the coolest and nobody could best me, not even Craig.

At the flats we waited for the girls. After a time, Anna and Ella came running up, sweaty. Anna was as mad as Craig had been.

Craig just thought this was funny by this point. "Good luck finding your way home," he called out as he dropped the journal. We headed back toward the house.

When we came flying out of the path and up the driveway, Mom came out steaming, "Where is Ella? They need to leave!"

Mom was always in an especially bad mood when our aunt and uncle visited. Ella and her parents didn't visit that often, but when they did, they usually brought us treats. Regardless, Craig and I knew we were in big trouble if we didn't get the girls home.

We headed back out. After a relatively short ride, we heard Anna yell out, "Oh no, the swine have found us!"

Craig spun around behind Ella and hit her in the back of the head while I laughed.

Ella tried to hit him but she didn't have a chance. She yelled instead, "Jerk!" She was such a spoiled brat. She deserved it.

Anna defended Ella, "You left us out here. I'm telling on you when we get home."

We circled the girls once more, before spinning out and taking off. We didn't go straight home to avoid a beating. When we finally made it home, Mom had her belt. "Don't ever embarrass me around those people!"

Craig and I couldn't sit the next day, then again, we got beat fairly often back then.

In retrospect, we should have been better brother's to Anna. I still have nightmares about Anna. Mom and Dad never protected us. I have survivor's guilt. I should have died. I should have gone to prison. I don't deserve the home and happiness I have now.

Shaking off the negative thoughts, I remind myself that my job now is to make sure that my kids, Anna and Craig, have the life their aunt and uncle deserved. My stomach has stopped hurting so I lunge at them once more. Craig and Anna immediately tackle me.

"Dinner is ready." Sally calls out. The kids rush for the dinner table.

Sally is a good cook, for east coast cooking. The food here is generally bland. I do like the seafood. I had a hard time with the change in cuisine at first as I was raised on spicy Mexican food. I found this little Mexican restaurant where I go every few weeks alone. The food isn't as good as back home, but they bring me unlimited tortilla chips and fresh salsa. Add a few beers and my mind transports me back home. Sally and the kids hate it. I don't mind going alone. My time to remember and mourn.

"Do you think you can get off for Anna's concert next Thursday?" Sally asks. Young Anna and Craig eagerly help themselves to hot rolls reaching across the table while shoving one another. "Manners." Sally corrects them.

"I work a turnaround next week. I am not going to make it." I hate missing the kids' events. I can't complain, though. When I was relocated, I was placed in trade school. I am now the frontline supervisor of extraction workers in the oil field. Good pay, good benefits, but I still have to do the turnarounds. Bill, one of my older guys, reminds me of my dad. He is kind of an ass, but I have to admit he is also my favorite.

Witness protection kept me in a safe house for quite a while before I landed here. I testified in a closed hearing to the judge. Not even Mom, the defendant, was in the room. After Mom fell, the dominos followed suit. The Syndicate took a big hit, but I'd bet the Syndicate remains virtually unscathed today. Protecting my kids from that world is my primary goal in life these days.

Sergeant Peters or Marshall Severa became my confidants and brothers while awaiting trial, giving me a new found respect for the law. Young Craig wants to grow up to be an officer. I could not be prouder. After the trial, I never heard from either agent again.

I don't really use the internet and I am not allowed on social media, but I did break the rules and googled Tiffany recently. She married and divorced. I like to think she never found anyone as great as me. I can't imagine her mourning both Ella and me at the same time. Leaving her was the hardest. She was my first love. She made me want to be a better man. She was the push that led me in this direction, without her.

A part of me would love to tell Sally and the kids all about my life, my old life. But this new life is far too precious.

I repeat my cover story to myself as a reminder, *I am an orphan who was raised in foster care. My trade school was paid for by the foster system. I am one of the lucky foster kids who has stability in adulthood.*

Sally thinks we should adopt a foster kid. She thinks I could really identify with the kids and help them find their way. The idea scares the shit out of me. I can only imagine the kid would read me as a liar right off.

At least I live near the best fishing in the East Coast, Chesapeake Bay. The kids and I love to go crabbing along the shore starting midyear. The striped bass are big and in good supply, but you can only keep one. On my best day, I caught and released 20. Sally cooks 'em up good. Sometimes she fries them and other times she steams them with veggies.

The transformation from the old Jake to this new Jake has broken me and rebuilt me stronger, for the most part, but the dark shadow of my past self remains as an open wound under the surface.